MacLean

MacLean

Philip McCormac

ROBERT HALE · LONDON

ISBN 978-0-7090-9167-7

Robert Hale Limited
Clerkenwell House
Clerkenwell Green
London EC1R 0HT

www.halebooks.com

2 4 6 8 10 9 7 5 3 1

Typeset in 10/13pt Sabon
by Derek Doyle & Associates, Shaw Heath
Printed in Great Britain by the MPG Books Group, Bodmin and King's Lynn

In loving memory of Joe McCormack
1935–2009

1

Tennant parked his Range Rover in a vacant slot in the small car-park. Stepping from behind the wheel he took a moment to scrutinize the other vehicles. There was a scattering of medium-sized vans and estate cars and 4x4s in hues ranging from dark blues to dirty whites. The only exception was a silver Mercedes with a personalized number plate – COL Y4.

Stretching his six-foot frame, Tennant shrugged his leather jacket into a more comfortable fit about his brawny shoulders and wiped his hand across his shaved head.

The sign above the warehouse announced: *Phoenix Fancy Fare – Wholesale Only – Belfast's Biggest and Best*.

Tennant walked across to the big double doors marked: CUSTOMERS. An entrance hall stacked high down one side with plastic pot planters and urns led into the warehouse. The youth on the till looked up at Tennant.

'Collymore?'

The youth shrugged and shook his head. For a moment Tennant considered giving the youngster a smack on the mouth. Deciding it wasn't worth the effort, he turned and walked through into the warehouse.

The aisles were stacked high with giant packs of toilet rolls, plastic buckets, toys, clothing, stationery and thousands of similar items indispensable to the running of modern society. Customers, loading trolleys in the overstocked passageways instinctively made way for the shaved head and leather jacket and the scowling face. Without knocking he pushed open the office door at the rear of the building and walked inside.

A woman in her late thirties sat at a desk strewn with paperwork Standing beside her was a younger woman, bent over and supporting herself with both hands on the desk. The two women looked up when the door opened.

'Collymore?'

'Yes, and who are you?'

'I'm looking for Colin Collymore. Where is he?'

The older woman narrowed her eyes. She had a pleasant face, softly made-up and well-groomed hair. She smiled brightly at him.

'I'm Mrs Collymore. If you'll tell me what you want, perhaps I can help you.'

The young woman straightened up, a slight frown on her face. Her hair was long and soft and hung round her face in appealing riotous strands. She had a vivacious self-possessed manner.

'It's Collymore I have to see. When will he be back?'

'Mr Collymore won't be back for some time. I'm dealing with his affairs. If you tell me what your business is with him I'll do my best to help you. Otherwise we're very busy.'

The last sentence was meant as a dismissal.

The bruiser was growing angry. His frustration and annoyance at not finding Collymore heightened. He thrust his beefy face towards the women.

'My business with Collymore is private. Just tell me where he is and I might just leave you in peace.'

Mrs Collymore shrank slightly in her chair as she heard the snarl in his voice. The younger woman had a quizzical frown on her face, almost as if Tennant was a source of mild amusement. Tennant felt his ire rising under her scrutiny. It was the younger woman who answered him.

'You'll find Colin at the Royal Victoria Hospital, Ward Ten. Visiting hours, two till four.'

Tennant's brow creased as he thought this over.

'What happened?'

'Colin suffered a stroke last Wednesday. He's recovering well and the doctors think he might be able to come home in a day or two. But it'll be some time before he is fit enough to come back to work again.'

Tennant's eyes narrowed. 'You taking over running the place?'

Perhaps it was because the young woman was showing no apprehension that Mrs Collymore recovered her confidence.

'Yes, we're in charge. Is it something personal you want to see Colin about, or is it business to do with Phoenix?'

A fan heater whirred in the background. The air smelled stale with an oppressive stuffiness. Tennant stared belligerently at Mrs Collymore. He put his hands on the desktop and leaned down towards the woman, asserting his dominance over her. Mrs Collymore shrank back into her chair. The younger woman watched with a look of mild boredom.

'It's business, Mrs Collymore. Your husband pays an insurance premium each week. He hasn't paid anything for over a month now and my boss sent me along to sort out any difficulties.'

He emphasized the last word, breaking it up into separate syllables as if the word carried some more sinister meaning. Mrs Collymore spread her hands, palms upward across the top of the paper-strewn desk in a helpless gesture.

'Mister . . .' she hesitated, 'you didn't give your name.'

'Tennant.'

'Mister Tennant, I've had to take over from my husband at short notice. I'm working my way slowly through the invoices. I'll be writing to everybody to explain the situation and all payments will be met. At the moment I can't do any more than that.'

'Look, missus, you don't understand, do you? I've come to collect. Your husband pays cash. Our collector calls every Monday. When he doesn't collect then I come round to sort out any problems. Understand?'

'You're like a financial adviser?' It was the young woman who made this contribution.

The full force of his scowl was turned towards her. At first he thought she was being flippant and this fuelled his rage, but she was looking at him with a face of open innocence. He glared at her suspiciously for a moment.

'It's insurance you're paying. My company insures your business runs smoothly; employees don't get roughed up; vehicles aren't stolen; customers don't get hassle and arsonists don't torch the place.'

'What's the name of your company?'

'Tennant, Tennant & Tennant. Look, you pay me in cash, now! I go away satisfied. Otherwise. . . .'

Mrs Collymore was shuffling through the folders. 'Mmm . . . Tennant, Tennant. . . .' she was murmuring as she searched.

The flat of his hand slammed on the desktop, crushing the piles of paperwork – the sound like a miniature explosion in the office. The woman flopped back in her chair. She stared up like a terrified animal.

'Missus, you still haven't got it! We protect your property. We protect your business. Without our protection you wouldn't exist.' The words were forced through tightened lips like missiles aimed at the cowering woman. 'Now just give me five hundred pounds in cash which is what you owe in back payments and then every week when our agent calls you give him one hundred pounds in cash, OK!'

'What happens if we can't pay?'

He turned his attention back to the younger woman. She slid her bottom on to the edge of the desk and her dress tightened over her thighs. Tennant thought she was somewhat on the skinny side. He liked his women with a bit more flesh. Sighing deeply, he shook his head.

'Just suppose Colly was here today when I arrived. I would have to be a mite severe with him, you know, like push him around a little; frighten him a bit . . . know what I mean?'

Behind him he heard Mrs Collymore gasp.

'It was you last month who beat him. He came home in a terrible state – nose broken – blackened eyes. He'd been to casualty to be patched up before coming home. That was you, wasn't it? You work for Orchid Brown.'

Tennant ignored her, he was leering at the younger woman. She stared back at him steadily. Something about her disturbed him. She was too cool, too calm, too indifferent to his menacing presence. She should be cowering behind the desk along with Collymore's wife. Instead, she perched on the edge of the desk with her hands pushed deep into the pockets of her pleated skirt regarding him as if he were some unwelcome salesman come to push his products.

'Now, do you get the picture? Mr Brown sends me along only as a last resort. I don't argue. I don't listen. I am not a reasonable man. I just act – violently! But don't get me wrong, there's no rancour in it. I'm just a hired hand doing a job. I don't usually rough up women, but I'm not too particular. I always get results.'

The women could not mistake the menace in his voice. He waited for their response. He moved away from the desk folded his arms and leaned against the wall of the office, waiting. The frightened woman in the chair was the first to break the silence.

'We haven't got that sort of money here. Colin keeps some at home but it's in the safe. Only he knows where the key is.'

'Go and get it. I don't mind waiting.'

Tennant was watching the girl. Women were nothing but objects of lust for him. He used them, abused them and discarded them. What their feelings were about the affair, were really of no consequence. They feared his violence and he bullied them till they obeyed him to the point of craven obeisance.

He moulded them to his will and, when he had reduced them to slaves, he grew bored with them and craved a new creature to work on. But this one was acting out-of-character. She had the power to make him feel uneasy. There was no trace of fear in her bearing.

Tennant suddenly wanted to tame this woman. She had some steel in her character and would fight back, but that would enhance the experience. He ached to start on her soon. In fact he did not know if he should wait. An example would have to be made of Phoenix.

He had roughed up women before and enjoyed doing it. But he wanted more than the administration of a mere beating. He wanted sex with this young bitch. Wanted to dominate her entirely. Wanted to crush her young body beneath him and show her he was master.

By now the fantasy was becoming a consuming itch. He wanted to do it and do it soon. Perhaps he could get the older woman to go for the cash and leave her alone with him. The young woman stood up.

'I've some money in my building society.'

She was staring hard at the older woman as if trying to communicate something to her.

Tennant was suspicious. His eyes flicked between the two women trying to catch some gesture – some expression that would indicate what they were thinking. The woman behind the desk still looked frightened.

'No Roshein, I can't let you.'

'It's all right Francie, you can easily repay me.'

Roshein. So now he had a name. He would have her begging him to do it to her. His loins itched for her – more than he had ever itched for any woman. But he said nothing. Concentrated on the words they were using.

Was she up to something? Collymore's wife had risen to her feet, her eyes pleading with Roshein. Tennant thought she was scared of being left behind with him, but he had no intention of letting Roshein out of his sight. The girl turned to him.

'I can pay you today out of my savings. Would that be agreeable?'

He pushed himself off the wall.

'Yeah, but we go together. I don't want any tricks till I have that money safe.'

11

2

Roshein unhooked a beige raincoat from behind the door.

'I'll see you later, Francie. Will I meet you at the hospital?'

The older woman nodded dumbly, her eyes pleading with the younger woman for some sign, some indication of what she was up to. Roshein turned abruptly, opened the door of the office and walked out into the warehouse.

Tennant followed her through the store, watching her arse move beneath the pleated skirt; the lust rising in him like a hot flood that needed release. They exited into the car-park. Tennant indicated his Range Rover and they climbed inside.

'Where to?'

'I have to go to home to get my pass book – Glenavon Street.'

As they drove through the streets of Belfast the young woman stared out of the window her skirt riding up her thighs. Tennant's eyes kept straying to the white exposed knees. The pressure of the seat pushed the backs of her thighs out making them look full and plump. By now his lust was almost uncontrollable.

'You married?'

She looked at him with some amusement.

'What, like Francie, and end up with some fat slob who has an orgasm every time he sees a Guinness bottle? Catch yourself on! I'm better off on my own. At least I have some control over my life.'

The drab buildings of the city unreeled past the car windows like an old black and white movie. Belfast was a small city and it did not take them long to reach their destination.

Tennant wanted her more than ever now. That flash of defiance against convention showed she had a wild and independent spirit. He was relishing the thought of breaking her. She would resist and that would enhance the subjugation.

Glenavon Street was a row of old terraced properties at the city end of the Falls Road. One or two of the houses looked unoccupied but most had curtains at the windows and all looked in good repair.

Tennant felt slightly uneasy to be in enemy territory. His own stamping ground was the Shankill Road, a loyalist enclave. Glenavon Street was bordering on the Falls Road, a republican area and bitterly opposed to anyone coming in from the Shankill.

He drove to the bottom of the street did a three-point-turn and parked facing back the way they had come in. As the girl undid her seat belt he grabbed her by the arm.

'No tricks! Don't try and make a run for it. I'll just keep going back to Phoenix till I get what I'm due.'

She shrugged unconcernedly. 'I won't be long.'

But Tennant was uneasy. He felt there was something awfully wrong about this situation. He liked to be in control, but she kept throwing him off balance.

'Stay there.'

He reached under the seat and brought out a handgun.

'Jesus, what do you want that for?'

He grinned at her. 'Just a bit of insurance. As you know I'm in the insurance game. This is hostile ground for me. I don't want to end up in the Royal with perforations in my kneecaps.'

Abruptly he swung out of the Range Rover and glanced up and down the street. It looked deserted. One man leant against a wall with only the small of his back making contact with it; a brown bottle in the distended pocket of his jacket oscillated in time with the man's teetering momentum. He talked ceaselessly, his slack lips never quite closing on the words. There was no one else in sight.

'All right, no funny business.'

She looked at him with her habitual amused expression. It was really getting to him. He pushed the hand holding the gun inside his jacket. His eyes kept scanning the houses, the top of the road, the drunken man.

The house had a maroon painted door. She unlocked it and entered. He followed close behind. At the end of the entrance hall he saw a stairway. The young woman moved towards the stairs and Tennant followed.

Now that they were indoors he pulled his hand from his jacket and held the gun loosely by his side – very tense and very alert. He was tempted to rape the woman here, but he knew he had to get his hands on the money first. Once he had that he would find some pretext to take her to a safe place and enslave her. He didn't like being out of his home territory.

They mounted the stairs. He watched her legs as she went up in front of him. He had to stop himself from reaching out and. . . .

'Don't try anything,' he said instead.

She made no reply. As she got to the top of the stairs she appeared to stumble and fall forward. She yelled out some word – it sounded like shite or Sheila, he wasn't sure which. Something clattered across lino on the landing and a bulky shape bounded straight at Tennant.

He was fast all right. He had earned his reputation for being fast and deadly. As the thing launched itself at him he managed to bring up his gun and fire one shot. But that did not stop the momentum. The thing was too big and heavy.

The dog cannoned into him like a sandbag and he went backwards flailing his arms and crashing down the wooden stairs. Man and dog fell together. He lost his gun as his hand cracked against the wall. They crashed to the floor.

The man landed awkwardly with the dog on top and his arm underneath. There was an agonizing wrench as the shoulder popped from the socket. He screamed and threshed about on the floor fighting with the dog – trying to keep it from his face.

He pounded with his good hand at the animal's head. He was badly hampered by his damaged arm. The dog was lolling on top of him and suddenly he realized it wasn't driving forward – wasn't attacking anymore.

He kept his body tense as he held the dog at bay. Very, very slowly he relaxed. He pushed at the dog's head. There was no resistance. The head just moved where he pushed it and rolled back again when he released the pressure of his hand. That one shot he had got off had done its work. For the first time he noticed the red sticky mess on his hands.

The adrenalin drained from him as he realized what had happened. Pain flooded in to replace it. He cursed long and hard. Now he had another problem to deal with. He was pinned to the floor by the dog's unmoving bulky body.

He struggled to get out from under the dead weight of the animal; grunting with the exertion, every movement intensifying the pain in his shoulder. The dog was an inert mass on top of him. His injured wing hampered him. As he shoved at the body every move he made was agony. The throbbing in his shoulder was numbing that side of his body.

At last he was free and he lay flat on his back for a few moments trying to gather his resources. Groaning with the agony from his dislocated shoulder he rolled over on his good side and managed to get to his knees. He hung there gasping waiting for the pain to abate.

Shuffling about on his knees he searched for his gun. In the dim light he found it lying on the bottom step of the stairs. He remembered the girl and looked up the staircase. She was nowhere to be seen.

'You're dead!' he screamed, staring impotently up the empty stairwell. He wanted to go up after the girl, wanted to beat her to death with his pistol, but knew he had to get away from the house. The shot might have drawn unwanted attention.

He thought he was going to pass out from the unrelenting pain in his dislocated shoulder. Every movement brought fresh agony. Fumbling with the front door he almost fell into the street. The doors of the Range Rover gaped open and a youth was going through the interior. The radio lay on the front seat. A second youth was hard at work with a wheel brace.

'Get away, you little bastards!'

Tennant staggered to the car and reached with his good arm for the kid kneeling by the wheel. The youth lashed out at Tennant with the wheel brace. Tennant felt red-hot pain. It felt as if his fingers were broken as the iron smashed into his hand. He snatched his hand back and tried to kick the boy. But the youth had retreated to the rear of the car and was staring at something behind Tennant. Tennant turned.

There were two of them. Shaved heads, leather jackets, dark glasses – almost mirror images of Tennant himself. They just stood there not speaking. Tennant felt the fear. For the first time in his life he felt helpless and scared.

'It's all right, let them keep the radio. I won't complain. . . .'

A short flick of the head and he heard the kids fleeing down the street behind him.

'What you doing bringing a nice car like that into this neighbourhood? You're just asking for trouble. Where you from?'

'I'm from out of town. I got lost. Those kids hurt me. I've got to get to a hospital. Look, I can give you money.'

With his undamaged hand he fumbled at his coat pocket. It was the wrong move. The other fellow had a gun pointing at Tennant. It looked big and dangerous and the man holding it looked very capable.

'Take it easy, old friend. Just tell us who you are and what you are doing here.'

'His name's Tennant. He's Orchid Brown's enforcer. Beats up old men and women who fall behind with their protection payments.'

The young woman stood just inside the doorway. The men didn't seem surprised to see her.

'Orchid Brown! You work for Orchid Brown? What the hell you doing over here? You trying to muscle in on this side of town? We have an agreement. You milk your area we milk our side.'

Tennant opened his mouth to reply. He knew he might be pleading for his life. But the woman beat him to it.

'He wanted names and addresses of people paying protection money over in this area. He threatened to shoot me. I was so frightened I agreed to help him.'

'She's lying. The bitch is lying. I . . . she . . . I thought she was on the game. We were quarrelling over money. I—'

The gun came up and hit Tennant across the face. He fell back against the car. He tried to bite down the groan of agony as his shoulder jarred and spasms of hot pain lanced through him. Sweat beads of fear and anguish leaked from his pores.

'Shut your dirty mouth.'

The blood mingled with the sweat that trickled down Tennant's face and dripped on the leather jacket. He stared dully at his tormentor.

'Get in the car. Tony, you drive.'

He lay on the floor of the Range Rover with the gun rammed hard into his ear. The gun wouldn't have made any difference. Tennant couldn't fight back – not with a dislocated shoulder and a broken hand. His body trembled as if he had a fever. His undergarments were soaked with the sweat of fear. He heard the window being wound down.

'So long, missus, this animal won't bother you again, or anybody else for that matter.'

The young woman watched the car drive out of the street. She turned back into the hallway and dropped to her knees.

'I'm sorry, Sheena, I'm so sorry.'

She cradled the dog's head in her arms. Tears ran down her cheeks and mingled with the dark blood oozing from the bullet wound in the dog's throat.

3

He stepped through the gates. Did not look back. Gerry was there – waiting, a big grin on his face. The gates clanged shut behind him. Gerry could not help himself. He rushed forward and wrapped his arms around him.

'Tom MacLean, you are a sight for sore eyes.'

He could not help smiling at his friend's enthusiasm. Looked at Gerry – at his premature balding head – his long fine nose and clean features.

'You and me, Tom we're going to get legless tonight. Then we're going to get us a couple of birds and we'll not see daylight for a week.'

'Go easy on me, Gerry. I've been away for two years.'

'Aw, you'll soon be back in the swing of things again. It'll be like old times. You and me, Tom, the mad muckers of Belfast.'

The car was an old Granada gleaming with care and polish. He threw his bag into the back and climbed into the passenger seat. Gerry, his face still wreathed in smiles switched on the ignition. They drove away from the prison, meeting very little traffic.

Gerry plugged in a tape – Chaos A.D. Sepultura – grinned across at Tom. Under the raw sounds of the heavy metal he began to relax; the drag of the last two years in the Long Kesh Prison beginning to fade.

He stared out at the passing countryside. Hedges, trees, field gates flashing by. Then houses, a few scattered here and there with bigger and bigger clusters looming on each side. He leaned over and turned up the volume. His head filled with the raucous voice rasping on about tanks and police and riots in the streets as if the singer had Ulster in mind.

Gerry was beating on the steering wheel and screaming out the words with the singer. He was happy. His friend Tom MacLean was back from his stint in Long Kesh. They would party. It was a good feeling. Then came the roadblock.

They slowed down and fell into the queue. The cars edged forward slowly. Around them was an army cordon made up of young squaddies cradling automatic rifles. The police screening the cars looked relaxed and bored.

The Granada moved to the head of the file.

'Name?'

'Gerry Hayes.' Gerry had his licence handy and reached it out the window.

'Where are you going?'

'Home.'

The constable had a square face that looked flat and grey beneath his peaked cap. Beyond them could be seen the soldiers in flak jackets with their SLRs. Their helmeted heads moved constantly as they surveyed cars and buildings. There was a moment's silence before the constable spoke again.

'Where is your home?'

'Can't you read? It's on the licence.'

Gerry was cocky. MacLean did not like that. Best be polite and answer all questions in the correct manner. Prison had taught him that. Authority had no sense of humour.

'Where are you coming from?'

Gerry smiled a brash smirk on his face.

'Long Kesh Prison.'

That was another mistake.

'Open the boot, sir.'

With an exaggerated sigh Gerry opened the door and climbed out and went round the back. MacLean heard the click of the boot being released.

He sat there trying to become invisible. Staring through the windscreen, not looking at the soldiers in their battledress and the RUC in their police uniforms and flak jackets, the dark metallic weapons in their hands the symbols of power.

Ulster was like that. The province was awash with guns and Semtex and rockets and homemade explosives and youngsters willing to set them off.

To be someone you had to have a weapon. He had done all that. He had served his time. Did not want to go back to prison again. So he sat still and listened to the policeman rummaging in the boot, staring at a squashed insect on the windscreen and cursing Gerry for being so cocky.

The boot slammed shut. Gerry came round the car and got inside.

'Bastards want us to pull over.'

The policeman was indicating a gap between the police Rovers. Gerry started the car and wrenched at the steering wheel. The car lurched away from the roadblock clearing the way for the cars behind. A policeman was beside the passenger door.

'Step out of the vehicle, sir.'

MacLean opened the door and got out. He stared at the man standing out of sight of the line of cars at the roadblock. He was middle-aged, in plainclothes.

'MacLean,' the man said.

MacLean said nothing. From the other side of the Granada he could hear Gerry protesting. The policeman was instructing Gerry on the search procedure.

'Hands on top of the vehicle – feet spread wide.'

The plainclothes man waggled his finger and MacLean walked tgwards him.

Detective Inspector Paul Anderson had put MacLean behind bars. He was clean-shaven with a handsome, open face and receding hairline.

MacLean stopped walking, observing the man in front of him.

'Good to be out, MacLean?'

MacLean nodded still not speaking. Waiting. He was wary. DI Anderson was clever and wily.

'You were lucky, MacLean. You went away for being a member of an illegal organization. I wanted to put you away for life – for murder.'

MacLean waited, watching the older man, not saying anything.

'For murder, MacLean.'

'I didn't murder anyone. All I did was deliver leaflets and *An Phoblach/Republican News*. I just made up the numbers for making your charge sheet look good. Another terrorist put behind bars.'

'Ah! You and I know different. How many was it, MacLean? What was your kill tally?'

'I did spit in a detective's soup once. I don't think it would have killed him.'

'Very funny, MacLean.'

MacLean knew it was coming. He fell back with the punch, grunted and went to the ground groaning as if it hurt. The boot hit his thigh and that *was* painful.

'I'll be watching you, MacLean. Make no mistake about that. I want your hide. I don't mind how it comes, either behind bars, or on a slab in the morgue. But mark my words I'll get you.'

He was watching the polished toecaps from beneath lowered lids.

Waiting for another kick. It didn't come. The boots moved away.

'On your feet, sir.'

The young constable was prodding him with his gun barrel.

I could take that gun from him and shoot that bastard Anderson.

He knew he could do it. The constable was young and inexperienced. A quick slice to the throat. Snatch the gun from his nerveless hands. Snap the safety catch off and spray the place with bullets. Jump in the police Rover. Drive out through the soldiers – bullets hammering into the bodywork. Go to ground. He was still a member of the Organization. They would hide him.

He stood up and walked back to the Granada. Gerry was leaning against the car white-faced, nursing his crotch.

'You can go now, sir.'

The policeman was opening the door of the Granada. MacLean slid inside feeling the bruise on his thigh as he did so. Gerry was easing inside also.

'Bastards!' he said under his breath, and groaned as he tried to ease himself in the seat.

Gerry kept repeating the word as he started the car and reversed up on the road again. They were waved through and the car drove past the soldiers.

The soldiers' gaze slid over them then ignored them, their eyes darting over cars and buildings, young eyes alert. There was danger everywhere.

They drove in silence, the good humour left behind at the roadblock.

4

'MacLean, how are you?'

'OK, glad to be out.'

Colin Thompson, white T-shirt tight showing off his muscular torso. Short blond hair. Round face. Broad flattened nose. He had done his time in Long Kesh.

'Brown wants to see you.'

The multicoloured lights of the darkened dance floor glittered and pulsed. Thompson's tall, bulky form loomed over him. MacLean finished his beer and stood.

It was supposed to be a quiet night out, clubbing with his friend, Gerry. He didn't want to see Brown, but when Brown summoned you went if you had any respect for your body. Gerry was sitting between the two young girls they were planning to bring back to the flat.

'What the hell!'

Gerry was standing now looking pugnaciously at Thompson. The blond man shot a glance at MacLean. Would he deal with this, or what?

'Gerry, it's all right. These are friends of mine,' MacLean said pushing Gerry back down in the seat. 'I'll see you back at the flat.'

Gerry still wanted to make an issue of it. MacLean knew his friend had consumed too much alcohol to be reasonable. He kept his hands on Gerry's shoulders.

'Please, Gerry, let me handle this.'

Feeling the steam go out of him Tom eased up and stepped back.

'Let's go,' he said to Thompson.

MacLean had to stand between Thompson and Gerry, willing the big man to move. Thompson was still eying Gerry not sure if he shouldn't hit him – a creep getting aggressive like that!

'Come on, let's not keep Brown waiting,' MacLean urged.

It was touch and go.

The big man glared from MacLean to Gerry, the anger tightening his face then turned and stalked back through the crowd of dancers. He was elbowing youngsters out of the way and getting ugly glares. They made it to the exit without starting any fights.

The BMW was sitting outside the club with the engine running. Behind the wheel sat Rob Segal, deep sunk eyes of a junkie with a straight slash of a mouth and tight greying hair. He nodded.

'MacLean.'

MacLean nodded back and got in the rear seat of the BMW.

Orchid Brown. Gang lord. Flat smoky eyes. In his thirties. Squat build wearing a neat tailored suit.

It was known Brown had a weakness for orchids. Grew them in a couple of large glasshouses, back of his house. Only it wasn't a house as such, more a mansion. He even exhibited the orchids at the Balmoral Royal Agricultural Show. Won rosettes. Displayed them in a glass case in the big house – the rosettes that was.

It was all hearsay for none of Brown's employees was ever invited to Brown's mansion. Only top policemen and politicians were ever invited into the gang boss's sanctuary. Brown mixed with men of influence. He also had a penthouse on the Malone Road and properties in Spain.

'MacLean, glad to see you back in circulation.'

'Good to be out.'

Brown didn't beat about the bush.

'I got a vacancy. You remember Bill Tennant?'

MacLean remembered Tennant. Hard and brutal – a woman beater. One of Brown's enforcers.

'He was found with a hole in his head. Mite careless of him. We're making discreet enquiries to find out who was responsible. Anyway, it's created a vacancy. You interested?'

'Mr Brown, I just did two years. I don't want another stretch. I gotta keep my nose clean.'

Brown reached across the large mahogany desk and picked out a fat cigar from a container.

'Help yourself.'

'Thanks, I don't smoke.'

'I look after my employees. No one gets pinched on my patch. I got friends in high places. I got solicitors. I got made-to-measure alibis. I got men as would perjure their souls for a fix. You don't need to worry about the peelers. You get lifted I guarantee you'll be out inside twenty-four hours.'

'It isn't that easy, Mr Brown. The day I came out of the Maze, DI Paul Anderson was waiting for me at a roadblock.'

'Anderson, eh, what was he after?'

'Me – seems he thinks I killed some people. Wants to take me down for it.'

For a few moments the gang boss was silent regarding the man in front of him.

MacLean was young – in his mid twenties. A good-looking young man with dark eyes and sensual lips.

'There was talk about you, MacLean. It was whispered you were a hit man. Specialized in taking out surveillance units. You were supposed to be good. Went in, did the job and came out clean.'

MacLean shook his head – looked suitably bewildered. 'I wish I knew who started those rumours. It sure caused me a lot of bother. I was political, that's all.'

'Mmm. . . .'

Brown lit his cigar with a gold lighter, the fragrance drifting through the air. He scrutinized the youngster across the desk from him.

'Bullshite, MacLean. You come to work for me. I'll look after you. I need a hit I provide the shooter, the car, the hideaway, the alibi.

'No matter what you say, you were good. Now that Tennant's gone I need to replace him. A grand a week, your own transport, free entry to all my places of entertainment. Six weeks' paid holiday a year. You're hired.' Brown waved his hand in dismissal.

MacLean was shaking his head. 'Mr Brown, I wish to God I could take you up on your offer. But I would be taking the job under false pretences. I'm no hit man. I can't even hit a snooker ball straight. With Anderson on my tail I would be watching my back all the time. In the end it might even draw his attention to you.'

The cold eyes regarded him across the desk for long silent moments. Slowly he nodded.

'Anderson, it all comes down to Anderson. I've tried to find that guy's weak spot. He's a saint. I can't get a handle on him. Everybody has a price or a weakness. For some it's drugs, for some it's women, for some it's young boys or young girls. I can supply them all. But Anderson – he's up there like a saint on a pedestal.' He shook his head. 'OK, MacLean, you change your mind, you don't hesitate. You come and see me. I'll risk Anderson.'

MacLean stood. 'I appreciate you asking me, Mr Brown. It's real flattering. I only wish I was up to it.'

Brown waved a hand in dismissal. MacLean turned and headed for the door. He missed the signal from Brown to Colin Thompson. Outside the office door MacLean heaved a sigh of relief. Thompson came out after him and closed the door.

'Let's go.'

Thomson slugged him in the back of the head as he reached the top of the stairs. He tumbled down, unable to stop from hitting the steps and the walls. But he was falling under control. The days spent training in the gym at the prison paid off.

His young muscular frame bounced and hurtled downwards. At the bottom of the stairwell Rob Segal waited. He had the baseball bat upraised, both hands gripping it ready. Behind Segal was another flight of stairs. As the bat came down MacLean went in under it and tackled the batsman like they were on the rugby field.

He heard the whoosh of expelled breath as his shoulder took Segal in the midriff. He somersaulted once on the stairs. The momentum catapulted Segal into space. Then he was up and taking long strides following the tumbling floundering Segal down the stairs.

As Segal crash-landed at the bottom MacLean jumped with both feet on to the sprawling man. Segal screamed.

Not pausing to see how his victim was faring MacLean used the squirming body as a launching pad. He crashed though the doors and kept on running. He didn't stop running till he was on Grenville Avenue.

Slowing down to a walk he adjusted his clothing and got his breathing under control.

The car slid alongside the kerb.

'MacLean.'

I got to change my name, he thought. *I seem to be the most popular guy in town.*

He had started running when the car pulled on the pavement blocking him.

'Get in, MacLean.'

He closed his eyes then opened them again.

DI Anderson was holding the rear door open.

5

'So you're working for Brown, now?'

'Brown, who the hell is Brown?'

He knew it was a mistake as soon as the words were out of his mouth.

Anderson sighed. 'I sometimes wonder if we speak the same language, MacLean. Orchid Brown, gangland boss. Has a hand in narcotics, gun-running, extortion, prostitution, protection. You name an illegal activity and you can bet sweet-smelling Orchid has his dirty paws in there somewhere. *Now* do you know who I mean?'

MacLean was shaking his head. 'Mister Anderson, I work for nobody. At the moment I'm unemployed. I sign on regular at the buroo in order to draw my weekly allowance that keeps me starving. Sometimes I wonder if I was better off in prison. At least when I was inside I got regular meals.'

'At the moment you're living with Gerry Hayes. We know Hayes sells pirated goods. He's not of interest to me. It's Brown I want.'

'Why don't you arrest this Brown if he's such a threat to society?'

'I have a top ten list of criminals in Belfast I would like to take down. Whenever I get close the evidence goes missing, or the witnesses end up dead, or have a fatal loss of memory. Some day I'll get close to Brown, and some day I'll make the charges stick. Until then I'm reduced to harassing punks like you.'

'Where am I on your top ten?'

For a few solid moments Anderson regarded the young man he had lifted.

'I want Brown. You can help me. The day I collar Brown is the day you drop off my radar screen.'

MacLean kept silent. He knew Anderson was lying. The detective would never let him alone. Anderson was on a mission to clean up Belfast City and Tom MacLean was part of the disorder the policeman was keen to sweep back inside prison.

'You going to co-operate, MacLean? With you on the inside of Brown's organization you would be my eyes and ears. I provide you with drop-off points and contacts. Once I've gathered enough evidence I pounce and, like I say, when that happens I lose interest in you.'

'Why are you after me? I did my time. I paid my debt to society.'

Anderson smiled then, thin-lipped smile with no mirth in it.

'Listen, you punk, I'm offering you a deal. You can take advantage of it and live your life without police harassment, or you can spend the rest of your life looking over your shoulder. I'll always be there, MacLean. Just like today. I have you under surveillance. I can make your life not worth living. Every time you make a wrong move I'll have you picked up. I have men who would give a slice of their pension to get you in a cell and interrogate you. There are official organizations that can whisk you off the streets and you would never surface again.'

'Just who are the criminals in this city? You're threatening me with unlawful imprisonment and GBH. That's kidnapping, blackmail and assault. And what the hell can I do about it? Who can I complain to? Where are my civil rights?'

'Civil rights! What about the civil rights of the soldiers you wasted?'

'Christ, you keep talking in riddles. If you are to be believed, I killed more soldiers than Rambo. I keep telling you I was in the political wing.'

'Wise up, MacLean. Are you going to play the game, or do I slap you down?'

'The only game I'm playing is to keep my nose clean and not land back in prison. You want to turn me into a snout of some kind. Well, I've heard about snouts. They end up with their hands and feet wired together, tattooed with a blowtorch. Can't you get it through your head? I want to get on with my life. Get a respectable job – settle down.

'In spite of what you think, I'm not a thug, or a gangster, or an assassin. I'm just an ordinary guy trying to lead an ordinary life. Somewhere along the line you decided to put me in prison on a trumped-up charge. I lost my freedom. I don't aim to lose it again anytime soon.'

'You disappoint me, MacLean. I thought you were smarter than that. The only way you'll survive in this place is to be on the inside. I'm offering you the chance to work for me – the law and order brigade. You'll get a hundred a week and all expenses.'

MacLean stared steadily across at the detective and was tempted to tell him Brown had offered him a lot more plus protection from the law. He said nothing.

'Just you remember this conversation, sonny boy. I pull the strings. If I jerk too hard you'll be left hanging high and dry. Think about my proposition. It's the best show in town.'

Still MacLean said nothing; kept his eyes on Anderson.

'You want me to drop you anywhere?'

'I want nothing from you. I want to go home, have a shower, wash my clothes and get the stink of pigswill off my body.'

Anderson took a small card from his top pocket. He reached across and placed it in MacLean's hand.

'That's my number. When you change your mind you ring that number.'

MacLean stuffed the cardboard square into his pocket.

'Can I go now?'

Anderson nodded. MacLean pushed open the door walked away from the car without looking back.

When he thought it safe he began the game of losing your tail. Up and down alleys; into side streets. Ducking into shop doorways and lurking till he judged it safe to go back out in the street again, scrutinizing the pedestrians still on the street this late. Watching out for cars that had been on the road when he dropped out of sight. Walking into pubs and looking for a back entrance. Pubs were not good in this respect. All were security conscious. Back entrances were barricaded against hit squads penetrating. When he was sure he was not being followed, he made his way back to the flat he shared with Gerry.

On the way he stopped in the late night convenience store and bought a *Belfast Telegraph*. Familiar faces of Ulster politicians pasted on the front page. We will not be moved.

Thatcher under pressure. Margaret Thatcher the British Prime Minister being harassed by her own politicians. He scanned the headlines. Whichever politicians ruled in Westminster would not change anything in Northern Ireland.

There was a noticeboard in the window advertising items for sale. He paused and pretended to study it. All the while he was watching the street, the image reflected in the glass. He couldn't help reading some of the ads.

Kittens – free to good home. Ford Fiesta for sale. Childminder. Odd jobs done – no job too small. Man with a van. Job vacancy. Warehouseman required phone 66549.

He walked back in the shop and asked for a pen to write the phone number of the job vacancy. The man in the shop gave him one of the wee pens so favoured by bookies. He wrote the number on the top of the newspaper, went back in the shop and gave back the pen. Then he returned to the shop entrance.

The street was clear. He walked the last few hundred yards still alert. Confident he had not been followed he turned into the high-rise block of flats and ran up the stairs. All his care to throw off a tail was wasted effort. When he stepped inside the flat they were waiting for him.

6

'MacLean.'

Gerry was sitting in the window looking at MacLean with a scared look on his usually cheerful face. The two girls were sitting on the settee smoking cigarettes with elegantly exaggerated flourishes and trying, not very convincingly to look unconcerned.

MacLean stood in the doorway still holding the newspaper. He ignored Gerry and nodded at the speaker.

Maurice MacElwain: wire-framed, tinted glasses shading his eyes; long, dark, wavy hair – leather fitted jacket. Expensive shirt, colour lavender. Faint smell of after-shave. Slight shadow of beard on his sallow cheeks. His men spaced around the room. Two hard-faced unfriendly men, shaven skulls.

'How are you, MacLean? You're looking good. Heard tell you kept yourself fit in the Kesh. Must feel good to be out.'

'Sure, good to see old friends again,' MacLean answered, not meaning a word of it.

MacElwain stood. 'Plunkett wants to see you.'

MacLean sighed. He knew what they wanted – it wasn't what he wanted. It would be pointless to say no. It wasn't a word Plunkett recognized, not from other people anyway. He nodded across to Gerry still sitting in the window, still looking scared.

'See you later, Gerry.'

His flatmate did not answer. MacLean went out sandwiched between the two heavies. When they arrived down at the entrance hall one of them went outside while they waited. The heavy returned and nodded to MacElwain.

'All clear.'

The Mercedes rolled up outside and stopped. They crowded inside.

'On the floor, MacLean.'

He obeyed. It would have been pointless to argue. They placed their feet on him. A small humiliation. It was because they did not want him to see where they were going. He suspected they were driving round in circles much like he had meandered around on the way back to the flat in order to throw off any tails. More likely it was to confuse him as to their whereabouts. After a fifteen-minute drive they stopped.

He heard large wooden doors sliding on rollers and the car drove inside. When they allowed him out of the car he could see it was a storage unit. Loaded pallets were stacked so high it hurt his neck to look up to the topmost reaches. Plunkett was waiting in a partitioned office. There was a desk and a computer unit and a row of filing cabinets. Plunkett was sitting on a metal chair waiting for him. A flick of his head dismissed MacElwain.

'How are you, Tom? It's so good to see you out again. Was it hard inside?'

The suit would have come from London. It had the cut and sheen of money. The shirt also was tailored. The man was immaculately groomed. Dark hair was brushed straight back. His face had that handsome Latin look. He held out his hand. MacLean moved forward and took it. The grip was iron. For a moment they tested each other's strength.

'You look older, Tom. More mature. It suits you.'

'I survived.'

The smile appeared exposing perfect white teeth.

'I never doubted it for a moment. You are a born survivor.'

He fished a gold cigarette case from the inside pocket flicked it open and offered it.

'I don't smoke. Quit when I was in prison.'

'Why didn't you come and see me, Tom? I thought I would have been first call.'

'The Kesh finished me, Louie. I don't want to go back.'

Carefully Louie selected a long, black-tipped cylinder and slipped it between his lips. MacLean watched as the cigarette case was put away and a lighter took its place. The man sucked at the lit cigarette. He turned his head sideways and blew the smoke away.

'You were good, Tom. You were the best. We never had anyone as good. You were a natural.'

'I'm burnt out, Louie. I'd be no good to you anymore.'

Plunkett smiled and smoke drifted from his nostrils as he contemplated the young man in front of him.

'You're just out of prison. Naturally you feel stale. But a guy with your talents never loses them. We need you, Tom but we can wait till you're ready. Take as much time as you want. Yes, we need you, but we can wait.'

MacLean was shaking his head. 'You don't understand, Louie. I mean it. I'm not the same bloke who went into Long Kesh. Two years in that place does things to a man. You start to think about things. Long nights with nothing to do but think. It screwed up my mind. I couldn't go back to the old trade again.'

'How are you for money? You need an advance? You're still on the payroll. We took care of your pa for you. We were sorry he passed away while you were inside. But we took care of everything for you, the funeral and all that. He had a decent send off. You're one of ours, Tom. We won't let you down. We're loyal to our members. We expect the same loyalty in return.' Plunkett reached out a hand and patted MacLean on the knee. 'Take your time. When you're ready come back to us.'

MacLean said nothing, the memory of his father's death stabbing low and hurting inside. A father who had disowned his son.

'*You'll never make anything of yourself,*' the scorn in the old man's voice lacerating.

Hurting inside because he couldn't tell his father what he did. It would have been pointless anyway. His father would never understand. Just like Plunkett would never understand how he felt now. Plunkett had sent him out as he had sent out others. Plunkett did not know how it was out there.

Man against man. Men trained by the state to kill. That was who they pitted him against. Trained killers of the state. Skilled in every art of taking life. Vulnerable points in the body, garrotte, poison, knife, explosives. In the world of covert surveillance there were no rules – no morals. Ruthless destroyers of life.

The men he was sent after were faceless enemies. Automatons trained to kill. Skilled in weaponry and unarmed combat, using every dirty trick to kill. Ambush shots in the dark – no warning – striking like serpents. Hidden. Shipped in to make the kill. Serpents – venomous, swift, deadly. Quickly shipped out again. Mutilated bodies left as a warning to the enemies of the state.

He had survived against them. He had left his own victims in the field. It had been his task to seek them out and slay them in turn. The dead bodies stretched out in the field – dark mounds decaying beneath the stars – decomposing – returning to the earth from whence they came.

No. He did not want to return to that. He was twenty-five going on seventy-five.

Plunkett would not understand, would not want to.

7

The flat was empty when he got back. He guessed Gerry would be out somewhere downing more drink. The girls would have fled as soon as the coast was clear. That is if they had any sense. It was tempting to go back out again and look for Gerry and get drunk with him. Instead he went to bed. Sometime in the morning Gerry stumbled indoors and fell unconscious into bed.

He fried the eggs and toasted the soda farls. The crispness of the bread enclosing the softness of the eggs made for satisfying eating.

While he ate breakfast he browsed through the *Telegraph*. Situations Vacant. Plasterers, bricklayers, plumbers. Every job seemed to require a trade. His own trade was not listed. He did not want to go back to that. Somehow he had to live. Couldn't exist on the money handed out by the British State. As he folded the paper he saw the smudged phone number he had written down last night at the newsagents.

Searching through the mess of Gerry's flat he found the phone beneath a pile of discarded clothes. A girl's voice answered. She sounded young. He surmised she was the receptionist.

'The job advertised. Saw it in the window in McCann's Stores.'

'Is the ad still in there?' She sounded surprised.

It hadn't occurred to him to check the date on the card.

'Thanks.' Broke the connection. He was turning away when the phone rang. He looked at Gerry lying mouth open, out to the world. Picked up the phone again.

'Sorry, we got cut off.' It was the receptionist he had just called. 'What's your name?'

'Tom MacLean.'

'Are you in employment at the moment, Tom?'

'No, I'm unemployed.'

He could almost hear the sigh.

'The buroo send you?'

'No, I already told you, I saw the ad in McCann's.'

'Ah, so you did. When can you come in for interview?'

'You tell me.'

'Are you free today?'

Free! No he wasn't free. Gerry wanted him to sell pirated goods. Brown wanted him as muscleman. Anderson wanted him as snout. Plunkett wanted him back at his old trade. No he wasn't free.

'Yes, I can make it today. What time?'

'Just come on in when it suits you. You're looking for Phoenix Fancy Fare. It's a factory unit off Slaney's Lane. You can't miss it. There's a carpark and signs all over.'

'Who do I ask for?'

'Roshein.'

'Roshein . . . Roshein who?'

'Just Roshein will do. I'm the only Roshein here. Are you strong and fit?'

'A bit.

'It is hard work. Moving heavy cartons around.'

'I'll give it my best shot.'

'See you then, Tom.'

He returned the phone to the cradle. Gerry was still sleeping undisturbed. Somehow he liked the way the girl said his name. Tom. Not MacLean. Plunkett was the only one who called him by his first name.

He went in the bathroom and shaved. Splashed aftershave, found a clean shirt in the wardrobe. Gerry's denim jacket. Jelled his hair. Critically examined his image in the mirror.

'What the hell! It's only a warehouseman.'

Gerry woke before he left.

'A shitty job in a warehouse! What are they going to pay? One hundred a week! I can make more than that in a day.'

'Gerry, I have to lie low. Got to keep my nose clean.'

Even Gerry, his friend didn't know what he did before he went to prison. Maybe he suspected but he didn't know.

'I've got to be seen to be in regular employment.'

'That thing with MacElwain, what was all that about? MacElwain, he's scary people.'

'There's things happened in prison. They think I know something about it,' he lied. 'I didn't know what they were on about. When they realized that they lost interest in me.'

'So they won't be coming back here again?'

'Look, maybe I should try for a place of my own.'

He wasn't certain they wouldn't come for him again. If he had a place of his own he might be harder to trace.

'You've changed, Tom. We used to have a laugh together. Go out clubbing, drinking. Since coming out of prison you don't seem to be the same man I once knew. Let's go out again tonight. Have ourselves a ball. Get drunk. Get us a couple of chicks and bring them back here. And maybe no one will spoil it this time. What do you say?'

'Wait till I see if I get this job, OK?'

The derisory look on his friend's face was not encouraging.

He was vague about what a warehouseman did. The girl had asked if he were strong and fit. He'd never been so fit. Two years in prison and a rigorous training regime in the gym saw him fit. He'd never been in such good shape; honed and ready for anything. Only he didn't want to go back to the old life.

The old Tom MacLean was history. The new Tom MacLean was just a regular guy. Nine to five – five days a week. Moving cartons around a store. He couldn't believe how excited he was. A regular guy. A regular job.

He let himself out of the flat.

Old habits die hard. He took a roundabout route to Slaney's Lane. Doubling back – checking his tail.

Phoenix Fancy Fare – Wholesale Only – Belfast's Biggest and Best.

He walked through the gate, noted the car-park – a smattering of 4x4s, estate cars and vans. Inside was a young woman at a till checking out an order. The fat merchant she was serving laughed with her over some joke. They looked up as he entered, and then ignored him.

He stood easy examining the aisles with the merchandise piled high. Lots of plastic goods, electrical stuff, videos, lighting equipment, bulk packs of batteries. He'd never seen so much stuff in one place before.

'Can I help you?'

She was smiling across at him. The fat merchant was wheeling his loaded trolley out through the big doors to the car-park.

'I phoned earlier. Tom MacLean.'

Her eyes widened in surprise.

'My, you are keen. Wasn't expecting you till much later.' She reached for a mike. A ghostly voice resonated through the warehouse. 'Malachy, would Malachy come to the till, please.'

When she smiled at him it was a genuine bright and pleased-to-see-him smile. Malachy slouched up to the till, lanky, about seventeen, in a brown working coat, grinning at the girl.

'Malachy, this is Tom MacLean. He's come for a job. Look after the till while I take him to the office. Shout if you need me.'

Malachy's grin changed to a scowl. The scowl was for MacLean.

She was slim with long, brown hair wearing a navy striped blouse with a brisk white collar, a tight black skirt and medium-heeled black shoes. She looked confident and assured.

'Come. We'll talk in the office.'

She led the way. Her calves were muscular and well formed. He watched her bottom as she walked ahead of him and felt a stir of excitement. An older woman was already in the office. Attractive, with well-groomed hair. There was a family likeness between them. The older woman smiled brightly at him.

'Mrs Collymore,' the girl introduced her. 'Her husband usually runs this end of things. He's away at the moment so you have us to deal with. We were hoping to take on another hand.'

He smiled at the woman, waited.

'Coffee?' she asked.

'Sure, strong, no sugar, white.'

Mrs Collymore jumped to her feet. 'I'll get the drinks, Roshein. You attend to Mr MacLean.'

She perched on the edge of the desk not behind it and smiled at him. He liked her relaxed manner.

'Tom, you mind I call you Tom? We're a small family firm so everything is informal. I'm Roshein. Mrs Collymore is Francie and Malachy you met at the checkout.'

His brow creased momentarily. 'Just the four of you to run this place?'

'Four?' It was her turn to frown.

'Malachy, you, Mrs Collymore and Mr Collymore.'

'Yes, I'm sorry, I'd forgotten about Colin – Mr Collymore. He's away at the moment and we don't know when he'll return. We need more staff, but it's hard to recruit at this level. We can only pay low wages to start with. There'll be overtime, of course, should you want to earn more.'

He made an indifferent shrug.

'What was your former occupation?'

'I've worked casual on a market stall. Friend of mine hired me. Then he set me up on my own. I. . . .' He hesitated as if unsure of how to proceed with the next bit. He had rehearsed the lies on the way to the store, trying to make it sound genuine. 'I was sold a consignment of goods that had been previously owned. I know it sounds naïve. In all innocence I put them on my market stall. I was rumbled and there was a raid.' He looked suitable crestfallen. 'You might as well know I did two years for it.'

That brought her eyebrows up into her hairline.

'I'm not asking for sympathy. I won't blame you if you end the interview now.'

Mrs Collymore had been busy somewhere outside preparing the drinks. She returned with a loaded tray and handed him a steaming mug along with a cheerful smile. She had good teeth. The make-up was subtle. She was a very attractive woman. He smiled his thanks, looked over the cup at the girl. She was not looking at him. She held her foot out at an angle rotating it and pretending to contemplate the shine on her shoe.

'Do you want this job, Tom?' Mrs Collymore had not moved away from him. She stood before him as she spoke. He stared into her eyes, softbrown and moist.

'Yes.'

She could see the truth of it in his eyes.

'Would you wait outside the office while I discuss this with Roshein?'

He stood in the warehouse smelling the plastic and the dust and the stale air, sipping the hot drink. He did not look back into the office. He was nervous. He had never been so nervous in his life. Even when they sentenced him to two years in the Kesh.

Inside the office the women were talking.

'You don't like him.'

'Francie, he's lying to us. Everything he's told us is a lie.'

'It's you, Roshein! Every male you meet is a liar or a cheat or a scumbag. For God's sake lighten up!' She giggled. 'He's cute. Make a change from that lumpkins Malachy mooning after you.'

'Jesus, Francie, you take the biscuit. And you're married anyway.'

The smile disappeared from the older woman's face. She sighed. 'Roshein, the man I married left me.'

'What the hell you talking about? Colin's just come out of hospital. He's not capable of leaving you.'

'That's the trouble, he's not capable.'

'What you mean?'

'That stroke he had, that changed him. Oh Roshein!' The tears welled up.

'Oh God, Francie, don't cry. You'll have me crying with you.'

Francie was mopping up the sniffles with paper tissues.

'The other night when I got back . . . he . . . he was in one of my dresses.'

'Colin, in one of your dresses! No, Francie, you're kidding me.'

Francie was still sniffling and nodding. In spite of herself Roshein was beginning to smile, but trying to hide it.

'You're a cow, Roshein. It's no laughing matter.'

'Oh, Francie, I'm sorry. I just can't help it. Which dress was it?'

'That green one that nearly shows my boobs.'

The sisters were looking at each other and burst out laughing.

'He had my make-up plastered on his face. Roshein, I could have died.'

'Francie.' Roshein put her arms around her sister and held her close. 'It's just the drugs he's on,' she assured her. 'He'll get better.'

'I hope so, Roshein. What if he turns up here some day like that?'

'Jesus, don't, Francie. What about your man, MacLean? Can we take a risk on him?'

'He looks manly enough.'

They were giggling again.

'What the hell! We've had nothing but junkies and winos apply for the job hoping to filch a few goods to feed the habit. We'll take a chance. He looks respectable enough. Agreed?'

'Agreed. But he's only on trial. One wrong move on his part and he's out on his ear.'

8

Roshein had told him the job was hard, unloading wagons, stacking shelves. He didn't find it hard. The lorries reversed into the loading bay. The driver jumped down and opened up the back. Then he would trundle large unwieldy pallets, as tall as a man, off the wagon. They were shrink-wrapped with some sort of clear plastic to keep the bundles together. MacLean had to bring out the pallet truck and manoeuvre the iron-wheeled truck under the pallet – jack it up and drag the whole massive package inside. Up to half-a-dozen pallets would come on one delivery.

Roshein was with him to instruct him.

'Count the pallets and only sign the delivery note if the numbers tally and are undamaged. Can I trust you to stick faithfully to that?'

He was given a Stanley knife to slit the wrapping and get at the goods inside.

Urns, plastic buckets, jugs, mugs, garden ornaments, toys, washing powder, tools, lighting equipment, video tapes, boxes of confectionery, toilet rolls. The stuff poured in and he sorted and stacked it. The goods poured out again via customer trolleys and he helped them load it in their vans and estate cars.

He was amazed at the amount of goods that passed through the doors. When a delivery came in he was sure there was no room inside the warehouse to store it, but somehow there was always enough space to stack it even if some had to go on the floor between the aisles.

'It's like Christmas every day here,' he remarked to Roshein.

'Tom, since you joined us it looks as if we have got busier. You seem to have brought good luck to Phoenix.'

They were wary of each other. He treated her with respect because that was how he always treated women. Also, he didn't want to jeopardize his position.

She was vigorous and businesslike, while Mrs Collymore was friendly and kindly, asking after his welfare and keeping him supplied with tea or coffee. MacLean had the impression she was eyeing him as a potential playmate. He wondered what Mr Collymore was like.

Malachy resented him and remained surly and uncommunicative. MacLean chose to ignore the youngster's hostility, was polite to the youth and got on with the job.

One afternoon he had stacked and priced himself out of work in the store. He did this on a regular basis, finding quicker and more efficient methods of performing his tasks. When he enquired of the women if anything else needed doing Mrs Collymore told him to take a seat in the office and instigated a coffee break.

'Tom, you work hard at this. We've never had anyone do so much in such a short time.'

He grimaced. 'Are you trying to tell me I've worked myself out of a job?'

'Good Lord, no. You're too valuable a find for us to let you go. For a time we've been toying with the idea of a delivery service. Taking orders out to shops and market stalls that maybe don't have the time or transport to come here. Do you drive?'

'Yeah, I drive.'

'It's Roshein's idea, so I'll let her discuss it with you.'

'It'll take a while to set up,' Roshein explained. 'I'll have to canvass the shops that don't use us and try to induce them to use the service. You could work inside the warehouse in the mornings and take out the deliveries in the afternoon. It would mean extra money in your wages.'

He sat across the desk from her as they roughed out the details.

'What do you do for enjoyment,' she asked suddenly.

'Enjoyment?' He repeated the word as if he had not thought about it before. 'Work out at the gym a few nights, videos, clubbing. Not much else.'

'Would you like to come and listen to me some night?'

'Listen to you? I listen to you all day here. What's the catch?'

She made a face at him. He grinned back at her feeling more at ease with her now she had offered the extra work.

'I'm part of a girl band – The Sham Rocks. We play at club venues. If you're not doing anything important tonight you could come along and listen to us.'

'I'd like that.'

He was nodding. Inside he was thinking, careful, don't get involved. Stick strictly to business hours. But he was committed now. Anyway, Gerry would come with him.

*

'Round the back, she said.'

They could hear the dull thunder of the music coming from inside the building. The two doormen looked like they wanted to punch someone. They glared their macho challenge at MacLean. He let his gaze slide over them not making eye contact.

'Looks a crummy joint.'

'No worse than some of the joints we been in.'

'What's she like this Roshein tart?'

'Not exactly pretty, but good to look at. Got a compact body and a great pair of legs.'

'Skinny?'

'No, not skinny. Tall for a bird but good arse. She's nice.'

'You falling for her?'

'Yeah, I've asked her to marry me. She said, yes, only she wanted to meet my family. I told her I'd bring my da. Don't let me down.'

'You bugger!'

They were round the corner out of sight of the bouncers. Gerry leapt on his pal. MacLean let him put a half nelson on him.

'Damn it, Gerry. You'll muss my hair.'

'I'll muss your face, you prick. What a thing to tell the girl.'

They broke apart, threw mock punches and then continued round to the back of the club.

'What're her mates like?'

'One's a sumo wrestler. One's a dominatrix. I think the drummer has a beard. She'll suit you, weirdo.'

MacLean hammered on the double doors at the rear of the building. After five minutes of banging and shouting they heard bars shoot back. The door opened a crack and Roshein peered out at them. Her frown changed to a smile and she opened up for them.

'I wasn't sure you'd come.'

MacLean grinned back. He pointed to Gerry.

'Me da insisted on accompanying me. Doesn't like me being out on my own.' Gerry punched him.

'Take no notice of him, Gerry. You look more like his kid brother than his father.'

She slammed the doors closed and bolted them. The music was louder now they were inside. MacLean was admiring Roshein looking so different in a short green miniskirt, low-cut white fancy blouse with glittery shamrocks sewn on. She looked so different from the woman in proper dress he knew at the warehouse. They stopped before another door. The noise was really loud now. Roshein turned to MacLean.

'Francie is here tonight. I'm sorry, but she insisted when she heard you were coming.'

MacLean shrugged. 'The more the merrier.'

She opened the door and the raw rock music overwhelmed them.

'I'll have to leave you with Francie. We're on next,' she yelled in his ear.

He nodded. The darkness, the loudness the crowd, he loved it. She took his hand and guided him around the room. Her hand was warm and cosy. It triggered a comfortable glow inside.

Mrs Collymore was sitting at a table near the front. She jumped up and kissed him and hugged Gerry. There were bottles on the table in front of her. It was impossible to talk. She just pointed to the drinks.

MacLean sat beside her and grabbed up a beer. Gerry sat on the other side and they were all drinking. With a wave Roshein left them to it. MacLean watched her white blouse, luminous in the dim lighting, till she disappeared. He sat back relaxed. He felt good.

The sound fell away allowing the compere to be heard. The voice throbbed into the room.

'They're here tonight again. Those glam girls you all want to take home with you. The greatest sound in rock bands. It's the Sham Rocks.'

They bounced on to the stage. Three of them. Teeth flashing white and legs right up to their navels. There was thunderous applause and whistles. Roshein slung her guitar. The electric thrum vibrated round the roon. She soloed for minutes, holding the crowd spellbound. Bass coming in suddenly, drums thudding and rolling. Roshein's voice hard and high.

The boy out there
Stumbling in the dark
The scream of grief
Tearing at my heart.

MacLean found himself sitting forward in his seat. Glanced at Gerry. Blinked. Had his arm round Mrs Collymore. MacLean couldn't see where his other hand was. Grinning he turned back to watch. Lost himself in the music and seeing his boss perform on stage.

41

9

He lost track of time. All his attention was on the girl band, mostly on the lead singer. After every number the crowd roared and clapped and whistled. Everyone was having a good time. He had never been fond of girl bands. Now he wondered why.

When the break came he was sitting dazed and happy. Beside him Mrs Collymore and Gerry were in a clinch, oblivious to all else. The DJ came on to fill in. Heavy waves of metal filled the void. Then Roshein was beside him smiling and taking his hand. Tugging him to his feet. He went with her.

She took him backstage and into a room cluttered with chairs and clothes and cracked and stained mirrors. The room smelt of perfume and body odour, cigarette smoke and hair spray. They stood in the room, the music muted suddenly, shy of each other.

'Well, what do you think?'

He smiled that slow easy smile. She was mesmerized, watching him.

'That really rocked. You were extraordinarily heavy.'

She smiled back at him took a step nearer.

'Gerry seems to be enjoying himself.'

He shook his head. 'I can't believe it. She's older than the chicks he usually dates.'

She laughed. It was a good sound in the little stuffy room. She reached for him. Arms up round his neck. She was tall, didn't have to reach far for his lips. They were like that for a long time. She eased back from him staring up into his eyes. Green eyes serious and murky could see the longing in there.

Don't get serious, he told himself. Just a fling, as they say.

'What do you want to do after the show?'

'Go home, get some sleep,' he answered. 'I have to be up early for work.' She reached out touched his lips with her finger.

'I could give you the day off. Saturday is never busy anyway. Francie and Malachy will be able to cope without us.'

'Us?' he teased her.

She regarded him steadily and with mutual need they embraced hard and passionate.

'Us,' she mouthed in his ear.

'Us,' he repeated.

It was at least another hour and a half before the show was finished. MacLean thought the encores would go on all night.

The DJ rescued them, drowning out the crowd with more loud rock. Sometime in the course of the night Gerry and Mrs Collymore disappeared.

MacLean fought his way to the door and into the corridor. The girls were lugging the instruments down to the exit. He was introduced.

Davina, bass guitarist, long and slim with outsize breasts. Elsa, drummer, East European, small, blonde with elfin good looks. The girls eyed him up and he could see the invitation in their faces.

'I can't find Gerry or Francie,' he told Roshein.

'Oh, they'll be around somewhere. Stay here with the equipment while I bring the van round.'

The drummer and bass guitarist stayed to help load the instruments and electronic equipment into the old Phoenix warehouse Transit then disappeared into the night trailing goodbyes.

He climbed into the front seat and Roshein drove away from the club. They turned into a tenement street at the end of the lower Falls Road and pulled up about halfway down. There were no streetlights. When she switched off the engine there was an eerie silence.

'You live here?'

'Yes. The band stores the equipment here. I live on the top floor. Before I take you up there's work to be done.'

They unloaded the band equipment into a downstairs room. There was the rattle of keys as she made everything secure. She led the way up a flight of stairs to a landing, turned and dragged him inside the living quarters. They were tearing at each other's clothing before they got to the bedroom.

He took no notice of the two men when they walked into the store. They spoke to Malachy at the checkout. The men were on the fringes of his awareness as he sorted, priced and stacked a delivery of batteries. Mrs

Collymore had called Roshein back to the office to speak to someone on the phone.

The men disappeared into the back of the store. It was a few minutes later he ran out of pricing tape. Malachy responded to his query with an offhand shrug and a sneer.

He had no idea why Malachy disliked him. He accepted the antagonism like he did the weather. It was there. He could do nothing about it. It splashed against his lack of concern like rain off a plastic mac.

He was unable to carry on with the job he was doing without the pricing tags so he went down to the office to seek Roshein's help.

The office was partitioned plasterboard with glass windows taking up at least half the panels. As he approached he realized something was seriously wrong. He stopped moving forward and quietly observed.

The office was a wreck. Drawers in the filing cabinets were lying open and paper scattered around the floor. He wondered he had not heard the noise of the disturbance. But then the music blaring out in the warehouse would have blotted out anything but the most piercing of sounds.

The thug with the broken nose and scarred eyebrows had Roshein's arm pushed up her back. He could see the agony on her face as the man pressed harder. His mouth was opening and shutting as if he were yelling.

The other big man was sitting where Mrs Collymore usually sat. Like his companion, he had a blunt, scarred face and a shaved head. Mrs Collymore was there also, perched on the man's lap. He was grinning and slapping her face from time to time. Blood was running from one nostril in a thin stream.

He knew he could not get involved in something heavy like this. He had to turn around and walk away. What was happening in that office was none of his business. He had to walk back up the store, ask Malachy to phone the police and then go home. This had nothing to do with him.

He opened the door and stepped inside.

Mrs Collymore was sobbing, Roshein was swearing. He listened to her language for a moment and was amazed at her command of colourful epithets. The men looked up at this interruption. MacLean held up the empty dispenser.

'I run out of pricing tags.'

'Get the hell out of here,' Roshein's 'boyfriend' snarled.

He ignored the man and looked at Roshein.

'Where do you keep them?'

She had stopped swearing and was staring at him, her face twisted in pain.

'You some sort of halfwit? Get lost!'

He moved further into the office. It was roomy enough to hold two desks and a row of filing cabinets. He tried not to walk on the paper files scattered on the floor.

'I wasn't talking to you, shitface. I was talking to the lady.'

The man's eyebrows met in the middle. He looked across at his mate sitting at the desk. The man was staring at MacLean his mouth agape. He had stopped hitting Mrs Collymore.

'This guy for real?'

MacLean looked at Roshein. She, too, was frowning at him shaking her head, warning him off. Her attacker was slowly releasing the pressure on her arm. It was plain he was genuinely perplexed at the newcomer's attitude. He was used to frightening people. When he walked into a room people moved warily out of his way.

'Willy, am I going to slap him, or are you gonna do it for me?'

'The man's tatie bread and don't know it.'

He released the girl's arm and stepped away from her. He had massive shoulders and arms. A gorilla.

'Man, I'm gonna hurt you some.'

He moved forward. MacLean tossed the pricing dispenser towards him. The bruiser couldn't help it. He ducked.

MacLean kicked him between the legs. It was hard and brutal. The man grunted and leaned forward grabbing his crotch. MacLean shifted slightly and kicked him in the mouth as the gorilla arched towards him. The head snapped back. Blood spilled from the broken mouth.

MacLean stepped closer and used a bunched right fist to hit the bruiser in the guts. As the man's mouth opened in a gasp of agony MacLean's left fist hit him on the chin. The teeth snapped together. The beaten man was staggering back. MacLean followed.

He was merciless, left fist, right fist. The head was pounded from side to side. His victim crashed against the filing cabinet. MacLean brought the heel of his hand up under the man's chin. The head bounced off the metal cabinet. The eyes glazed and he slid to the floor.

He did not need Roshein's warning gasp to tell him the second thug was coming for him. The scrape of the chair and the footsteps were warning enough. He whirled, dropped to a crouch and launched himself at the heap coming towards him. His head crunched into ribs. The whoosh of sound as the air was driven from the man's lungs was very audible.

MacLean kept powering forward. They crashed into the desk. The man screamed as his spine smashed against the edge of the solid wood desk. His face was contorted in agony. MacLean disentangled. As the injured thug lurched forward, MacLean punched him hard in the stomach, and then brought his knee up into the face. The man went down with a bump that shook the flimsy walls of the office.

'Jesus!'

Roshein was staring at him with her hand across her mouth. MacLean smiled at her. She slid slowly to the floor and sat there staring at him with wide-open eyes.

10

'We need blankets, or large sheets of some kind, and parcel tape.'

Roshein was kneading her arm, the one that had been halfway up her back. She stared at him blankly.

'You watch over these goons while I fetch the things I need.'

When he returned she was standing over the men with the metal top of the shredder in her hands.

'It was all I could find,' she said apologetically.

'You gonna shred their shirts or what?' He couldn't help it.

She glared at him. For a moment he thought she was going to throw the shredder at him. He held up the tarpaulins he had taken from the shelves in the store. They were still wrapped in plastic.

'I couldn't find blankets. These will do as well.'

Quickly he was ripping open the packets of tarpaulin sheeting. They were bright blue the colour of a summer sky.

'I'll need your help.'

Mrs Collymore came around the desk. She had been repairing her make-up and hair. Her face looked red and swollen from the slapping she had taken. She kicked the man who had been slapping her.

'Bastard!'

MacLean was spreading the sheeting on the floor, Roshein was helping.

'Where did you learn that?'

'From my time as a market-trader. We used tarpaulins to keep off the rain.'

'No, you fool – to fight like that.'

He had known what she meant in the first place.

'My father ran a boxing club. I was his star pupil.'

'You're a compulsive liar, Tom. Why won't you ever tell me straight about you?'

He was rolling the first thug on to the tarpaulin. Blood splashed on the blue, livid and ominous. He grunted with the effort. Roshein was pulling at the man, gripping his ankles.

'Can I help?' Mrs Collymore asked. 'I don't like standing here like a helpless female.'

MacLean looked at her thinking that was exactly what she looked like.

'Watch outside the door. Anyone looks like coming in here you keep them away.'

He was busy wrapping the unconscious man in the tarpaulin, grunting as he rolled him over and folding the sheeting neatly and tucking in the surplus. Next he handed the parcel tape to Roshein.

'Here, I'll turn him over as you tape the tarpaulin in place.'

Gangster No. 2 was making moaning noises as he came round. Without waiting for instructions from MacLean, Roshein got up and smashed the shredder on top of his head. Gangster No. 2 stopped moaning. Grunting with the effort they eventually had the two mummies prepared. Using scissors MacLean cut holes in the tarpaulins so the unconscious thugs could breathe.

'Go get the van and drive it around to the back door.'

Roshein grabbed up the keys and went out.

'All clear, Francie?' he called.

'Wait a minute.'

She went into the warehouse and came back in a moment or two; gave him the thumbs-up sign. He grabbed one of the mummies and dragged it out of the office and over to the back door. Unbarring the door he glanced outside. The Transit was turning the corner. He rolled the mummy outside, and then went back for its companion. It was only a moment's work to drag the second tarpaulin bundle outside and on to the loading platform. Roshein had the van reversed and he waited for her to come round and unlock the back doors.

Again he grunted with the effort as he hauled the blue caterpillars into the van. Francie was peeping anxiously from the doorway.

'Hold the fort till we get back,' he called to her.

Her anxious face disappeared and the door was slammed and barred. Roshein was in the driver's seat.

'Where to?'

'The Royal.'

She looked at him and frowned. 'To the hospital, you mean?'

'That's it, the Royal Victoria Infirmary, or as near as you can get.'

She shrugged. 'I won't ask why we are taking two cocoons to the hospital, but so far you seem to know what you are about.' She drove across the car-park and stopped at the entrance gates when she thought to ask, 'What if we hit a road block?'

'If that happens we abandon the vehicle and report a stolen Transit van.'

She nodded, let in the clutch and eased the Transit out into the road. As she drove he watched to see how she was holding up. So far, in spite of all that had happened, she had kept her cool. He could see her colour gradually returning.

'Who were they anyway?'

'A couple of Orchid Brown's men. We owe him protection money.'

'Orchid Brown! Christ, you are in trouble. He can't afford to let you get away with this. Once these guys tell their story he'll have you put down.'

She was silent. He could see her biting her lip.

'I guess it was my fault. If I hadn't intervened you'd have come to an arrangement and paid him what you owed.'

She still didn't answer and they drove in silence. At the hospital they drove into the car-park. They kept going around the back of the hospital. Ambulances were parked about the place. They reversed into a space by a door.

'Here you can't park there!'

He wore a peaked cap and had a small moustache and looked as if he hated everyone in the world. MacLean wound down the window.

'Laundry pick-up. We're here for the contaminated disposals.'

'You're in the wrong bloody place, you fool! It's around in block A. You can't miss it. Got a green door.'

'Sorry, we're the new crew. Nobody told us anything.'

'Bloody cretins,' the man growled, then indicated the direction they had to take. MacLean waited till they were out of earshot.

'Just remember you belong here,' MacLean advised Roshein. 'Don't look guilty. Act natural.'

'You've done this before?'

'Yeah, hundreds of times,' he joked. 'They must have moved the green door.'

While she drove she hummed the words to Green Door, and old fifties song.

He grinned to himself. She recovered fast.

No one took any notice of the van as it drove up. They carried the blue bundles inside and left them in the corridor.

On the way back to the store she pulled up in Neeson Avenue, a quiet side street. She rested her elbows on the steering wheel and buried her face in her hands. He could see her hands trembling.

'Look in the glove compartment. Should be a bottle in there.'

He found the half-bottle of Bushmills whiskey.

'That's all we need for you to be pulled up for drunk driving,' he scolded.

'Give me the bloody bottle,' she snapped.

He watched her unscrew the cap and take a long slug. Whiskey fumes contended with the stale smell inside the cab. She offered the open neck to him. He shook his head. Took the bottle from her and screwed back the lid.

'You're wrong you know.' She was looking at him as she spoke.

'What about?'

'Back there about not intervening. Someone had to hit back at those thugs.'

'Mmm . . . it's done now anyhow.'

'What now?' She was still looking at him.

He didn't look at her. Stared out the window. Realized she was waiting for guidance from him.

'We'd better get back. Your mum will be worried.'

She started to laugh then, said, 'My mum', and carried on laughing.

'What's the joke? I miss something?'

'She's my sister.' Still giggling. 'Wait till I tell her.'

He grinned back at her.

'She'll sack me.'

'Not after today, she won't. We can't afford to let you go now. And anyway she's sweet on your pal, Gerry. She'll not want to upset him.'

He frowned. 'I thought Mrs Collymore was married.'

She sobered. 'Yeah, her husband is Colin Collymore. He is part-owner of Phoenix. Orchid Brown's men put him in hospital. They beat him up and put pressure on him. Shortly after that he had a stroke. He's not really recovered from that. So what happened today was inevitable. They were never going to leave us alone.'

'I guess.' He was thoughtful.

She started the engine. Began driving.

11

Malachy gave MacLean a baleful look when he saw him arrive back with Roshein. MacLean was too preoccupied by other worries to take much heed of the youngster's jealousy. When they entered the office Francie flung her arms round MacLean.

'My hero.'

She kissed him hard. MacLean was out of his depth – bemused. Roshein grinned over at him. He was waiting for her to reveal his gaffe about thinking she was Roshein's mother. She just smirked and watched him squirm.

'What now, superhero?' she asked.

He managed to disentangle from Francie. Her perfume was overpowering.

'Coffee, anyone?'

'Yes please.'

Francie smiled at him fondly and disappeared in the direction of the restroom where the kettle and sink were located.

'I think the best course is to sell the warehouse and get out while you still have a whole skin. It'll be a few days before those two beefcakes can contact Brown and maybe another few days before he decides to take any action.'

'Sell up because some gangster wants protection money?' she said, indignation evident in her voice. 'This is our living.'

'You can always get another job. And there'll be the money from the sale of the business.'

She was shaking her head. 'It won't work. How long do you think it'll take to sell this place? It's got to be put on the market. A price will have to be figured out. A price for the property and then the stock will have to be factored in. Then we wait around while we find a buyer. And, if it leaks out why were selling, no one in their right mind would want to buy

51

a business with Orchid Brown shafting it.'

Everything she said was true.

'Lock up and walk away.'

He nearly laughed out loud at her lugubrious expression.

'That is a joke!' she said, and was silent for a while. 'What if I went to the police?'

'The police? And what would they do? You know why Orchid Brown has operated for so long without running foul of the peelers. He has some of them on his payroll. He'll be kept informed of every move against him. And even if you reached a copper who might be inclined to take some action, what are they going to charge him with?'

'Assault and extortion.'

'Roshein, think it through. The police are well aware of what Orchid Brown does. They've never been able to pin anything on him. Those two heavies he sent would deny everything and, don't forget, we put them in hospital. If they wanted they would be the ones filing assault charges. But they won't do that. Brown will just deny everything and wait for the police to drive away and then he'll send someone else. Brown will be out for revenge. This time it won't be two goons he sends; the men that come again will be much harder and will come expecting trouble. They won't scare so easy.'

Francie came in with a tray of drinks and a packet of digestive biscuits. Roshein told her MacLean's proposal to sell up.

'The business is in Colin's name. I suppose I could persuade him to put it on the market.'

Roshein gave her the same look she gave MacLean when he first proposed the sale.

'Francie, we're not selling up. There is another way.'

MacLean and Francie waited.

'We hire our own thugs.'

MacLean was smiling.

'Well?' she challenged him.

He was shaking his head a bemused expression on his face. 'You're declaring war on Orchid Brown?'

'If that's what it takes.'

It took him a moment or two to realize she was serious.

'I'm not sitting round like a scared little girl letting some gangster tell me how to run my business. If he wants a fight I'll give him one.'

'Roshein, you don't know these people. They're completely and utterly ruthless. You told me they put Francie's husband in hospital. With the same lack of compunction they'd just as soon put him in the morgue. Those two heavies Brown sent today – they're way down the scale of brutality. There're men out there who will strip a man naked and spend days killing him. The ones who come after you will not be human. These guys are from Planet Primitive. They're scary men. Nothing you have ever experienced will prepare you for the terror these men induce.' He paused and she stared at him defiantly. 'When the police find a body in a field they never reveal the full forensic evidence. They tell you the man died of numerous stab wounds. They don't tell you of the days of agony the victim spent skewered on a meat hook while his captors carved him up. As far as these sadists are concerned the man they are working on is of no more significance than a cow or a pig in an abattoir. In fact, the animal in the slaughterhouse probably suffers less. Most times it is knocked unconscious before being butchered. The human butchers are vying with each other to see how much pain they can inflict before the victim dies. Those are the monsters who will come after you. The fact that Orchid Brown will pay them is of no consequence: they do it just for the pleasure they get from inflicting pain.'

There was silence in the little office.

'So, we just roll over and let them do what they want? There is no law but the law of the gun. This is not a civilized, law-abiding country we live in. This isn't part of Great Britain. It's a lawless island somewhere in the Atlantic.'

'Roshein, I ain't going to argue that point. This is Ulster. This present war has been going on for twenty years or more. It has brought all the ugliness of the human race to the fore. You have the paramilitaries and you know how they operate. Every day you read of bombs going off, or shootings. Then there are dozens of branches of the Crown security forces each pursuing their own ruthless agenda and working hand in hand with the paramilitaries. There is the RUC also using the paramilitaries to further their own ends. Then there are the ordinary criminals like Orchid Brown.'

He paused for a moment trying to find the arguments to persuade her of the insanity of going up against the vicious criminal gang of Orchid Brown.

'A man I met in prison explained Ulster to me by quoting a verse from the Bible. It was from Revelations.

"And I looked, and behold a pale horse: and his name that sat on him was Death, and Hell followed with him. And power was given unto them over the fourth part of the earth, to kill with sword, and with hunger, and

with death, and with the beasts of the earth."

'The beasts that were released from Hell settled here in Ulster. They stalk our streets and feed on blood. They are like the hydra. No matter how many you kill there are more to take their place. This is their ground and they are at home here.'

'You paint a terrifying picture, Tom MacLean. You're telling me I don't stand a chance of surviving this coming confrontation.' Suddenly she looked weary. 'I'll make up your wages and pay you off. You'll get a bonus for today's work.'

'What're you going to do?'

'I've told you what I'm going to do, Tom. I know people out there, too. I don't know what it'll cost me, but I'll hire them to protect my business. No man tells me what I can do and what I can't do. They beat up my sister's husband and he'll maybe never recover. They come in here and kick around two helpless females. But for you being here, God only knows how it would have ended. I didn't declare war on Orchid Brown. He declared war on my family and me. Well, I won't roll over and give in to tyranny. We worked too hard to build up this business. You think I'm going to hand the profits over to a fat pimp like Brown?'

She suddenly stood. Her face was set. Her eyes were flashing fire.

When he was in prison he had begun an art history course. He had come across a painting by French artist, Eugene Delacroix: *Liberty Leading the People*. The centrepiece was a stalwart female brandishing a flag. She was clambering over a raft of dead bodies. Behind her came a throng of men armed with a variety of weapons. When he studied the female in the painting he knew he would have followed her also. She inspired heroism. She inspired great deeds.

At that moment MacLean, looking at Roshein, had a feeling that up to that point since leaving prison he had a choice in what direction his future lay. That choice was slowly narrowing.

12

'The first thing is to get any vulnerable people to a place of safety. They've got to go into hiding.'

She was frowning at him. 'Tom, what the hell are you on about?'

'When this thing starts they'll pick off the weaker members first. The victims.'

His eyes flicked towards Francie. She was over by the filing cabinet sorting out the scattered files and was not aware he was referring to her.

'You said Colin Collymore was away. Then you told me he had been beaten and was just out of hospital. They'll look for him. Thrashing him will put pressure on you. Your sister is also a target.' He flicked his thumb over his shoulder. 'Malachy has to go also.'

Francie had paused in her tidying and was looking up at him. Roshein was staring also. She folded her arms across her chest and regarded him silently.

'Are you telling me to do these things, or advising me?'

He sighed. It was a deep and regretful sound. Both women were watching him. He had known this moment was inevitable. At each phase in his life he had found himself at a crossroads. Like ten years ago when he had knelt by his brother's coffin.

Ignatius MacLean, 14, shot on his way home from school.

Thomas MacLean looking at his twin's face, fixed in waxen death through tear-blurred eyes. At the funeral service for his dead brother the priest had based his sermon on a particular passage from the Bible:

And shall not God avenge his own elect which cry day and night unto him, though he bear long with them? I tell you that he will avenge them speedily. Luke 18: 7-8.

The priest had paused and fixed his stern gaze on the congregation.

'That is the message I bring to you today. God is the final arbiter. It is not for any of you to take it upon yourselves to presume to do the work of God. Leave your anger and vengeance here along with the coffin of this young boy. Let the bile of anger be buried with him. Let the vitriol of vengeance in your hearts lie hidden in the grave along with this pure innocent soul that we have come here today to send on a journey to a better life. I am sure if Ignatius MacLean could speak he would echo my words of tolerance and peace. . . .'

There was more of the same. But the youngster who had come to bury his twin brother was not listening. Already his heart burned with what the priest had referred to as the bile of vengeance. It was at that crossroads he had taken the fatal steps along the road of retribution. It had been a bitter, fraught journey. One he regretted but, looking back he knew it was inevitable he would take that road.

Here in *Phoenix Fancy Fare – Belfast's Biggest and Best*, the crossroads loomed again. The deep sigh he gave seemed to come from his very soul.

'I'm telling you.'

That was it, he was committed. There would be no turning back.

When she smiled at him, that wide smile that transformed her from an attractive young woman to a beautiful, desirable creature; he was lost. All reservations faded. Her eyes were sending messages that sent tremors through him. He tried to look away, but it felt too good. He was hooked. He was committed.

It seemed then the office faded. The woman scrabbling on the floor after pieces of paper slipped out of view. There was just the two of them looking and knowing. He realized she was saying something to him and he snapped back in focus.

'What about you? Won't your family and friends be in danger?'

He nodded slowly. Thought of Gerry. Would have to warn him.

'I'll attend to that. You will have to shut the store. Put a closed notice up – due to bereavement, holidays, anything.'

Her sister was slowly standing knowing something momentous was happening, not sure what.

'Francie, you and Colin are going on holiday,' he told her. 'I want you to leave now. Go home and tell Colin.' Taking over; taking control. 'Don't let anyone know where you are going. Just go.'

Francie was standing up now, looking scared, switching her gaze from him to Roshein and back again.

'What's happening? I need to know.'

He took her gently by the elbow and brought her across to her desk. She was looking at him like a lost little girl. Her world was spiralling out of control. He could see the fright in her eyes.

'It's going to be all right, Francie. We have to close down the business for a time while we take care of the nasty men who want to shut us down permanent. Things might get rough for a while. It's best you take Colin to a place of safety. They've harmed him in the past and they'll want to do it again.'

'Can't I stay here and help?'

'Francie, the weakest member of the Phoenix organization is Colin. From what I gather he's just come out of hospital. Someone needs to take him to a place of safety. You're the best one fitted to that task. You do that and there'll be one worry out of the way. It's a front closed down that we don't have to watch out for.'

She reached up and kissed him on the cheek. 'Keep my little sister safe,' she whispered in his ear.

'Don't worry; I'll take good care of her.'

They watched her gather her things and make ready to depart. She looked at him uncertainly.

'Your friend Gerry . . . he and I . . . we . . . he spent that night at my house.'

He gazed back at her soberly. 'Gerry – it's possible because he's a friend of mine he might be in danger also.'

Gerry hadn't told him where he went that night, possibly because Mrs Collymore was an older woman and married.

'At your house, Francie, what about Colin?' Roshein asked, not shocked but curious.

'Colin didn't seem to mind. He was watching videos in the sitting room dressed in my underwear.' She smiled nervously at MacLean. 'I'm sorry, it's the way he is; since the stroke. In the morning we all sat down to breakfast like the best of friends. It was all right, Roshein. Colin liked Gerry. Invited him back again.'

'Ker-ist!' Roshein expelled a noisy breath.

'You . . .' MacLean paused, trying to frame his query without further embarrassment. 'Would you like Gerry to join you wherever you want to go?'

She nodded slowly still looking at her sister avoiding looking at MacLean. 'We have the holiday cottage in Donegal. We could go there.'

'I'll tell Gerry. Get him to ring you.'

'When will I see you, Roshein?'

'It's best you go straight away. I'll ring you when I can.'

Francie looked at MacLean, made as if to speak, changed her mind and walked slowly out of the office. MacLean looked at Roshein.

'It's Malachy's turn. Just tell him it's temporary. We'll be open again in a month.'

13

Detective William Moultrie glanced round the room filled with desks and police personnel. There was a pulsating sense of noise and motion. Satisfied no one was paying him any attention he picked up the phone and dialled. At the other end Orchid Brown picked up the handset.

'Yeah.'

'Found two of your boys last night.'

Silence. The detective waited patiently. He held out his manicured hand and critically examined the nails.

'Where?'

'Royal Vic. We were called. Two men had been badly beaten, trussed up like Christmas turkeys and delivered to the back of the hospital. They're still at the hospital. We have uniform watching over them.'

'Call off the watchdogs. I want to see those men myself.'

Detective Moultrie smiled. 'I'll have to pay someone.'

'How much?'

'A couple of grand should cover it.'

'You're a greedy bastard! I can spare you five hundred.'

Moultrie put down the receiver with the satisfied look of a man whose solicitor had called and told him his elderly aunt had died and left him an inheritance. The constables at the hospital would disappear for fifty apiece. He was whistling a lively tune as he vacated his desk.

'Those parcels we found at the hospital last night,' he told his superior. 'The doctors reckon they're recovered enough to be interviewed.'

'All right, but don't waste too much time on it. Looks like a gang-related incident. They'll tell you nothing.'

'We'll see.'

By the time he got to the hospital, Moultrie had worked out a safer and cheaper method of removing the constables watching over the injured hoods.

'I'll give you guys a break while I interview those mummies.' He flashed a twenty-pound note. 'Have a drink on me. Don't hurry back. I'll need time to work on these guys.'

They were eager to be let off tedious guard duty and the twenty ensured they did not ask questions. Detective Moultrie watched them go then used the hospital phone.

'All clear.'

The bodyguards came first, big men in dark suits, shaved heads, eyes shifting round the hospital corridor. One of the minders looked uncomfortable holding a flowerpot. It held a single orchid. Seeing only Detective Moultrie waiting, Orchid Brown came directly up to him; stared at the detective with his flat smoky eyes. Moultrie nodded and pointed to a door. One of the bodyguards handed the detective an envelope. Moultrie stuffed it in an inside pocket.

The bodyguards went first. Cased the room. Orchid followed his goons into the ward. The detective kept watch outside in the corridor.

The two men were a mess. Faces discoloured by bruises and cuts. One had his head heavily bandaged. They stared with miserable expressions at their boss.

'Tell it!' he snapped. 'And no crap.'

They had sorted out their stories in advance. They had only just arrived at Phoenix when five men jumped them. Armed with baseball bats they had been beaten unconscious and knew nothing more till they woke up in hospital.

'We fought hard, boss. Downed a couple, but there were just too many of them.'

'You recognize any of these people?'

'No, boss, They were all masked like with balaclavas.'

Orchid listened to the tale, no expression on his face. The patients glanced at each other nervously and did not meet Brown's eyes. He stood beside the man with the bandaged head.

'That looks bad, Tolland. Does it hurt much?'

Reached out, gently touched the head with an outstretched finger. The bandaged head flinched from the touch like it had been a hot poker, looked up at his boss with a frightened expression.

'Bad enough, the quack was worried my skull was fractured.'

'Fractured,' Orchid mused.

There was a plastic water jug and a beaker standing on the bedside locker. Orchid picked up the jug. Held it to his nose and sniffed.

'Is this fresh?'

The man in the bed shrugged then winced as his hurts kicked in.

'Dunno, boss, I could do with something stronger.' The man in the bed beginning to relax as he noted the mild concern of his boss.

The jug was replaced on the top of the cabinet and the gang boss waggled a finger at the man with the orchid. When Orchid turned to the man in the bed with the bandaged head he was smiling slightly.

'Brought you a gift. This is an orchid. Grew it myself. Do you know how delicate orchids are? They need a lot of care and attention. Got to be grown in a hothouse. Had a gardener once.' Pause. 'Left the glasshouse open one night after we had a frost warning. Lost a whole crop of delicate orchids.' He shook his head at the memory. 'When I finished with him there was just enough left to bury in the rose bed. Gardeners say roses like blood. You can buy it, you know. Blood fertilizer. It doesn't tell anywhere about human flesh and blood and roses. But I can recommend it. Blood-red blooms.'

The gang boss paused again, lost in thought. Turned to the man carrying the orchid. Took it from him. Placed the pot carefully beside the water jug. A long black pipe jutted up from the compost alongside the stem of the orchid. The gang boss stepped back a pace, reached out and pushed the pot a fraction to one side. He took his time. Moved the pot again, touched the single bloom with careful fingers. Stepped back to admire the effect. The man in the bed watched, his apprehension diminishing. Brown suddenly frowned.

'What's this?'

He reached forward and pulled out the metal bar planted alongside the orchid and bounced it off the bandaged head. Tolland screamed and sank down in the bed, the white of the bandages becoming stained with red.

'Shut him up!'

One of the minders reached out a gloved hand and placed it over the blubbering mouth. Slapping the iron cosh against the palm of his hand Orchid made his way around the bed to the second patient.

'Waldron, you can tell me what really happened. Forget that shite about being ambushed at Phoenix.'

Waldron tried to sink down in the bed beneath the covers. Orchid judged where the man's knee was and brought the bar down with vicious force. The victim opened his mouth to scream and the iron bar was rammed into his mouth cutting off the sound. Orchid bent over the struggling man, gagging on the bar halfway down his throat.

'When I remove this little persuader you start talking. Talk sensibly to me and you might get out of this hospital alive. Now, where were you when you received the beating and who was responsible?'

Orchid removed the bar and sat on the edge of the bed and waited. His victim was swallowing convulsively, his mouth gaping open. Some of the compost from the flowerpot had adhered to the cosh and transferred to the interior of his mouth and throat. He was trying to cough up the bits of grit. He did not take his eyes from the iron bar as it was slapped rhythmically against his boss's palm.

'Honest to God, boss, it was at Phoenix it happened. There was a guy there,' He kept spitting bits of grit and gulping as he spoke. 'Young man, dark hair. Took us by surprise. We were distracted with the women.'

'What women?'

The man looked blank for a moment then recovered.

'The women in the office. We asked about Collymore like we were told. They told us he was off sick. We began roughing them up. This guy sneaked up on us. Smashed Tolland on the head. I jumped him but was hindered by the woman I was mauling. He put me down before I had a chance to defend myself. It all happened so quick, boss. We thought there was only the women to deal with.'

'Phoenix,' Orchid said then repeated, 'Phoenix. What is Phoenix?'

'Fancy goods, big warehouse. I did that round once,' one of the heavies spoke up. 'Had to come down hard on the owner, Collymore – a fat pig.'

'What happened to him?'

The man shrugged massive shoulders. 'We roughed him up. Didn't fight back. Just lay there and cried like a baby. Tennant told him we'd be back and he needed the cash, or there'd be more of the same. It was sometime after, Tennant went missing.'

Orchid sat for some time thinking then turned suddenly to the man in the bed. 'You recognize this guy who took out you and Tolland?'

'Never saw him before in my life. Youngish, dark hair was wearing some sort of dustcoat. Could be he worked at the place.'

'Phoenix,' Orchid Brown said thoughtfully. 'I think it's time we took a closer look at this Phoenix.'

14

There was an eerie sense of quietness around Phoenix when the 4x4s pulled into the car-park. There were several vehicles parked in the bays. A group of customers was gathered at the front entrance in earnest discussion. They turned to watch the newcomers. Car doors opened and a crew of very large and ugly men spilled out on the tarmac. They crowded round the rear of each vehicle and were handed baseball bats.

The customers standing about at the entrance to the warehouse edged nervously from the front of the building. Trying to look as if they were not hurrying they sidled towards their respective vehicles.

'You men, stop there!'

They stopped moving, nervous – sphincters tightening. Like a guard of honour the batsmen came forward and lined up, glaring balefully at the cluster of men who were now wishing they had not come to do business at Phoenix that morning. The trapped men shifted nervously from foot to foot fearfully watching the goons with the bats.

Colin Thompson, Orchid Brown's second-in-command, wearing a short bomber jacket stepped forward and tested the doors of the warehouse. They rattled but remained closed. He saw the notice pasted and paused to read it.

> *Temporary closure. Due to unforeseen circumstances Phoenix Fancy Fare is forced to close for a short period. When present difficulties have been resolved Phoenix will contact each of our valued customers individually. Please accept our apologies for any inconvenience caused.*
> *Colin Collymore.*

When he finished reading, Thompson kicked savagely at the doors and swore loudly and profanely. His followers glowered at the group of unfortunate men and women who had arrived that morning to trade with Phoenix. They shifted uncertainly and tried moving unobtrusively towards their vehicles. Thompson stopped kicking the door and turned to his men.

'Keep them there while I make a phone call,' he growled, then tore the notice from the door.

They shifted their grips on the shaft of the bats and circled around like dogs herding sheep.

'Back up against the wall!' one of them ordered.

The men stumbled back to cower against the front of the building. Thompson strode across to one of the cars and instructed the driver to take him to the nearest payphone. The driver found one on the outskirts of the trading estate.

'Damn place is closed. Got a notice on the door,' he mouthed into the phone when he got through. Then he read out the notice to the person on the other end of the phone. 'What do you want us to do? Shall we break in?' A pause while he listened. 'No, there's nobody here at all. Just a crowd of punters. Caught out like us. Looks like no one knew about the closure.' A slow and cruel smile appeared on his face. 'Interrogate them? Find out if anyone knows anything? Sure, sure, I can do that.'

Back at the warehouse the Phoenix customers were still lined up and scared, their guards looking eager and willing to break heads. Thompson began smiling at some anticipated pleasure.

His captives waited apprehensively watching his arrival. They stood against the front of Phoenix warehouse like suspects in a police line-up.

Thompson glared at the row of men. Amongst the crowd trapped in front of the warehouse were a couple of women. They looked just as frightened as the men. 'Anyone know anything about this closure?'

There was a rumble of voices, indistinct, a shifting of feet, a nervous movement of bodies.

'Look, we're nothing to do with Collymore,' a large man with fleshy, pallid face spoke up. 'You can't keep us here. We have businesses to tend to.'

'Him.'

Thompson pointed to the man who had spoken out. One of the batsmen stepped forward and swung hard into the man's midriff. He grunted loudly and went down holding his stomach. He stayed on the floor groaning. Thompson raked his eyes along the row of frightened faces.

'What's going on?'

'We don't know no more than you, mister. We're all in the same boat.' The man who spoke was nervous his hands fluttering on the ends of his arms like a cluster of fat caterpillars.

'That's right,' a voice piped up. 'It was open yesterday.'

'Anyone know anything about this Colin Collymore?'

'Sure, he hasn't been here for a while now. Had a stroke. Been in hospital.'

'Who runs it then?'

'His missus runs it along with her sister. Some youngster works here with them along with a new man just started.'

They were eager to help. The man who had been hit stayed on the floor moaning softly.

'Shut him up!'

The moaning man got a kick in the face. He screamed and a bat thumped against the back of his head. The noises stopped. Thompson thought about the information he had gleaned from the helpful people lined up against the front of the warehouse.

'Listen, you pricks,' he called, when he was finished. 'I want names and addresses and phone numbers of all the people who worked here.'

There were murmurs of protest.

'I have to get back to my shop. I'm late as it is. I have customers waiting. I can't let them down.'

'Shut up!' Thompson screamed.

They were immediately silent. It did not stop the men with the bats stepping forward and laying about them indiscriminately – hitting heads, arms, legs. When they stopped beating, except for the odd sniffles and moaning, the silence was almost complete.

'Any more lip and we start breaking legs. You'll have to be carried to your lousy shops on stretchers. Start digging out those names and phone numbers. And be quick about it. I haven't got all day to hang around a damn warehouse talking to a bunch of pricks.'

'I tell you, mister, we don't know them other than by their first names,' one brave soul ventured 'I think the kid was called Malachy. Other than that we don't know no more.'

For a moment Thompson was tempted to jump in amongst the terrified men and start beating them. He balled his fists in anticipation and glared at them. They could feel the menace coming off him and shrank back against the warehouse.

'Get the hell outa here! Go on, scram,' he yelled, and started pushing the frightened men towards the car-park.

His gang took their cue from their boss and lashed out eagerly at the helpless victims as they scurried to escape. As the last of the vehicles exited Thompson walked over to his own car. A man with a badly scarred face wound down the window and peered out at his boss.

'Spider, see if you can find a way into this place. I need info on the people that work here.'

Ten minutes later Spider returned from around the back of the building carrying a file which he handed to Thompson.

'That's all I could find, Colin, names and addresses of the employees. It's all in there. There's not many anyway.'

Thompson opened the file and studied it. Coming to some decision, he turned back to the cars.

'We'll try this Malachy McClendon, Dormer Avenue. It's the nearest. OK,' he yelled. 'Let's go. We're moving out.'

Vehicles roared and snarled into life, the procession of vehicles exiting the carpark. The noise faded into the distance. A slight breeze wafted across the empty tarmac picking up waste paper and dust and taking a couple of carrier bags through a weary dance of artless abandon.

15

MacLean found Gerry in Parson's public bar with a pint of Guinness in front of him and a plate of pork pie. A half-empty bottle of sauce stood on the small, round, wooden-topped table along with the drink and pie. Gerry was studying a horse-racing rag. He blinked owlishly at MacLean. They were surrounded by the murmur of voices, occasional bursts of laughter and the clink of glasses. The place felt warm and cosy and miles away from the dark world of Orchid Brown and his thugs.

'What the hell you doing here at this time of the day?' Gerry asked. 'Did Roshein give you the sack?'

'Yeah, sure, she found out my best friend was shagging her married sister.'

Gerry's face reddened. 'She told you that?'

Despite the seriousness of his errand MacLean could not help smiling at his friend's discomfiture.

'She reckons you're too old for her sister. Asked me to have a word.'

'Damn you, Tom.' Gerry looked down at his drink. 'Can I get you anything?'

Gerry trudged to the bar while MacLean nibbled at the pie. It was smothered in brown sauce. He made a face, put back the piece he had picked up and wiped the sauce from his fingers with Gerry's paper napkin. When Gerry returned he sank half the Guinness in one slug. Gave a satisfied gasp and tackled the pie, no sauce. 'When are you seeing Francie again?'

'She's real nice, Tom. We had a good time together. That was a great night. The club the music and . . . and afterwards Francie took me home. At first it was a bit scary. Her old man, he's weird. All got up in women's lingerie. I was a bit nervous, but he didn't seem to mind me taking his missus to bed. Tom, I really like her. I know she's older than me but that don't matter, does it?'

Gerry was staring earnestly at him, seeking his approval.

'You're a lucky man, Gerry, finding someone like her. She is a lovely woman.'

'You were only teasing, Tom, about getting the sack?'

'It's worse. The company's closed down.'

Gerry's eyes widened. MacLean bit into the salty meat of the pie and chewed while he regarded his friend.

'How would you like to go on holiday, Gerry?'

'Holiday? You know I go to Ibiza each year in July. Never miss. Why would I want to go again?'

MacLean told him. Told him why Colin Collymore was the way he was. Told him about the men who came to the warehouse demanding protection money.

'The kid, Malachy and me, we managed to throw them off the premises. But they swore they would come back. And they will. They'll swamp the place with foot soldiers and beat the shite out of anyone they find. So we have to close down and go into hiding. The Collymores have a cottage in Donegal. We're sending Francie and Colin there. She asked about you, if you would like to join them.'

'She did?' Gerry looking pleased – suddenly frowning. 'Donegal, there's nothing in Donegal, only rocks and donkeys.'

'So, go donkey-trekking. Christ, Gerry, it'll be like a love nest. Just think of it. You and Francie spending all that time together. Sun, sand, shamrocks and shillelaghs. And Colin cooking breakfast for you.'

'You think I'm weird, Tom, wanting her and with him there as well?'

'To tell the truth, Gerry, I'm jealous. I got to make do with the sister. She's tough as old boots and so demanding. No, I think you got the best of the bargain.'

'Tom, I never know when you're ribbing me. What about you? Where will you go?'

'Oh, I can disappear. Slip down to Dublin for the duration. Don't worry about me. Just you go off to Donegal. Have a great holiday.'

Gerry was dreamily staring off into the distance. MacLean knew he had sold the idea. He pushed a slip of paper across the table. It had Francie's home phone number written on it.

'Phone her.'

Gerry grinned at him. 'I've already got her phone number.'

When he got to the house in Glenavon Street, Roshein peered out of the top window with a phone in her hand. She pointed to the phone indicating he had to wait while she finished. He leaned against the door and watched the street.

There wasn't much going on. Little kids playing football. They stared at him curiously. He was a stranger. Before long someone would know an unknown man was calling at No. 27. He was relieved when a few minutes later he heard footsteps clattering down the stairs. There came the rattle of the key then Roshein was dragging him inside to the hall. She pushed the door closed then hung around his neck. When they came up for air she smiled at him anxiously.

'Well, what about Gerry?'

'He'll go. He seems pretty keen on your sister.'

Her face lightened. 'Thank God for that. Poor Francie, she'll have two men to look after.'

'Half man, half woman.'

'Don't.' She batted him playfully. 'I never did take to Colin, but I feel sorry for him now.'

'It's another debt Brown has to pay.'

When she had secured the front door she headed back upstairs dragging him with her.

'The good news is I recruited some people to help out.'

'I'm impressed. What did you offer them?'

She grinned. 'I offered them shares in Phoenix. Told them the turnover along with the potential for expansion. They're curious enough to want to know more.'

'What does Francie think of you offering out the business like that?'

She shrugged. 'I didn't ask. But is it better to have no business, or own part of a successful company? She has no choice but to agree. Anyway I own half shares in Phoenix.'

'You do? I didn't know that.'

'A few years ago when Phoenix went through a rocky period I baled them out but only on proviso that I came on board as a silent partner. At the time I thought it was a good investment for me and also for Colin and Francie. Then all this business with protection money blew up. You see, Colin kept it from me about this Orchid Brown thing. Otherwise I might never have come in with him. It was only when the Income Tax began querying our returns I twigged money was being siphoned out. When I put it to Colin he had to confess where the money was going. We had to make a deal with the tax office. We paid them a lump sum and they walked away from the investigation.'

'Jesus H. Christ! How did you juggle all that?'

She grimaced. 'It wasn't easy I can tell you. Anyway it's time for a little relaxation.'

Again her arms crept round his neck. When they finished kissing she murmured throatily, 'What'll it be – bed or booze?'

'Why not both?' he mouthed, into the thick perfume of her hair.

'It'll be late tonight before our men arrive. We have time.'

16

'Spaghetti bolognaise?'

MacLean shrugged. For a brief time he had lived with a dark-haired third generation Italian. He had drooled over her pasta dishes. *Spag bol* was her speciality. Garlic bread, red wine and the main dish – succulent and rife with flavour. He would relish every mouthful.

The sex had been good too. She was fervent Catholic. When they first went to bed she had insisted on removing the gold crucifix from around her neck.

'I cannot make love with Jesus watching.'

The religious emblem discarded on the bedside cabinet; the gold chain making a tiny rattle. With the shedding of the cross and chain she shed her inhibitions. She was insatiable; initiating marathon feats of sexual gymnastics that left him exhausted and replete.

It had lasted a couple of months before she had cooled. He had probed wanting to know what had gone wrong. It was not he who was at fault. Her religious upbringing had caught up with her. She had been to confession. The priest had told her to amend her sinful ways. No more sex. Pasta without the sauce of love to sweeten it. The memories were poignant.

'I make my own sauce,' Roshein boasted. 'You're going to love this. Open the wine.'

Cabernet Sauvignon. He dragged the reluctant cork from the bottle and poured the blood-red wine. Roshein smiled at him from beside the stove, steam rising from the pan, her face glowing from the heat of the cooking. She looked domesticated and desirable in blue and white striped apron and a large ladle in her hand.

'Can I do anything else?'

'Lay the table. Cutlery in that drawer. Give me the plates. I'll put them in to warm.'

The phone rang. She was torn between tending the cooking and answering the phone. She lifted the pan of pasta from the electric ring. Picked up the phone.

'Hello, Roshein here. A pause while she listened. 'Yes, thanks for phoning. I'll try to get there as soon as I can.' She turned to MacLean, her face drained of colour. 'Malachy, he's in intensive care in the Royal. That was his mother.'

'What the hell happened to him?'

Malachy drove a scooter to work. MacLean imagined the youngster had been in an accident.

'Some men came to the house and took him away.'

She stared at him her eyes wide and pained.

'Brown,' he said, 'Orchid Brown. It's started already.'

'I'll have to go and see the boy. His mother sounded in a dreadful state. I'll have to go and see what I can do.'

'No you won't.' He was shaking his head. 'They'll be watching the hospital. They know you'll come running. They'll pick you up and then you'll join Malachy in a hospital bed.'

'I can't just do nothing. Malachy has bugger all to do with this business. He's just an innocent youngster caught up in my troubles. His mother . . . he's all she's got. I have to go to them and do what I can.'

'Roshein, listen to me: you can't go near that hospital.'

'Look, it's a public place. What can they do? Kidnap me in front of all those doctors and nurses? They have security people there as well. I'll be perfectly safe.'

'If you must go then I'm coming with you. Perhaps I can divert them or at least keep you safe.'

'We can't both go. The guys I recruited will be coming here later. One of us needs to be here to welcome them and tell them what they're getting into. It would be best if I'm here to receive them, but perhaps I'll be back in time. I . . . we arranged a signal so I know it's them. Before they set out they'll call on the phone. They'll let it ring three times then ring off. When that happens they're five minutes away. You go downstairs and open up for them.'

He wasn't happy. She could see his worried look. Cupping his face in her hands she pulled him to her and kissed him.

'It'll be all right. I can take care of myself. I'll be careful.'

Grabbing up her jacket and keys she made for the door.

'Don't forget; let the phone ring three times and by coincidence there'll be three of *them*. You introduce yourself and tell them what the deal is all about. You know as much about it as me. Whatever happens, keep them here till I return.'

He felt a sense of foreboding when she was gone. To keep his mind occupied he turned to the stove and continued cooking the meal she had left unfinished.

It was ten o'clock when the phone rang. He stared in apprehension as it rang the stipulated three times and then stopped. At last something was happening. He went downstairs and opened up poking his head out and looking both ways. Within minutes he saw three dark figures approaching. He opened wide and they filed inside murmuring greetings. He led the way upstairs. In the living quarters they examined him non-committally.

'Where's Roshein?'

MacLean sighed and told them what had happened.

'I'm worried it might be a way of tricking Roshein out of hiding and into the clutches of the people who are causing all this bother.'

'Why'd you let her go?'

The speaker had a head of straw-coloured curly hair. He was young and was growing a straggly moustache and an untidy matching beard confined to the lower part of his chin.

'Perhaps we should introduce ourselves,' MacLean suggested.

The hairy youth nodded. 'Dennis Mallet.'

The second man was older with dirty fair, collar-length hair. Designer stubble covered most of his lower face.

'Charlie Mitchell.'

The last of the trio looked too young to be here in this company. He did not look much older than Malachy.

'John Lamb.' Dark, mousy, untidy hair along with the obligatory whiskers sparsely distributed on cheek and lip.

'So, why did you let her go if you were suspicious?'

Christ, he was thinking, were these the best Roshein could come up with? They all looked as if they would be more at home strolling around a university campus than plotting with Roshein to take on a gangster like Orchid Brown.

'I don't know how well you know Roshein, but when she decides to do something it's hard to deflect her. She was hoping to be back soon. Asked me to fill you in.'

He reached for the red wine he had opened previously in anticipation of the meal with Roshein. Somehow drinking it without her had not appealed to him.

'Drink anyone?'

Three heads nodded their acceptance. He poured them generous measures, one for himself. They found seats around the room and sipped the wine and waited.

'Because of this trouble with Malachy, Roshein asked me to stay behind because she knew you would be turning up. She didn't want you to arrive and find no one here. As Roshein has probably told you she is part owner of a large wholesale warehouse supplying fancy goods to shops and market-traders. Phoenix Fancy Fare was pretty prosperous and doing well till a certain gang who prey on businesses took it upon themselves to offer insurance against accidents, labour problems, arson, theft and so on and so on. For some reason Phoenix either fell behind with the payments or the owner, Roshein's brother-in-law, objected to paying. Whatever the problem, he was beaten up and hospitalized.'

His guests listened in silence. He sipped at the wine finding it dry and tangy on his tongue.

'Roshein and her sister Francie were keeping things afloat with the aid of the youngster, Malachy, the one now in hospital. She advertised for help and I came along. Shortly after I started, two of the gang came in the warehouse to rough up Roshein and her sister. I intervened before I knew the background. When I learned who the gang boss was, I realized Phoenix was in big trouble. I advised selling up, or getting out, but Roshein decided to fight back. She wants to recruit you to help her. Now tonight, as I told you, she got a phone call to tell her Malachy, her teenage employee, is in intensive care at the Royal Vic. Nothing would dissuade her from rushing across to the hospital.' He stopped talking and waited.

'What happened to Malachy?'

'My guess is that Brown's thugs abducted him and gave him a hiding to teach Phoenix a lesson. Pay up or else.'

The phone rang. All four stared at the instrument. For a moment no one moved. The ringing was persistent. MacLean picked it up. The voice was harsh – abrupt.

'Your Transit van is parked at the Phoenix warehouse. There's a package in the back needs attending.'

The connection was broken. The purring in his ear was like an electric insect boring into his brain.

'What is it?' someone asked.

'I think they've got Roshein.'

17

His guests were standing watching him – waiting.

'Let's go and get her then,' the eldest of the trio, Charlie ventured.

'It's a trap. Just as they lured Roshein to the hospital to visit Malachy, this is just a variation of the same.'

They were moving to the door.

'Sit on your ass, fellow. We'll go fetch her.'

'Wait.'

They stopped, looked at him, their eyes unfriendly.

'I have no transport. You take me and drop me near. I'll go in and check it out on my own.'

Charlie Mitchell nodded. 'OK then, if that's what you want.'

They waited while he grabbed his jacket then followed him downstairs. Cautiously he opened the front door and cased the street. All seemed quiet. One by one they slipped outside. They filed down one side of the street alert and watchful. The car was parked on waste ground. Two youngsters emerged from the darkness as they approached.

'OK, mister, we minded your car for you.'

A clink of coins and the kids faded.

Their transport was the Range Rover that had once belonged to Orchid Brown's enforcer, Tennant, now deceased. The vehicle was changed beyond recognition with false number plates and dodgy respray.

MacLean knew nothing of this piece of history. If he had, his estimation of the men he was travelling with might have gone up somewhat. At that point, as far as he was concerned, this trio of misfits were serving only as the taxi to Phoenix and whatever unpleasantness awaited them there.

'Pull in here,' he ordered.

The hirsute youth, Dennis Mallet was driving with MacLean sitting beside him in the passenger seat. His companions were in the rear. Mallet dutifully eased to a stop at the kerb. They were a short distance from the warehouse.

'I'll go on in and see how they're playing it. Follow me in fifteen minutes. But be careful. These guys play rough.'

The youngest member of the gang, John Lamb reached over from the back seat. He was pushing a bulky car phone at MacLean.

'Take this. You get in trouble and you call. Don't worry about the number. Just press call. It'll automatically come through to my phone.'

Surprised, MacLean hefted the unwieldy phone. 'If nothing else I can brain anyone who gets in my way.'

As he reached for the door Mallet stretched over and opened the glove compartment. He took out a heavy rubber torch and offered it to MacLean.

'I'd rather you used this.'

MacLean took the torch. His original negative estimate of Roshein's recruits was beginning to be reversed. With the phone stuffed inside his jacket and the sturdy torch in his hand he stepped from the car.

Knowing the warehouse would be staked out, MacLean began a circuitous route to his destination. As he worked he was sharp – alert. Parked cars were scrutinized, dark doorways likewise. He was doubling back then taking shortcuts. At one stage he disappeared down a back entry behind a row of houses. Except for a noisy mongrel he spotted nothing suspicious. From the end of the street he could see the warehouse, a dark hulk in amongst other irregular buildings.

The Transit was parked with its rear end towards the front doors of the warehouse. Except for the silver Mercedes with the personalized number plate – COL Y4, which had been taken up to Donegal carrying Gerry and Mr and Mrs Collymore, the Transit was the only other vehicle connected to Phoenix Fancy Fare.

Roshein used the van to drive to and from work. She used it also to fetch and carry goods when deliveries to the warehouse were delayed or interrupted. It was also used to ferry The Sham Rocks' musical equipment to and from their gigs. It was old and had rust holes in the bonnet but it ran smoothly. Now it sat ominous and isolated in the Phoenix car-park.

MacLean stared at the vehicle trying to find some hint as to what was in store for him when he approached it. He wondered if he were the real target of the gangsters. After all, it was he who had hospitalized Brown's enforcers.

The caller had said a package needed attention. Was Roshein the package? A mutilated, blood-soaked corpse would act as a warning to all the businesses paying protection to Orchid Brown. Don't mess with the system. You paid Brown and stayed in business; you didn't pay and you end up dead.

Orchid Brown would have accountants working for him to estimate how much he could squeeze from each customer. He employed thugs to enforce his demands. The owners of Phoenix had fought back and kicked Orchid Brown's men off their property. Brown could not let that happen. If word of it got about that one of his clients had given the boot to his enforcers, it might just start a little wave of rebellion that could grow into a full-blown uprising.

No, Brown could not allow that to happen He would come down hard. It would be a lesson to all those people who were minded to do the same. Scraping up the bodies would be hard to ignore. Brown had to stamp on Roshein's defiance and had to stomp down hard.

MacLean scanned the buildings around him. Could see nothing out of place. Listened to the night sounds – the distant roar of a car engine – the ghostly rattling of a train. The dog he had disturbed still barking. He heard a car engine approaching and pressed back into the shadows. He frowned. It was the Range Rover he had travelled in.

Moving slowly, it crept along the chain-link fence that surrounded Phoenix Fancy Fare. Pulled up just past the gates and sat there engine idling. He was aware of a grudging respect growing for these unlikely allies.

The car phone Lamb had given him was a stroke of forward thinking. Now, if the Transit was under surveillance the Range Rover parked in the road was drawing attention away from it. With this thought in mind it gave him the confidence to walk swiftly across to the wrought-iron gates. The chain and padlock that usually held them secure were missing. He pushed and the gate opened easily. Quickly he slipped inside and walked cautiously towards the van.

He stood in the shadow of the van, eyes scanning the yard – the buildings. Could see nothing to rouse his suspicions; nothing to disturb the quietness of the night.

Slowly he squatted staring at the shadows beneath the van. He was sweating when he took out the torch and switched it on. Lying on his back he played the beam of the torch underneath – petrol tank, axles – fuel pipes and cables – searching for anything amiss, wires interfered with, new wiring or pipes, something taped to the underneath. Searching for signs of an explosive device.

He crawled round to the front and wriggled underneath the engine compartment, reached up and sprung the bonnet. During his examination keeping a peripheral look out for a sudden run of feet, the movement of bodies rushing through the night towards him. His helpers in the Range Rover would probably see anything before he did and give him warning. Probably the phone awkwardly pressing into his side would ring.

Lying beneath the van the beam of the torch probed up into the engine compartment. Plenty of room beneath the bonnet to hide a bomb. He could see nothing suspicious.

Wriggling from underneath the van he lifted the lid and scraped the prop in position, carefully scrutinising everything in there. Battery, compressor, plugs, carburettor, liquid reservoirs – nothing suspicious. The cab was next.

His torch illuminated the interior and played over the seats straining to see down to the floor. He pulled the door and flung himself clear. All he could hear was his own heavy breathing. Stood up again and peered inside. Everything seemed normal.

There's a package in the van needs attention, the voice on the phone had said. That left the body of van. Whatever it was he would find it in the back.

He stood at the rear of the van and wished he had a suit of armour. If he called up the army they would have the resources to deal with suspicious vehicles. Protective armour, remote control robots and, as a last resort, controlled explosions.

The door was the roller shutter type. Normally it was secured by a padlock. That was missing. He reached out and lifted the metal latch. Slowly he heaved at the door and sweated.

Scraping noisily against the guides, the door squeaked upwards, curling on to the roller at the top. The gap widened to about six inches and he was still alive. Nothing had blown his head off. He bent his eyes to the level of the narrow opening, swept the torch inside and stopped. For frozen moments he stared inside.

'Oh, my God!'

18

The Range Rover drove up to the gates. John Lamb jumped out and pushed them open for the vehicle to drive inside. They could see MacLean at the back of the Transit, kneeling on the ground in an attitude of prayer his head resting on the tailboard.

The Range Rover wheeled around the car-park and pulled up behind him, headlights illuminating the rear of the van. Lamb had walked across the yard and was saying something to MacLean. Charlie Mitchell jumped out of the car leaving Dennis Mallet in the driver's seat with the engine running. Charlie peered into the interior of the van the headlights of the car making the inside bright.

'Dear God!'

He reached out and pushed the shutter door up as far as it would go and climbed inside. MacLean raised his eyes and watched.

She was lying naked, face down. Charlie bent over. He reached out and felt the body. Looked down at his hand.

'She's still warm. Covered in grease.' He moved to her head. 'Christ, her hair's gone! The bastards shaved her bloody head. Damn it, she's still alive!' His voice grew excited. 'There's a pulse.'

MacLean was climbing inside now. He'd been afraid to look. He knelt at the other side of the body opposite Charlie. With a pang of anger saw the bald, blood smeared scalp where someone had brutally shaved her skull. Reached out felt the stuff messy on her skin. Smelt it. Some sort of vile-smelling animal fat.

'What have they done to her?'

'Help me turn her over,' Charlie responded.

With her body smeared in grease it made handling difficult. Their hands kept slipping but in the end they moved her.

'I can't see any injuries. No sign of wounding. She's breathing all right. My guess is she's been drugged. We'd better get her to hospital. Find something to wrap her in. What the hell is this stinking stuff they've slathered her with?'

They wrapped Roshein in a car rug. She gave no indication of consciousness, her limbs flopping around limply as they handled her. The greasy substance spread everywhere. They carried her gently like a grown-up version of a helpless child to the car.

At the hospital she was taken from them and wheeled off for treatment, nurses wrinkling their noses at the smell given off by the coating of grease. Then it was a matter of waiting around in the corridor. Pacing up and down. Drinking vile coffee from a dispenser. The doctor who came to see them was young, good-looking and fresh-faced.

'She's going to be all right,' he assured them. 'Can you tell me how she ended up covered in pig fat and drugged up?'

'We don't rightly know ourselves. I work for her. She got a phone call to tell her another employee had been taken to hospital. That was the last we saw of her till we found her unconscious. You saying she was drugged?'

'That's why I'm asking you what happened. We think it was heroin. Is she a user? I couldn't find any needle marks.'

'Not as far as I know. I've only known her a few weeks.'

'Roshein didn't touch drugs,' Charlie Mitchell cut in. 'Whatever happened someone else drugged her. You say she's going to be all right? Apart from the heroin were there any other things done?'

'As far as we can tell she's not been sexually interfered with, if that's what you're thinking. There seems to be no physical damage. Her head was shaved rather crudely. Then she was drugged and smeared in fat.'

'Thank you, Doctor,' MacLean said.

'Anyway, I informed the police. It's expected when drugs are involved.' The doctor smiled at them nervously. 'I think they've just arrived.' He was looking past them.

MacLean whirled. Detective Inspector Paul Anderson was standing in the corridor steadily regarding the little group of men.

'MacLean,' the detective said, as he walked forward to join them. 'Now what sort of company is this I find you consorting with? Charlie Mitchell & Co. There was you telling me you wanted to keep your nose clean, and here you are hanging out with Charlie Mitchell and John Lamb. Now I wonder where Dennis Mallet is. Probably hijacking a car somewhere.' He shook his head in mock reprimand. 'I didn't know you were acquainted with these notorious rogues.'

MacLean said nothing.

'So what have we here? A young woman taking an overdose while indulging in some sort of kinky sex games involving lard?' Again, shaking his head as if in disapproval. 'The younger generation! Like to tell me what your part in all this is, MacLean?'

As MacLean opened his mouth to speak the detective held up his hand. 'Let's do this in private. Can't have you conferring with your shady comrades to get your stories right.'

The door opened again and two constables walked through. Anderson turned to them. 'Keep this pair here while I interview this piece of gaol-bait.'

Anderson led MacLean back out of the corridor and into a side-room. There was a large yellow flip-top bin nestling in the corner. One wall was taken up with sink and draining board. A black leather couch was against another wall with a curtain rail running around for private examinations. There were two chrome and plastic chairs. Anderson hitched a hip on the couch and motioned MacLean into one of the chairs.

'Talk, MacLean, and it better be good. I have enough to send you back to prison if I so chose.'

'Aren't you going to read me my rights?'

'MacLean, you haven't any rights. Just now I have you on suspected drug trafficking, kidnapping, and associating with known criminals.'

MacLean stared stolidly back at the detective. 'You're a bastard, Anderson.'

'You know, I've been told that so many times I have to keep checking my birth certificate to reassure myself. Now talk and tell me the truth. Over the years I've built up a certain expertise in detecting liars.'

MacLean looked down at the floor. He knew Anderson was waiting for him to make a mistake. He decided to tell the truth, or as much as was safe.

'The woman's name is Roshein Rafferty. She is co-owner of a fancy goods company called Phoenix Fancy Fare. I started work for her a couple of weeks ago. She was pleased with my work and she asked me back to her place last night to discuss expansion plans for the company. She was talking about starting up a delivery service. We were there to thrash out details.

'In the course of the evening she got a phone call telling her one of her employees was in hospital. She left me at her house to wait for her while she went to see him. Then some friends of hers arrived. You just met them. I'd never seen any of them before that. While we were having a drink there was a phone call telling me to go to the warehouse as there was a package needing my attention. Those fellows volunteered to drive me. When we got there Roshein was inside the van stripped naked, her head shaved and unconscious. God knows what all that's about. We rushed her down to the hospital. And then you arrived.'

He paused, waiting for comment from Anderson. When the detective did not respond he risked a look. Anderson was regarding him steadily.

'Well, that matches what we already know. But there's something you're not telling me, MacLean. Why did they do it? Who did it? And why did they phone you?'

'I don't think they phoned me especially. They phoned the house where Roshein lives. I happened to be there and answered the phone. I swear to you, I don't know what's going on. I've only been working at the firm a few weeks. I . . . I wanted a straight job. I didn't think I'd get employment so easily, what with a prison record. You know how it is. I only work for the woman, for God's sake. How do I know what my employer does in her spare time?' He was shaking his head. 'It seems to me like some bizarre game is being played. She was stripped naked, smeared in grease and her head shaved and then pumped full of heroin. What sort of sick ghouls do those sort of things to a woman?'

'I'm impressed, MacLean. You're a liar, a good liar, but a liar just the same. I don't believe a word of it. There's something fishy going on here and you're right in the thick of it. For now I'm letting it go, but you'll be hearing more from me. Now, get out of here while I interview these other monkeys.'

19

MacLean waited outside the ward till they finally allowed him in to see Roshein. She looked pale and somehow diminished in the bed. The door opened and Charlie and John followed him inside. The nurse was protesting that only one visitor at a time was allowed. The two men reassured the nurse telling her one was Roshein's brother and the other was her lawyer.

'How are you?' MacLean asked.

She smiled weakly. 'I feel like shite. You were right. They were waiting for me when I pulled into the hospital. There were three of them. Grabbed me – bundled me into a car. My hands were tied and I was blindfolded. Never removed the blindfold and stripped me naked. I was sure it was a gang rape thing. But instead they asked me questions: who worked at the warehouse, and who roughed up the two men sent to collect protection money? I was determined not to say anything. They told me it didn't matter. There was some talk about a truth drug. I would tell them anyway. Then they injected me. After that things got fuzzy. You'll have to tell me what happened after that.'

'I had a phone call which told me where to find you. Charlie here and his friends came with me. We found you unconscious in the back of the van. They'd smeared you in some sort of fat.'

She pushed back the covers. 'I'm getting out of here. Get my clothes for me.'

'Your clothes are missing.' He looked discomfited. 'You were naked when we found you.'

She swung her legs over the edge of the bed and sat there regarding the men gathered around her. With her shaved head and the shapeless flannel nightdress she looked childlike and vulnerable. MacLean thought she looked remarkably similar to pictures he had seen of refugees from a

Hitler death camp. He wanted to reach out and wrap her in his arms and comfort her.

'I'm getting out of here.'

'Roshein, do you think that's such a good idea? The doctors want to keep you in for observation.'

'Damn it, go and get me some clothes!'

'Look—' MacLean started to speak.

'I'll go,' John interrupted. He went out.

'Help me stand.'

She held out her hand. MacLean took it and she used him to pull herself to her feet. She held on to him. They were very close.

'Never a dull moment, Tom. You regret starting at Phoenix?'

'The only thing I regret is not stopping you when you wanted to go to the hospital.'

Her face clouded. 'What about Malachy? I never got to see him.'

'Only his mother is allowed in. They've managed to stabilize him. He's out of danger. I told his mother what happened to you, or at least as much as she needed to know. Told her you'd be in touch as soon as you were feeling better.'

John arrived back carrying a bulging laundry bag. He emptied the contents on the bed. Skirts, dresses and blouses along with shoes and socks tumbled out. He grinned at Roshein.

'Hadn't time to go to M&S.'

She looked at the assortment of clothes. 'John, you never fail to amaze me.' She sorted through the clothing, then turned to the men watching her. 'Could a girl have some privacy?'

They piled out the door and waited self-consciously in the corridor. When she emerged she looked pale and weary. She had dressed in jeans and a striped blouse. MacLean thought the yellow cardigan she had buttoned over the top did not suit her at all. As she stepped forward she swayed and put her hand to her head. MacLean was instantly by her side.

'Roshein, are you sure this is wise? Maybe you should wait another day at least before discharging yourself.'

'Tom, I just want to go home.'

With Charlie on one side and MacLean on the other they escorted her to the lift. John was waiting by the lift doors pressing buttons.

'Dennis will bring the car round and meet us out front.'

The lift arrived and they boarded. As the doors closed, a police officer stepped into the corridor. He was speaking into his handset.

'Party of three males and one female going down in the lift.'

Parked in the car-park of the hospital DI Anderson received the call.

'Alert the mobile patrol. Tell them to keep an eye on the front of the building. Watch out for any vehicle approaching for a pick up.'

More static and talking.

'Dark-blue Range Rover approaching. Has parked in front near entrance.'

Voices talking mixed with static.

Anderson spoke into the handset. 'Tell them to describe the driver.'

The description came back. Young, male, fair hair and untidy beard.

'Dennis Mallet right on cue. All right, move in now. Keep vehicle blocked in. Just delay them a while. Routine vehicle check. I want to be in position to follow when they leave.'

'We're being followed,' Dennis observed.

'Yeah, I know,' MacLean replied. 'Any idea who it is.'

Mallet was driving and looking in his mirrors. 'I'd make a shrewd guess it's the peelers.'

'OK, take me to Phoenix. I'll jump in the van and lead them away. Maybe with us split up we might manage to confuse them. Whatever happens, get Roshein home safely.'

A few hours later, after driving to Lisburn and back to Belfast, a round trip of roughly thirty miles, and stopping to fill up with petrol, MacLean parked the van back at Phoenix. The police tail had followed him there and back. He hoped it had given the Range Rover a chance to evade the police surveillance.

Locking the van he began walking. It was early morning and the streets were busy with traffic and pedestrians as the people of Belfast commuted to work. Within a short time he had dumped his tail and got on a bus that would take him close to Roshein's house in Glenavon Street.

They were all there when he arrived. Roshein with slightly more colour in her cheeks was sipping coffee. There was the strong odour of fried food in the house. MacLean realized how hungry he was.

'While I was eluding police tails, you lot have been breakfasting. Is it all right if I grab a bite to eat?'

John Lamb held up a hand. 'Stay where you are, Tom. I make the best fried breakfast in Ireland. Would an Ulster Fry be to your liking?'

MacLean nodded gratefully. The famous, artery-clogging breakfast would do him nicely. He was ravenous. Slumping into a chair he turned to Roshein. She was regarding him over the rim of her coffee cup.

'What now, Tom?' she asked.

He realized they were all watching him, Roshein, Dennis Mallet and Charlie Mitchell. John Lamb, the youngest member of the group had gone in the kitchen to cook his Ulster fry. He gazed back at them soberly.

'That depends on you, Roshein. After all that has happened you can see what you are up against. Malachy in hospital and you kidnapped and drugged up. That was just a gentle warning. If you don't toe the line and pay up when next they come they'll be playing for keeps. You figured out why they covered you in grease?'

She shook her head. 'All I remember as they ladled the foul stuff on me was what they were saying. I was terrified at the thought of what was going to happen to me. They were telling me this is how you prepare a pig for roasting.'

He nodded. 'They were telling you what would happen next if you don't be a good little girl and cough up the protection money.'

'What, roast me like a pig?'

'Yes, Roshein, that's exactly what they were telling you. The police will find a burnt-out car with a charred body in it. So, you tell me what you want to do. My advice is to quit now and pay up.'

20

There was a prolonged silence after MacLean's statement. Roshein sank back in her chair staring at him with a pensive expression on her face. MacLean could not tell what she was thinking. It was John Lamb who broke the silence by poking his head inside to enquire what MacLean wanted to drink with his fry-up.

'You have any Bushmills?' MacLean asked, then looked at Roshein for confirmation.

She nodded, 'There should be a bottle in the cupboard under the sink.'

The youngster was grinning broadly. 'Tom, you have bizarre tastes, but whatever turns you on.'

He went back in the kitchen and after a few minutes reappeared with a bottle of Bushmills and tumblers enough for everyone. Charlie Mitchell took it on himself to pour the drinks.

'Water, soda, ice, anyone?'

MacLean requested soda and Dennis asked for water. Roshein refused the whiskey. She was still nursing her mug of coffee. Charlie went to the kitchen to fetch the whiskey mixers, on the way meeting John Lamb with a heaped tray of breakfast for MacLean.

'Well, if it tastes as good as it looks then you might justly claim to cook the best breakfast in Ireland,' MacLean remarked, as he eyed up the eggs, bacon, sausages and fried bread. 'I have a flatmate whose idea of a good breakfast is a dish of sugary cereal.'

He took a slug of the undiluted whiskey while waiting for Charlie to return with the soda and went to work with his knife and fork. While he ate he spooled back the events of the last twenty-four hours.

'When Anderson saw you guys at the hospital he seemed to know you. You fellows got form or something?'

His three companions looked at each other before returning his gaze. 'We're no angels, if that's what you mean,' Charlie told him. 'So far we've managed to keep one step ahead of the peelers.'

'What do you do, if that's not too indiscreet a question to ask?'

'Whatever offers an opportunity to make a quid or two,' Charlie offered vaguely. 'We cater to the criminal classes. You need a fast car, Dennis will fix you up. Even drive the car sometimes. Need a shooter for a robbery, or a bit of Semtex to blow a safe. Whatever the guy needs we can supply. We provide anything from a complete computer system to counterfeit money. John here will crack any security system and hack into any computer and phone network. We all have our talents. What do you do?'

'Have you done time?' MacLean asked, evading the question.

The trio grinned at each other. 'Some, when we were younger.'

Christ, thought MacLean, when they were younger! They must have started their criminal careers when still at school.

'Now, we're a bit smarter. Nothing we do is traceable back to us. You see, we don't actually commit the crimes. All we do is supply the hardware and the technical expertise. If necessary we dispose of any swag. Also, if someone needs an alibi we can supply that. So you see, the peelers may suspect us of being involved in a particular crime, but they can never pin anything on us.

'Anderson has had us all in at some time or other and applied the third degree. He's pretty sharp is Anderson, but he can never trace anything to us. It's a battle of wits between the law-and-order brigade of Ulster and us. Anyway, mostly they're too busy chasing the paramilitaries to devote any amount of manpower to dealing with us petty criminals.'

MacLean pushed the empty plate away from him. He sat back and gave a contented burp.

'Pardon,' he apologized. 'John, you were quite right. That was the best breakfast I've had since I left home as a kid.'

His glass of whiskey was empty and reaching for the bottle he replenished it with another generous measure.

Throughout this exchange Roshein had said nothing. She was sitting huddled on a big comfortable settee piled with scatter cushions. With her shaved head MacLean was thinking she looked curiously alluring and altered in some unique way.

The upstairs floor of the house had been converted to a self-contained flat with bedroom, bathroom, kitchen and living room. The furniture was mismatched but of good quality. Bookshelves lined one wall. It was carpeted throughout with deep pile beige carpet. Large comfortable upholstered chairs made up the seating. A big TV in one corner watched over everything like an all-seeing eye. MacLean had never seen the TV switched on. By the window a small coffee table held the telephone and directories.

'Roshein, I can see you deep in thought. Care to share your thoughts with us?'

She turned her head and stared at him. MacLean could see the colour had crept back into her face as she sat among friends in the comfort of her own home and drank the hot coffee.

'Those people, they can do what they like,' she said eventually. 'When Colin was threatened and then beaten by a couple of their thugs I advised him to go to the police. Colin refused to do so. His words were, 'I don't want Francie to find me some morning lying in the front garden with my guts spilled all over the lawn.' The truth is, Colin hadn't got the money to pay his arrears for the protection they offered him. What we weren't aware of at the time is that on top of everything else, Colin had a gambling habit. He was losing more money than Phoenix was making. The strain of it all was too much and he became ill. Then he had a stroke. I suppose the stress must have brought it on. Just after Colin had his stroke, a man came to demand the arrears built up while Colin was going through his difficult patch. His name was Tennant.' She fell silent at that juncture.

MacLean was thinking of the job offer from Orchid Brown. He had wanted MacLean to replace Tennant. The enforcer had been murdered and MacLean was offered his job.

'This Tennant, I heard something about him,' he said. 'Wasn't he bumped off? If another gang is muscling in on Brown they might be too busy fighting amongst themselves to bother about us.'

The other men in the room were nodding thoughtfully.

'I was responsible for his death,' Roshein said unexpectedly.

That got their attention.

'When he came to the warehouse demanding money I lured him over here on the pretext of paying him off. As you probably know this is Provo territory. There's a network of spies and informers. When Tennant arrived, an alert must have gone out. At least that was what I was hoping. The boys don't take kindly to men like Tennant. He was lifted and that was the last I heard from him. He was found dead a few days later.'

She left out her own part in Tennant's downfall.

MacLean was unaware he had been holding his breath during the latter part of Roshein's narrative. He began to breathe again then took a slug of whiskey. The men in the room were staring at Roshein with concerted attention.

'When the peelers questioned me about the events of last night I told them I believed it was people from Orchid Brown's organization who kidnapped me and attacked Malachy. I explained that they were asking for protection money that I couldn't pay. They asked me if I could identify the men I was accusing. When I told them they were wearing balaclavas and that I was blindfolded, they told me without a positive ID, as they put it, then there was no point in trying to pin the crimes on Orchid Brown.'

When she finished speaking there was silence as each of her listeners thought over her story. Before anyone could speak, Roshein continued, 'I'm just a helpless victim caught up in a gangster's crooked racket. At any time he can increase his demands and bleed my business dry. Where does it all end? If my band The Sham Rocks become successful and start earning big money, will these crooks want a percentage of that also? I feel like a fly trapped in a jam jar with the lid screwed on tight. I'm battering against the glass, but there's no way out unless I can smash the jar, or someone lets me out. The people who might let me out are the police and they're helpless, or unwilling, to do anything for me. I'm on my own in this thing. Orchid Brown may put me under, but I won't go down without a fight.'

'You're not alone, Roshein.'

She stared over at him, her eyes full of gratitude and something else that made him realize what had really pressed him into siding with her. He was aware of the others in the room muttering that they too were joining forces with them.

With the sense he'd come to the crossroads and stumbled in a direction over which he seemed to have no control, MacLean smiled over at Roshein and raised up his glass. Around the room glasses were raised.

'There's an old proverb I think would be appropriate to this moment,' Charlie said. He had a mischievous look on his face. 'The last kick of a dying rat is always the worst.'

They were laughing and drinking the toast. Four men and one woman committing themselves to take on a gang of mobsters.

21

'Now we're committed,' Charlie said, 'we need some sort of plan. Anyone got any ideas?'

For a time no one responded to his question. A deep silence prevailed.

'Let's start with the basics,' John said at last. 'Orchid Brown is the problem. We have to make him back away from Roshein and her family and her business at Phoenix. In order to do that we have to frighten or damage him so much that in the end he comes to believe it's not worth all the aggro.'

'Can you see Brown being frightened off? He's a tough, ruthless gangster.'

'Yeah, it's not going to be easy. Brute force won't do it. And anyway, we haven't enough muscle to damage Brown in that way. It'll have to be something subtler. We need to probe somewhat and find out where he might be vulnerable. Like all men, he'll have strengths and weaknesses. Does he have a family? What about girlfriends?'

MacLean was shaking his head. 'You don't know Brown. If you killed his pet dog and his favourite girlfriend he'll put it down to collateral damage and keep on coming after you. He has none of the customary human feelings like compassion or fear. The only thing he respects is power and money and brute force. And Orchid Brown is an expert in manipulating all three to his advantage.'

'Could we lure him somewhere like I did with Tennant and dispose of him that way?'

The four men looked at Roshein and thought over her suggestion.

'Brown goes nowhere without his bodyguards,' MacLean asserted. 'I'm sure you all know the type – big, brutal and more than likely tooled up. There are only us five gathered here. Somehow I can't see us taking on Brown's crowd.'

Charlie moved to the telephone table and fetched a notepad.

'Let's make a list of all the things we know about Brown. Maybe somewhere there's something we can use.'

The group exchanged what sketchy knowledge they had of the gang boss while Charlie made notes.

'Gangster,' Charlie read off the list, 'activities – protection rackets, brothels, nightclubs, betting shops, drugs. Not married but has an assortment of girlfriends. Other family – don't know. Hobbies – growing exotic orchids. Well, there's not a great deal there. Any streetwise urchin could have told us as much.'

'This man loves his power, loves his wealth, loves the fear he brings on,' MacLean said thoughtfully. 'As far as I know no one has ever crossed him and lived to tell the tale. Or, if they have survived, it's more than likely they're in a wheelchair, or on a life support machine. Bodyguards surround him day and night. How can you hurt a man like that?'

He got up and began to pace about the room. His companions watched him. They sensed MacLean was turning something over in his mind trying to get it straight before putting his ideas into words.

'We all agree we can't get to Brown himself.'

They nodded watching him attentively.

'Why don't we take a leaf out of Brown's book? What if we go after Brown's business assets and hit him where it'll hurt the most?'

'What are you getting at, Tom?' Roshein asked. 'You think we should go into the protection racket and offer Brown's businesses protection?'

'Brown has a number of businesses – mostly illegitimate admittedly, but businesses all the same. That's where his strength comes from. That's where he gets the money to pay his thugs and shell out bribes to the police. Suppose those businesses began to suffer. Bookies are held up and the tills raided – same with brothels. The men collecting protection money are waylaid and relieved of their cash collections. Nightclubs – that would take a bit of thinking through. And with his involvement in the drug trade we can waylay the dealers. As well as all that he's probably into buying and selling illicit booze. We hit him any which way we can.'

He had their full attention.

'Putting the squeeze on the racketeers,' Charlie said. He was shaking his head looking bemused as he spoke. 'Ripping off the gangsters. Playing them at their own game. Christ on a crutch, that's some leap of imagination.'

MacLean gazed round at his companions trying to gauge their reactions to his proposals. The whiskey and lack of sleep were beginning to take effect. John was yawning, his mouth wide open. Dennis was looking bleary-eyed and his head kept nodding forward. Roshein looked wan and wretched. The only one who had maintained some degree of alertness was Charlie.

'Hell, let's call it a day, or a day and a night,' he suggested. 'You all look done in. We're all whacked after a hard day's night We go our separate ways for now and meet again to discuss our plans.' He eyed each one of the men. 'I won't take it amiss if you have second thoughts about all this. But in case you don't, let's say we meet again this evening, or if you want longer to think about everything we can make it tomorrow.'

They got to their feet and stretched wearily. MacLean went downstairs to let everyone out and make the place secure again. When he came back upstairs Roshein was still in the same huddled position on the settee.

'Is there anything I can do for you?' he asked.

She grimaced. 'Grow me a head of hair and pour a dose of headache mixture into me. Then I might begin to feel human again.'

'I wouldn't worry about your appearance. Actually that shaved head is quite sexy. Are you sure you're going to be all right? I'll have to leave you now till the next meeting of the gang.'

'Where are you going, or shouldn't I ask?'

He shrugged. 'I have to find somewhere to live. I'm worried they might know about Gerry's flat now. I'll have to move out of there. I'm sure I'll find a cheap doss-house willing to take me in.'

'Would you think me a bold girl if I suggested you could move in here for now?'

Surprised, he frowned and pursed his lips in thought.

'OK, but only on one condition.'

'What's that?'

'We consider it purely as a temporary move. Right now you're probably feeling wobbly and vulnerable. When you've recovered your normal self you might regret having invited a stranger into your home.'

She managed a wry grin and he could detect a spark of her old self returning.

'Would that stranger mind putting a wobbly, bald female to bed? I feel as if I could sleep for a week.'

They both were of the opinion they were too tired to be interested in anything other than sleep. However youth is resilient. Eventually, exhausted and replete they fell into a deep sleep.

22

The black taxi was parked across the street from the betting office. Dennis Mallet, the driver was wearing a cloth cap along with heavy rimmed glasses. In the back sat two men. The paintwork of the taxi was filthy as if it had been driving along muddy country tracks. Dirt had adhered to the windows making it difficult to make out the two passengers in the back of the cab. They might have been clergymen for they were dressed in dark clothing.

All was normal inside the betting shop. Flickering TV screens brought results and races to the punters peering up at the images and consulting newspapers and betting slips. Cigarette smoke drifted up to be sucked at by an ineffectual fan making a faint whirring sound lost in the hum of TV clatter and punters conferring over racing form and betting odds.

No one took any notice of the youngster sitting on one of the padded benches arranged around the walls of the shop. He had an unwieldy car phone pressed against his ear and a peaked cap pulled down low across his eyes. If anyone did take notice they would assume he was getting betting information direct from the racing track. In fact he was in contact with the cab parked across the street. John Lamb was giving a running commentary on the number of people inside the bookies.

'About fifteen punters in here now. The next race starts shortly. Their attention is on the TV screens waiting for the latest prices. If it's all clear in the street, any time in the next few minutes is as good a time as any.'

In the cab, John's voice was coming over the speaker sounding like the voice of a taxi controller. MacLean was waiting for the report from the young woman idling in the street some distance away. Roshein was standing with a parcel under her arm and was also was talking into a car phone.

'Street clear except for a green van. Can't see the driver. Probably making a delivery and is inside one of the shops.'

The information coming in from Roshein was also audible inside the taxicab.

'Go!'

As MacLean barked out the order he pulled the balaclava down over his head. Beside him Charlie was doing the same. They spilled out of the taxi and were running across the road. Both men carried sawn-off, pump-action shotguns.

Seeing his accomplices coming across the road John was at the door and opening it as if in the act of leaving when the two men burst in.

'Everybody down!' MacLean screamed.

Charlie stepped away from MacLean and aimed his shotgun at the row of TV sets that also by coincidence housed a video camera already sussed out by John. The report of the shotgun was deafening. Customers were diving to the floor. The suddenness and the shock of the shotgun blast that destroyed the TV system was terrifying and demoralizing.

MacLean was at the serving hatches. He shoved the barrels of the shotgun into the glass that separated the clerks from their customers. The window disintegrated in a cascade of glass fragments. When the glass showered the men inside the booth they were already cowed by the first blast from Charlie's shotgun. Their hands shot into the air without being asked.

'Stay still!' MacLean yelled. 'No alarms or heroes today.'

MacLean pushed a canvas sack in through the broken window.

'Fill that with cash,' he yelled. 'Now! Now! Now! Hurry! Hurry!'

As he bawled out his orders he waggled the shotgun about inside the window. 'Come on! Come on! I've not got all day.'

Two of the clerks grabbed the sack and began emptying cash drawers. Thick wads of banknotes were stuffed into the sack. Their hands were shaking so much some of the money escaped and sack and fluttered to the floor.

'Hurry!' MacLean screamed again. 'All of it! Don't hold out on me.'

With trembling hands the men pushed the sack toward the masked robber. The canvas bag was spilling over with banknotes. MacLean had to jerk hard to pull the bulging sack through the broken window. Clutching his swag MacLean turned and was moving swiftly towards the door.

Charlie was walking backwards after him threatening the men in the shop with his shotgun. There was no sign of John Lamb.

The raiders were outside and running across the street towards the taxi. The rear doors of the taxi were lying wide open. As they tumbled inside, the vehicle took off. The two robbers were frantically trying to pull shut the doors behind them. Before they reached the end of the street the doors were shut and the black vehicle turned the corner and was lost to sight.

Several streets away the taxi pulled into the kerb. Two passengers alighted. They were wearing dog collars and carrying what looked like snooker cue cases. The taxi driver got out of the cab and strolled in the opposite direction from that of the two priests. He was carrying a large canvas holdall.

Not far down the street the clerics got into a blue Ford Focus hatchback. The young woman who had been talking into the phone outside the bookies' was in the driving seat. The car engine was already running and, as soon as the two priests were inside, the vehicle drove off.

No one took any notice of the abandoned taxi until later in the day a nervous pedestrian phoned the police and reported it. Within an hour of being notified, the police had cordoned off the street and evacuated the inhabitants. Any abandoned vehicle in Northern Ireland was treated as a potential car bomb.

The EOD, Explosive Ordnance Disposal unit, was summoned from the army barracks at Lisburn. Another hour passed before the bomb disposal crew arrived on the scene.

The mud-splattered taxi sat innocuously in the street while police and army conferred.

'How long has the suspect vehicle been there?' the captain from the OED asked.

'We think it's been here a few hours,' the RUC sergeant replied. 'There was an armed robbery in Edison Street just a short distance away. That happened at 15.30 hours. Witnesses say the robbers used a taxi to get away. If this is the vehicle used in the robbery then it's been here since shortly after the robbery. That means it's been there well over an hour, or at most an hour and a half.'

'Damn! You think they put explosives in the getaway car?'

'Highly likely, sir. The explosion would destroy any forensic they may have left behind.'

'Mmm . . . I guess we'll have to use the Wheelbarrow.'

The colonel issued instructions to his team of technicians. A ramp was quickly erected behind the army truck. There was the whirr of an electric motor starting up and a low wagon emerged from the lorry and trundled down the ramp and on to the roadway.

The wagon was the size of a large lawnmower and was fitted with a couple of booms or extending arms. These could be fitted with a camera, or shotgun, or any gadget that might be useful in the defusing of explosives devices. There were shouted orders and the Wheelbarrow rattled along the tarmac towards the abandoned taxi.

The officers watched anxiously while the small machine halted directly behind the suspect vehicle. Police and army personnel were taking shelter in doorways or crouching behind their vehicles.

The arm holding the shotgun was positioned in line with the lock on the boot. The sudden sharp blast as the shotgun was fired made the officers twitch nervously as if in the expectation of a much bigger explosion. Nothing more alarming than the boot springing open occurred.

The EOD captain peered through his field-glasses in an effort to see for himself what the boot contained. The camera on the robot was working also and scanning the interior of the boot.

'What the. . . ! Some sort of flower. It looks like a flower pot.'

The operator was manipulating the grab on the robot to pick up the object. A small plant pot was pulled out and deposited on the tarmac. By now the colonel had donned his bomb suit – a heavy, awkward outfit with steel breastplate and extensive padding. A bulky helmet protected his head.

Shuffling forward he approached the suspect vehicle. The robot was resting motionless. On the road beside it, making a colourful splash of brightness, sat the plant pot with a single bloom rising from the packed compost. The EOD captain bent over and studied the object. Cautiously he reached out and, using a plastic rod much like a thick knitting needle, gently probed the compost.

'I don't think this is a device. As far as I can tell it's just a harmless plant,' he relayed back to his colleagues.

He then made an extensive check of the taxi – peering inside and carefully opening doors.

'False alarm. The damn thing is clean.'

The colonel picked up the flowerpot and carried it back to the waiting officers. He bowed to the police sergeant and handed him the flower.

'A present for your girlfriend, Sergeant.'

The police officer grinned as he took the offering.

'An orchid! My, she will be impressed.'

23

Most or almost all information relating to criminal operations in Ulster passed through DI Paul Anderson's department. The detectives under Anderson investigated muggings, car-jacking, robberies, burglaries, drugs or any crimes not thought to be linked directly to paramilitary activities.

Details of the robbery of the bookies' shop in Edison Street came to the detective's notice the day after the robbery. He read the report, categorizing it as the usual criminal action till he came to the discovery of the taxi linked to the robbers and the finding of the flowerpot in the vehicle.

'An orchid!'

The discovery of the flower was sparking connections in his head.

'Find out who owns the bookies' shop that was robbed,' he ordered his sergeant, Gordon White.

The information was not long in coming back.

'Casement Holdings.' There was a thoughtful look on the detective's face as he mulled over the details of the case. 'The biggest shareholder in Casement Holdings is Orchid Brown. His shop is robbed and the robbers leave an orchid in the getaway car. Now, unless Brown is robbing his own shops I have a hunch something odd is happening here.' He stared speculatively at DS White. 'What do you make of it, Gordon?'

'Coincidence maybe. Don't forget the taxi used in the robbery was stolen a few days ago. The orchid may have been in the car when it was nicked. Then again, one of the robbers could have bought the flower for his girlfriend and in the haste to escape forgot to take it with him.'

'Mmm . . . maybe.' The DI did not sound convinced. 'Is it coincidence that an orchid was left after a robbery committed in a business owned by Orchid Brown? My instincts tell me otherwise. Any CCTV?'

After some inquiries DI Anderson discovered the police did not have possession of the relevant tape. He phoned the betting shop and was told security staff had taken the tape. A few more phone calls tracked down

Casement Holdings. Security was at present making an assessment of the tape, but a copy would be made available to the police.

'Get someone over there straightaway,' Anderson ordered. 'I want that tape.'

Later that morning DI Anderson and his sergeant were viewing it. They had watched the robbery a couple of times and were rerunning the sequence once more.

'That punter there.'

Anderson stopped the tape and pointed to a figure caught in the act of walking into the shop.

It was John Lamb with a large car phone held against the side of his head and a newspaper held up in front of him as if he were reading off something into the phone. He was wearing the traditional sports cap with the long peak pulled down low. The effect of the large phone and the cap and the newspaper effectively blocked sight of his face, making any identification impossible.

'He sits down keeping his back to the camera. He has the newspaper held up which hides his face. And that cap keeps his face in shadow. Now watch. He walks to the door and opens it just as the robbers burst in. See how he stands back to allow them unhindered access. The armed robbers burst inside and one of them points his shotgun at the camera and fires, effectively ending any transmission. After that they grab the takings and escape in the taxi.

'I'll bet my pension, Phoneboy is accessory to the robbery. Using his phone he's relaying information to the gunmen. He would judge the best time to make the heist. My guess is at the tail end of a race being shown on the TV when everyone's attention is on the screens. Phoneboy opens the door for the gunmen and the robbery is carried out with perfect timing and efficiency.' DI Anderson was shaking his head and making a wry face. 'Planned to perfection. They go in late in the day when the last race is being run and the takings are at maximum. Phoneboy is in place to co-ordinate the robbery and open the door for them while at the same time astutely covering up his identity. The robbers likewise are unidentifiable with their balaclavas. The only clue is the stolen taxi and the pot plant.'

The sergeant was rewinding the tape. Anderson sat back with a thoughtful look on his face.

'Gordon, I want a report on my desk of every armed robbery and hold-up in the last few weeks.'

'What is it, boss?' Gordon asked.

'I'm not sure. I need to know if similar crimes have occurred involving Brown's business interests. And, most importantly, I need to know if orchids were involved in any way '

'*Slainte!*'

MacLean raised his glass filled with whiskey. Roshein grinned across at him and raised her glass. Charlie, Dennis and John did likewise.

'*Slainte!*' their voices roared out the Gaelic toast.

Flushed with the success of the raid on the betting shop, the gang had gathered in Roshein's house to celebrate. On the floor were neat bundles of notes lined up in rows. The canvas bag that had contained the stolen money lay discarded to one side.

'I've counted it,' Roshein said. 'Whoever guesses the correct amount will get a free canvas bag to carry home their share.'

There was a buzz of laughter around the room.

'Two million is my guess,' called Dennis.

Again the laughter sparkled. They were on a high. The banter continued for a while. 'You could use it to pay Brown off,' MacLean suggested.

'Wouldn't that be something?' John crowed, 'Paying protection to Brown and using his own money to do so.'

'Whatever,' MacLean said, 'it is a start. Now we have to plan job number two. The sooner the better! Once Brown cottons on to what is happening he'll beef up security at his places of business. We can't rest on our laurels. We have to hit hard and often, and keep one step ahead all the time. In theory it should be impossible for Brown to watch all areas of interest.' He shifted his attention. 'How is your info coming along, John?'

For answer, the youngster pulled a sheaf of papers from his inside pocket.

'Herewith is the list of all Brown's known interests. As you said he has fingers in a lot of crooked schemes. However he also has legitimate businesses. I suppose they are to launder money coming in from his rackets.'

John handed over the printed sheets. MacLean spent some minutes examining the contents. At last he looked up.

'John, you're a genius. What the hell you're doing with a bunch of crooks like us baffles me.'

John was grinning and looking more than pleased at the compliment.

'When I was a youngster I saw what being a law-abiding citizen meant in Belfast. My old man was a totally honest and decent man. Paid his taxes when due and boasted, "in all my life I've never owed the tinker the tailor or the candlestick maker". One night he had taken a few drinks too many. It gave him the courage to mouth off at a policeman. He was taken into custody. When next I saw him he was a mess. His eyes were blackened. His nose was broken. There was even blood in his ears. When I asked him what happened he looked at me with his bloodshot eyes and said, "Son, the law in Ulster is no respecter of persons. I spoke out of turn and discovered the lawmaker is a lawbreaker". I resolved then that being an upstanding law-abiding citizen did not pay. I was only fourteen when I decided a life of crime was the only life for me.'

'Damn it all, John.' Charlie was looking at his protégée with some surprise. 'You never told us that before – I mean about your da.'

John shrugged. 'It wasn't something I was proud of.'

'I suppose we all have a tale to tell,' Charlie observed. 'What about you, Tom? You haven't told us much about yourself at all.'

'That's because there's nothing to tell. I was wrongly convicted of handling stolen goods and sent to prison for two years. Like you say even being innocent doesn't protect you from the law.'

'Christ, that would have been a bitter pill to swallow. Is that how you learned to rob a betting office?'

'There's nothing to learn about that. You just burst in with a big gun and shout, "Hand over the money!" Men have been doing that for hundreds of years. There's only one man I know who does not need a mask and a gun to take money from people.'

'Who's that?'

'The Chancellor of the Exchequer, that's who.'

'Ah-ha! No wonder they sent you to prison – making accusations against a minister of the Crown like that,' Charlie exclaimed triumphantly. 'We have a political dissident here. John is a by-product of law and disorder. Dennis we know about: he was born a criminal. Before he was weaned he was out stealing cars.'

Dennis raised his glass and grinned. He was a youth of little words.

'Roshein is a vigilante out to take revenge on the men who shaved her head.'

'Charlie, it's your turn,' Roshein countered. 'What are your reasons for turning to crime?'

Charlie took a sip of his whiskey then flicked back his shoulder-length hair before replying. 'To my great shame I have no valid reason. I just enjoy the thrill of the chase. I get a kick from winning.' He looked astutely at MacLean. 'However, I could not have gone into that betting shop on my own. I was terrified out of my brain. In spite of the terror turning my insides to mush I felt I had to follow when you jumped out of the taxi. You didn't hesitate. You went straight in there screaming and terrifying everyone in there. If I was scared stiff, they were even more so. You were so aggressive and convincing I began to wonder if you hadn't done that sort of thing before.'

'When I was a kid I used to watch all those old gangster movies. You know, the black and white stuff? That's the only training I had,' MacLean said. He picked up the sheets of paper John had handed him and bent over as if absorbed in the information. 'We must plan our next job.'

He missed the exchange of glances between his comrades in crime. They had a sneaking suspicion there was something he wasn't telling them.

'Drugs . . . there's always big money in drugs. That'll be our next hit.'

24

The shopping centre was busy. Streams of people wandered through. Tubby matrons clutching bulging shopping bags, young mothers pushing babies in pushchairs, elderly men shuffling along with fags drooping from slack lips, youngsters of both sexes loud and intimidating, men in suits holding briefcases like badges of office.

No one took much notice of the young man loitering near the toilets. Pinkie Nelson was feeling good. The day's dealing had been brisk. Even after he paid the security man he would still make a fat profit. When he got back to his flat he would snort a little coke and dream.

Two youngsters caught his eye and he nodded towards the gents' toilet. Inside, the money quickly changed hands and the plastic packet disappeared inside the youngster's parka. In a few moments Pinkie was back at his station again and available for the next punter.

Selling drugs was a profitable business if you knew the right contacts. His source, as well as supplying the coke, also gave protection from anyone trying to muscle in on Pinkie's pitch. That had happened once.

A new dealer began operating in the same precinct and was charging lower prices in an effort to squeeze out Pinkie. And it was working, for Pinkie's sales dropped. When he had gone to replenish his supplies, this drop in sales had not gone down well with his dealer.

'What's this, you buying from someone else?' the man in the flash car asked. A big fist reached out the car window and gripped Pinkie by the shirt. Pinkie was yanked hard against the car door.

'My profits are down, I got competition,' Pinkie said, frightened by the strength of the grip on his shirt. He felt as if the big man could pull him through the window the way a ventriloquist's dummy is stuffed into a suitcase.

'Don't give me that shite,' the man snarled, and shook Pinkie like he would the ventriloquist's dummy. 'Get in the back.'

The hand released him. Pinkie wanted to run like hell away from the big man, but his legs were trembling too much. He stared at those mean eyes and could not move. He had heard that rabbits when caught in the beam of torchlight froze in helpless terror and then could be picked up by the scruff of the neck. He imagined the man grabbing him and throwing him inside the car like the terrified rabbit.

The man jerked his head towards the rear of the car. He had never spoken to the man in the back, the one who handed out the package of drugs and took the money. His heart was pounding hard against his ribs. His throat seized up and tears came to into his eyes.

'Get in!'

He urinated down his leg just before he unfroze enough to get into the car. The man in the rear seat did not turn his head as Pinkie climbed in beside him. Pinkie tried to observe the dealer without seeming to. He saw a slim, well-dressed man with dark good looks. The man ignored him.

The car purred through the streets with a very frightened drug peddler in the back. When it pulled on to a piece of waste ground and rolled smoothly to a stop Pinkie knew they were going to kill him. Sweat was rolling down his face, mingling with his tears.

'Empty your pockets.'

It was a minute or so before the order registered. Pinkie was too frightened to move. He began to plead his case.

'I tell you someone else is working my patch.' Pinkie's voice had a hoarse, whispery quality as he tried to get his throat working.

For the first time the good-looking man glanced at him.

'I said, empty your pockets.'

Pinkie began to do as he was told. He worked feverishly emptying all the pockets. Small packets of whitish powder, dirty hankie, rolled up bundles of banknotes, a flick-knife all tumbled on to the seat.

'Count the money.'

Pinkie knew exactly how much was there.

'Four hundred,' he whispered.

'How many packets?'

'Thirty-six.'

While this was going on the big man in the front lit up a cigar. Tobacco fragrance drifted into the rear of the car. Pinkie's leg was cold where the urine had soaked his trousers. He shivered suddenly.

'Put it back.'

Pinkie sat immobile – terrified to move. The man sharing the rear seat with Pinkie leaned forward and spoke to the big man in the front.

'You think he's simple?'

'Yeah, his mother was an ape and his father was the zookeeper. He is the issue of an illicit union.' The big man snorted in what might have been a chuckle.

The handsome man turned back to Pinkie. He pointed a slim finger at Pinkie's possessions piled on the seat beside him.

'Put it back in your pockets.' He spoke slowly, emphasizing each word as if speaking to a child.

Pinkie's hands trembled so much he spilled some of his possessions on the floor of the car. The man stared out the window indifferent to the fright he was inducing.

The car started up and did a circular turn around the waste ground, the tyres making more noise than the smooth running engine. No one spoke as the car sped through the streets. It stopped at the place Pinkie had been picked up.

'Get out.'

Pinkie had to sit on the pavement when the car drove off. His legs would not hold him. He was not sure what it was all about. It was not until two days later he found out how it worked.

The policemen were coming from both entrances into the shopping mall. Pinkie froze against the wall trying to make himself invisible and waiting for the opportunity to slip into the toilets and shed his cargo of drugs. Before he could make his move, the police were past him and suddenly the rival dealer who had been selling on Pinkie's patch was fleeing down the mall.

He cannoned into a pushchair, spun round, somehow managing to stay upright. He was still running when he saw more policemen coming in the opposite direction towards him. He veered away and barrelled into Woolworth's.

Police were coming from all over. Pinkie was so surprised he forgot for a moment all about running for the toilets to offload his drugs. By the time he regained movement in his limbs and turned to flee, he was face to face with the big man who drove the flash car that collected his money and supplied the drugs. The man was grinning at him baring a row of uneven, yellowed teeth.

Pinkie stayed where he was. The big man stayed near, leaning against the wall. With his bulk and ugly face he looked as if he had just stepped out of a boxing gymnasium and wandered into the shabby shopping mall. The man was staring down the precinct towards the entrance to Woolworth's. His vigilance was rewarded and the police emerged with a noisy, struggling man. It was the rival dealer.

Handcuffed, with a brawny policemen each side of him, the man was being hustled out from the store. His handlers were not being too gentle with him. Blood was running from his nose and mouth. He shouted abuse and called on passers-by to assist him.

His hands were cuffed behind him. The more he shouted the higher the policeman forced his arms. All the time they were shoving him along towards the exit.

More police emerged from the store and were joined by colleagues who had lain in wait for the dealer to be herded their way. Grinning, laughing and congratulating each other on a good result they sauntered in the direction the prisoner had been taken.

Pinkie turned to question the big bruiser. The place where he had been standing was vacant.

That had all been some time ago. Since then Pinkie had no more bother with competition. He sold his little packets of oblivion to an ever-increasing clientele. Out of the profits he paid the security staff to leave him alone. The bulk of the money he collected went to the big man in the posh shiny car. No reference was ever made regarding the arrest of the rival drug dealer.

There was plenty of money left over for Pinkie. He also had a girlfriend he rented out for sex. Life was good. Sex and drugs were profitable enterprises.

25

Pinkie was unaware he was being observed. Earlier in the afternoon John Lamb had sidled up and purchased a hit. John looked suitably scruffy to arouse no suspicions as to his intentions. He wore an old pair of cord trousers and a patched anorak. He looked decrepit enough to be sleeping rough. Pinkie had plenty of the type as regular clientele.

Having established the identity of the dealer John left the shopping mall and went outside into the delivery yard. Dennis Mallet was parked there with a change of clothing in the car. John discarded his disguise. When he emerged in the mall again he looked like a student, even down to the Queen's University scarf. From inside a shop selling stationery he was able to observe Pinkie without himself being seen.

The mall stayed open late to catch trade from workers on their way home, consequently it was mid-evening when Pinkie left his station. He was feeling very satisfied with the day's dealing. There were fat wads of banknotes secreted all over his person. The big man in the large shiny car would be pleased with his consistent performance.

The gang kept Pinkie under observation all week. They saw how he kicked his girlfriend out in the street to solicit while he stayed in their grubby flat, watched videos and fed his habit.

The young girl had to earn the money to buy her own fix from him. Pinkie was no fool. He was too shrewd a businessman to pass up an opportunity to earn a profit even if it made his girlfriend into a whore.

Then the breakthrough came that the gang were waiting for. One evening, after arriving home, Pinkie remerged from his high-rise flat. Normally, once he arrived home he stayed put. Thursday night was different. Dennis Mallet was on duty till midnight when he was to be relieved by Charlie. He phoned Charlie as soon as he saw the dealer come back out into the streets again.

'Keep with him. I'll phone MacLean and then I'm on my way. Maybe our dealer is popping out for a fish supper.'

With the lights switched off on his stolen Ford Fiesta, Dennis followed the dealer.

Pinkie did not go far. Nonchalantly he leaned against a graffiti-decorated gable wall and waited. Dennis parked a few hundred yards away. They did not have long to wait. A dark-coloured Daimler drove into the street.

Pinkie saw the car and moved to the kerbside, waiting before the car slid to a halt. He had pulled out a bulky parcel from under his anorak and handed this through the lowered window. There was a slight pause and a large padded envelope was handed back out to him. A few words were exchanged then the dealer turned and began walking back in the direction of his flat. The Daimler pulled away from the kerb. Dennis was on the car phone as he started after it.

'Charlie, it looks like the target has made contact. He's exchanged gifts with someone driving a Daimler. It's pulling away now and I'm following. I think we've found the main man.'

Next morning the gang met up at Roshein's house. Everyone was there, but it was Dennis's show.

'I tailed the Daimler the rest of the night. He made twenty stops. At each pick-up someone was waiting. An exchange was made. The dealers I guess were handing over the cash and receiving drugs in exchange. Very little time wasted. I made a note of every place they made a drop-off. Finally they ended up at the Tin Man Night Club in Mason Street. Two men got out – one a giant of a man and the other slim and well dressed. I couldn't make out any more details than that. The big man was carrying a bulky sack. They disappeared into the club and didn't come out again.'

Dennis looked tired and, during his debriefing, kept yawning.

'Dennis, well done,' MacLean commented. 'You did the right thing following the car. That sack would have been stuffed with money – the payments from all those drug dealers. The Tin Man belongs to Orchid Brown. This has got to be our next hit. Dennis, can you remember the exact route the car took?'

'Sure.' Denis yawned opening his mouth wide. 'I know those streets like the back of my hand.'

'Draw up an itinerary. When you've done that we'll retrace the route and set up a place to ambush them, the later in the night the better when they will have collected most of the money. But right now you need to get off home to bed for a good kip.'

'Don't you want the route now?' Dennis asked, his voice distorted as he yawned again.

'Nah, it'll keep. We need to take our time planning this one. The next collection those guys will make should be the same time next week. That gives us time to organize a little hijack.'

'How much do you reckon that dealer would collect in a night?' John asked.

'From what I know of drug dealing and the number of dealers they picked up from,' Charlie answered, 'it'll be well over ten grand, maybe more.'

'Ten grand,' John mused. 'A fellow could have a grand holiday on that much money.'

'Don't forget it has to be split five ways.'

'Even so, it's still a lot of dosh.'

MacLean exchanged glances with Roshein. They grinned at each other.

'This is only the beginning. Brown has an empire. Everything he does is cash-based. We're going to keep siphoning off that cash. By the time we've finished with him, Brown will wish he'd never messed with Roshein and Phoenix.'

MacLean had Dennis drive him through the streets of Belfast on the route taken by the men in the Daimler. Roshein insisted on being with them, as did Charlie and John. Every now and then they would stop and MacLean would leave the car and wander about looking at buildings and entries and streets assessing the viability of each place for an ambush.

On a couple of nights he repeated the same procedure asking Dennis to stick as close as he could to the time schedule the Daimler had taken that night.

'We've got to stop the car cold. It has to be boxed in or immobilized. These fellows in the car will in all probability be armed. But they'll be careless. I imagine no one has ever attempted anything like this before. Our best weapon is surprise. Right up to the moment it happens they must remain oblivious to any threat. Then we spring the trap. If everyone plays their part and sticks to the plan it should run smoothly and come Friday morning we'll be several grand the richer.

'Charlie, I need a handgun – can you fix that?'

'You're talking to the right man, Tom.'

26

A series of minor crimes was committed around Belfast within the space of a few days. A large delivery van was stolen along with a smaller panel van from a locked yard. Someone broke into a works compound owned by Belfast City Highways Department. The foreman in charge of the yard was not sure what, if anything, was missing after the break-in. In another incident a high-powered motor bike was stolen from the forecourt of a major bike importer.

These were considered unimportant occurrences when set against the war crimes that were being carried out in the city. Shots were fired at a police patrol and an officer seriously wounded. The army investigated two suspicious packages left unattended. Firebombs went off in a big city store. The body of a man was found on a patch of waste ground. Numerous cuts had been sliced into his flesh. His had been a particularly prolonged and painful passing. Vehicle theft, break-ins and murder were shunted to one side while the security forces fought the ongoing war.

For some members of the Belfast community crime was a way of life. They flourished beneath the umbrella of the general disorder within Ulster. The more disruption the war caused the less attention they were likely to draw from the forces of law and order.

Ben Orwell lived a lavish lifestyle. His penthouse in Belgrade Street was extensively furnished with the best that money could buy. He entertained a string of glamorous young women at his opulent residence. He had no trouble pulling females. His obvious wealth, along with his Mediterranean good looks, attracted women. They suspected he had a dark side to his nature and this gave him added allure. They would be correct in their assessment of his character for Ben worked for Orchid Brown. His job was to manage the network of small drug dealers servicing communities all over Belfast.

What made him invaluable to his boss was his ability to instil terror among the dealers he serviced. No one crossed Ben twice. He was cold, calculating and ruthless. His most potent weapon was his driver and minder Cannibal Bates.

Bates was a giant of a man. He had hands almost as big as hubcaps. His wrists were bigger than most men's biceps. Taking great pride in his enormous strength, he used bare hands to kill or maim dealers who stepped out of line.

It was rumoured he had once killed a man by squeezing his skull in his immensely strong hands till the bone cracked and the brains oozed out like the filling in a meat pie. The story went he had taken the spilled brain, fried it and used it as sandwich spread. Hence his nickname, Cannibal. There was no one alive who could verify the story.

Another asset Orwell possessed which helped him run his operation in such a ruthless way, was his indifference to the misery his hateful business created in the ghettos of Belfast. If anyone had been brave enough to point this out to him, such a connection would have been incomprehensible to the drug dealer.

Ben Orwell was first and foremost a businessman. His operation existed to make profit. That the fallout from those operations should be human misery did not appear on the company balance sheets.

Margaret Thatcher, the British Prime Minister would have approved of his business principles. Market forces were operating. She would have been able to use Ben Orwell's business methods as an example of supply and demand. *Laissez-faire* was operating effectively amongst the misery and poverty of her turbulent province.

Thursday night everything was going as usual. The Daimler that Ben favoured purred smoothly from pick-up to pick-up. Piled on the back seat were bundles of padded envelopes with numbers corresponding to amounts of money. The dealers handed over their grubby packet of banknotes to the driver, Cannibal Bates. Bates handed the package to Ben Orwell in the back seat. Ben marked the bundle with the dealer's name and dropped it into a large sack before handing over the padded envelope containing the drugs.

Ben Orwell never communicated with the dealers unless they expressed a desire to speak to him. The whole operation was run like a slick machine. Money in – drugs out.

At the end of the night they delivered the night's takings to Orchid Brown at one of the clubs he owned. Someone else checked the cash against the drugs issued. Anyone found trying to fiddle the system was brutally and efficiently removed from service. Just another unsolved murder in the City of Death.

During the course of that same afternoon, a large delivery van pulled up at the junction of Mullen Road and Jarvis Crescent. A couple of workmen alighted and set up control barriers that blocked off part of the road. Just enough of a gap was left for vehicles to pass through. A workman's tent was erected over a manhole. By the time these preparations were complete the evening was drawing down.

Making a show of consulting blueprints the two workmen surveyed their preparations. After checking their watches they fetched amber lanterns from the van and placed these around the site ready for the coming darkness. Satisfied with their efforts they drove the large delivery van around the corner and parked in Jarvis Crescent.

Later in the evening the radio installed in the cab of the large van crackled into life. The workmen listened to the instructions. Acknowledging the message the men climbed down from the cab and extended the barriers across Mullen Road, completely blocking it to any oncoming traffic. A large and distinct diversion sign was placed before the obstruction with an arrow directing oncoming traffic into Jarvis Crescent. When these preparations were completed one of the workers climbed back into the cab of the van while his companion waited at the junction.

Traffic was sparse at that time of the night. While the men waited, only one car approached the makeshift diversion. The driver turned into the crescent and drove round to the other end emerging on to Mullen Road without too much inconvenience. The workmen waited for further developments.

Cannibal Bates grunted as he saw the roadworks and the diversion sign on Mullen Road. He obediently slowed down and turned the car into Jarvis Crescent.

'Shite!'

A large van was drawn across the road and had obviously got into difficulties trying to make a turn in the narrow road. The driver's mate was standing at the rear of the van gesticulating and yelling directions to the man in the cab. Cannibal slammed on the brake and halted about twenty yards from the stalled van. He wound down the window.

'Get that fucking van out of the way!'

The man on the ground turned around and gave the driver of the Daimler a one-fingered salute. The brute's face reddened. He opened the door and was ready to get out and pound the man to a pulp.

'I'll tear his fucking arm off and beat him to death with it,' he snarled.

'Leave it!'

The authoritative voice from the backseat restrained him. His neck turned a deep crimson and his collar seemed too tight. Consumed with incandescent rage he moved the gear stick into reverse. His eyes blazed with fury as he stared through the windscreen at the defiant man who had insulted him. Behind the Daimler a panel van pulled up. With all his attention on the man in the road Cannibal did not see the vehicle draw up behind him. The big car reversed into the van.

27

'Shite! Are they all fucking idiots around here?' Cannibal raged.

He twisted round in the seat to see what he had hit. No one was getting out of the van to remonstrate with him, which was just as well for by now Cannibal was in a murderous rage. Ben Orwell was twisting round also to view the obstruction.

A powerful motor bike came whizzing round the corner and into Jarvis Crescent. The cyclist pulled alongside the driver's door of the Daimler. The helmeted rider pulled a revolver and pointed it at Cannibal.

'Out! Out!'

A mike had been rigged on the rider's helmet to amplify his voice. The shouted order boomed loudly enough for the two men in the car to hear.

From the panel van a hooded figure jumped down and ran to the rear door of the Daimler. As he reached out for the car door Ben Orwell retained enough presence of mind to slam his hand on the locking lever. The hooded man wrenched futilely at the locked car. Flame belched from the revolver. The report from the gun was shockingly loud. The glass in the rear door disappeared in a shower of splinters. The raider on foot reached in, fumbled with the lever and the door swung open. He ducked back to allow the motor cyclist a clear line of fire into the car.

'Throw the bag out!'

Ben Orwell sat immobile shocked by the suddenness of the attack. The gunshot that had shattered the window had also shattered his usual cool.

'Throw out the bag, now! I'll shoot to kill next time.'

The threat galvanized the drug dealer. He gripped the black plastic sack and dragged it to the door letting it drop to the tarmac. The bag was open and the raider could see the envelopes of cash almost filling it. As the bag tumbled from the car the masked raider who had come from the Transit reached down to grab it.

Inside the car Ben Orwell was recovering. With the bag of cash distracting the raiders he stretched out his hand and dipped into the pocket in the seat before him. There was a metallic gleam from the object he dragged out.

'Down!'

The command came from the man on the bike as he shouted to the raider by the car. Obediently the hooded man dropped on top of the bag of money. There was a flash and a bang from inside the car. The bullet ploughed a furrow along the biker's helmet. The big gun in the biker's hand belched fire again and the drug dealer was flung back across the seat.

Before the echoes of the shot died there was a roar like an injured bull from the front of the car. The door was already open and the enraged driver emerged. Before the biker could bring his weapon to bear Cannibal lowered his head and charged.

Bike, rider and attacker spilled on to the road in a tangle of limbs. Cannibal kept up his enraged bawling. His great blunt fists were battering at the gunman. In the wild attack the biker lost his revolver.

Cannibal pummelled mercilessly. The only thing saving the biker from being battered unconscious was the protective gear he was wearing. Futilely he punched the man mountain on top of him. He might as well have hit the side of the Daimler. Foam was dribbling from the enraged driver's mouth as he kept up his relentless attack.

The biker jerked his knee up into his attacker's groin. The big man grunted but was not distracted from his attempt to smash the man on the ground into a pulp. Grabbing the big man by the lapels of his jacket the biker pulled Cannibal down towards him and at the same time jerked forward as he tried a head butt.

On the front of the helmet was a narrow brim made of toughened plastic. The plastic cut into the bridge of Cannibal's nose and sliced deeply into the flesh. It was a hard and vicious strike. Cannibal reared back from the cruel pain that all but blinded him. Blood spurted freely from the deep wound.

The chauffeur roared out in pain, momentarily letting up on his brutal attack. The biker immediately pulled the bodyguard back down and repeated the head butt this time catching Cannibal on the chin. Fresh blood erupted from this new and savage wound.

'Aaagh!'

Cannibal reared up and raised his hands to shield his face from further damage. A gloved hand came up from the ground and smashed into the bruiser's throat. Cannibal's mouth was open wide as he tried to draw breath from his damaged windpipe.

The big man's nose was ruined from the helmet strike and blood was flowing freely from the two deep wounds on his face. A flap of bloody skin hung down from his chin torn loose by the sharp rim on the helmet.

He roared like a wounded bull, but in spite of his injuries returned to the attack and once again began to strike the man pinned to the ground by his great bulk. The biker had his arms raised in a vain attempt to fend off the brutal battering. The big man was berserk. His meaty fists pounded like hammers on the leather-clad biker. It looked like a one-sided contest with Cannibal the favourite to win the fight.

Fortunately help arrived for the biker as his associates came to the rescue. One was holding a length of pipe and he swiped this across the top of Cannibal's head. The big man roared some more and swung round to deal with this new attacker.

On the other side another man used a wheel brace to hit Cannibal along the side of the head. The bodyguard grunted and began to sway. The wheel brace rose and fell once more while the pipe wielder swung again and his weapon bounced from Cannibal's head. With a great groan the bruiser rolled from atop his victim.

Released from the weight of his attacker the biker scrambled to his feet. He kicked viciously at the bruiser. His heavy motor-bike boot caught Cannibal on the side of the head. The big man groaned loudly and tried to roll away from his attackers.

'The drugs,' the biker yelled. 'Get the rest of the drugs from the car. Hurry! Hurry!'

Leaving off their attack on Cannibal the men ran to the car and pulled out the second sack containing the drugs. This sack was almost empty. In the meantime another raider grabbed the bag with the cash from the roadway.

The biker pulled open the lid of the helmet box attached to the back of his downed bike and pulled out a pot plant. Leaning inside the stalled Daimler he set the flower on the front seat. Then the raiders turned and fled past the large delivery van still effectively blocking Jarvis Crescent.

On the other side of the van a black Volvo Estate had reversed up the crescent and was waiting with engine running. For a few moments there was frantic activity as the raiders scrambled aboard. Doors slammed shut and the car took off.

Behind them they left a scene of utter chaos. A panel van and a Daimler saloon were parked nose to tail. Lying on its side a powerful motobike leaked petrol. Ahead of the stalled vehicles a large delivery van was wedged across the road.

A big man with blood pouring from deep wounds in his face crawled to the Daimler. Painfully he stood and groped inside the back seat. Suddenly he straightened up and howled as if he were a beast roaring a challenge. Wildly he cast his eyes around the stalled vehicles. He caught sight of the motor bike lying on its side. Any normal man would have struggled to get the bike upright. Cannibal plucked it from the roadway like it were a kid's pedal bike.

With some difficulty he managed to kick-start the motor bike into life. He manoeuvred around the delivery van blocking the road and accelerated to the end of the crescent. Reaching the junction with Mullen Road he exited and accelerated at speed. With blood flowing freely from his wounds and consumed with revenge for the attack, he was hell-bent on pursuing the raiders. It was a hopeless task. The men who had stolen the night's takings and shot Ben Orwell were long gone.

Traffic did not pile up at the blocked road. Motorists in Belfast recognized gunshots when they heard them. There was a quick exit from the scene as vehicles turned around and sought an alternative route. Some hours later the police arrived, followed in turn by the army.

28

MacLean rolled over in the bed and tried to sit up. He groaned as he made the effort.

'What the hell time is it?'

No one answered. The place beside him in the bed was empty. He flexed his neck and moved his limbs around experimentally. His body felt as if he had been through a cement mixer. He slid to the edge of the bed and sought for his clothes. Pulling on shirt and trousers he left the bedroom and headed for the kitchen.

'Hello.'

There was still no answer. He was obviously alone in the house. The clock on the kitchen wall indicated eleven o'clock. His stomach rumbled with hunger and he began to rummage for food.

He filled the kettle and put it on to boil. A bowl of muesli and fruit juice followed by five slices of Ormo thick-slice toasted and two boiled eggs later he began to feel as if he could join the human race again. With a mug of coffee he stretched out on the settee and began to mull over last night's events.

When the job was planned he was well aware of the reputation of the two men in the Daimler. Both Orwell and Bates were known criminals. Bates had done time for grievous bodily harm before being taken into Brown's organization. The big man carried no weapons but relied on his brute strength to eliminate his victims. He was a brute with a killer instinct.

His boss, Ben Orwell, had been a hit man in a murder gang. No one knew how many he had killed, but between the two gangsters in all likelihood they shared at least a dozen murders. That was why he had asked Charlie to supply a handgun. He'd had the feeling the men they were to tackle might prove a lot harder than the bookies' clerks on the last job.

The Browning 9mm Parabellum Charlie had come up with had proved its worth. The fact that Orwell was shooting at him from the interior of the car had saved him from a bullet in the head.

The door of the Daimler had not been fully open when the gangster grabbed his handgun and fired. MacLean had been bending down for his own shot at Orwell and subsequently the bullet had struck his helmet. Even so, the shock of the bullet bouncing off his headgear had startled him momentarily. He had fired quickly but accurately at the armed man in the car. Hesitation would have been fatal. His old skills, though rusty, were still there.

Charlie had reacted well also when MacLean yelled at him to drop to the ground. So easily one of them could have been killed or badly wounded. The whole team had worked well together. John and Dennis had set up the road diversion while Charlie had followed in the stolen panel van. He smiled as he remembered Roshein's chagrin at not playing a more active role in the heist.

'Just because I'm a woman you don't think I would be any use in the heat of the action.'

'No, no, not at all. I need someone reliable in the getaway car. Even if we have to abort the robbery, knowing you are waiting for us, at least we have a safe, secure exit. There wouldn't be much point in making the raid if in the end we can't ferry away the loot.'

She still wasn't happy with her role and made further protest.

'I thought Dennis was the driver for the team. He's more experienced than me.'

'Look, we need two men at the roadblock. A man and a woman would look kind of suspicious doing road repairs. Charlie will be in the panel van coming from behind to block the Daimler from reversing out of the crescent. He'll also be on hand should I get into trouble. We both need to be armed. Charlie knows guns. Ben Orwell and Cannibal Bates are killers. They'll both be armed. Would you be able to shoot a man coming at you with a gun?'

He was lying to her for Charlie would not have a gun: only MacLean would be armed.

She had bit her lip and stared back at him sullenly. 'Would you be able to shoot someone?'

'Damn it, Roshein, we all have a role to play. Would you just accept your part in this without bitching about it? We need a reliable getaway driver. He has to be there on time and not panic when things get hectic.'

Roshein's tightened lips showed him he had hurt her feelings. His own anger had been simulated. He did not want her to be anywhere near the two gangsters when the action started. He knew the vicious reputation of the two men.

On the days leading up to the raid she had been cool towards him. He had not attempted reconciliation. There was too much on his mind as he prepared the hijack.

He wished she were here now. The sound of the front door had him sitting upright. With some trepidation he listened to her footsteps on the stairs. He took a sip of coffee and was surprised to find the cup empty. Then he just sat there watching the doorway.

At first he did not recognize the young woman stepping into the room loaded down with shopping bags. She had platinum blonde hair and was dressed in a stylish coat. He blinked in surprise.

'Roshein!'

Without answering she deposited the bags on the floor and stood hands on hips and gazed at him boldly? She looked so different with the blonde hair he could not help staring, unaware his mouth was hanging open.

'Well, what do you think, you gormless bogman? Does it suit me?'

Slowly she pulled at the belt on her coat and let it fall open. Underneath she was wearing a green silk dress with thin straps looped over bare shoulders. The coat slid to the floor. The dress was of soft clinging material that showed off all the contours of her body. It left nothing to the imagination. He felt his desire rising. They had not made love since the tiff over her role in the robbery.

'Gorgeous!' He spoke breathily as if emotion were overcoming him. 'You're the reincarnation of Marilyn Monroe.'

She squealed delightedly and took him by surprise as she skipped across the short distance between them and threw herself at him. As she landed on top he tried not to flinch as his bruised body took her weight. He wrapped his arms around her. She was clinging to him like a drowning woman embracing a lifeguard. When at last they surfaced she stayed where she was and gazed into his eyes. They were misty and soft with a slight glazed look.

'I bought some sexy underwear. Would you like to see me in it?'

'Later.'

'Later than what?'

'After I've taken you in the bedroom and removed that green dream you're wearing.' He reached up and stroked her hair. 'It feels so real. But I didn't mind your shaved head; I fancied you no matter what.'

'Is it just desire you feel for me, Tom?'

'Won't that do just for now?'

She pouted. 'Well, I desire you too, Tom MacLean. You'll have to carry me into the bedroom. My legs have gone weak on me.'

Still holding her he struggled to his feet. This time he could not hide the grimace as he felt the aches and pains.

'Oh, Tom, are you all right? Charlie told me what happened. He said you were lucky to be alive. Tom, I couldn't bear it if anything happened to you.'

'Just a few bruises. I tangled with the Apeman from Ardee. He tried to batter me to death. But I'm still fit enough for a bout with you.'

He felt her aims tighten around him. She buried her face in his neck. When she spoke her voice was muffled.

'I don't care what you think of me, Tom. I love you, and that's all that matters.'

29

Orchid Brown gazed with morbid curiosity at the man sitting opposite. Cannibal had come straight to him after the hijack. The big man was a mess. He had barged into the club brushing aside the bouncers on the door. With his size and ruined face no one was inclined to argue with him.

Runnels of blood had dried on his face. A deep gash had split his nose and Brown thought he could see the bone. Part of the chin had been sliced and a flap of bloody skin dangled like a bizarre goatee beard. The front of his jacket was discoloured by blood that had dried to a burgundy stain.

Brown listened as the big man related the events of the night.

'You say Ben is dead.'

'I think so. He was lying in the back of the car with a hole in his chest. There weren't much I could do for him. I figured the police would be on the scene soon and they would take care of him. So I left him there. Then I took after those bastards on the motor bike they left behind. When I couldn't find them I came here.'

'So the police didn't see you?'

'Nah, I was long gone.'

Brown puffed thoughtfully on the cigar. He had offered one to the injured man but the big fellow refused. Brown was filled with grudging respect for his brutish employee. With the injuries inflicted on him a lesser man would have collapsed, or staggered off to seek help. Cannibal had got up and chased after the hijackers.

'You say they were all masked?'

'Yeah, except for the guy by the van. The biker with the shooter had on a helmet. The guy with him was wearing a balaclava.'

'Would you recognize this geezer again?'

'You bet.' Cannibal pointed to his temple. 'He's in here. When I catch up with him he's dead.'

Brown nodded thoughtfully. He pressed a switch. Almost immediately the door opened and Colin Thompson entered.

'These guys that pulled that robbery must have form. I reckon they'll be on police files. Here's what we do.'

When he finished instructing the two men Brown made a call to Detective William Moultrie.

'I have a man here been attacked and seriously injured. He caught someone breaking into my office. The burglar hit him with a fire extinguisher and got away. He reckons he can identify the intruder. Would it be possible for him to come down there and you show him some pictures?' The answer must have been in the affirmative. 'Sure,' Brown said into the mouthpiece. 'I'll have my man bring him in first thing in the morning.'

When Brown put the phone down he gazed with wonder at the wounds on Cannibal's face.

'God's truth, Cannibal you certainly weren't pretty before, but now you look bloody awful. Take him round Doc Wilson,' he instructed Thompson. 'Get him patched up.'

The big man stood up. 'I want them guys, Orchid. I want them real bad.'

'You and me both. You ID him down at the cop shop and we're on our way to catching them. Don't forget you need to lodge a complaint. That makes it all official for our man in the RUC.'

Sergeant Gordon White walked the length of the two vehicles and peered in the windows of the stalled Daimler. Standing at the rear of the van his boss DI Paul Anderson surveyed the scene.

'One dead body. Vehicles abandoned. A diversion set up that no one authorized. What went on here? Any idea who the stiff is?'

'Ben Orwell,' Sergeant White called out. 'He's a known drug dealer. Served time a few years back for manslaughter. From the looks of it he was shot at close range. As far as we know it was just a single shot. There was a revolver found in the car that had been fired once.'

'Mmm . . . is that the weapon that killed him? And why was he in the back seat? Did he have a driver? If so, where is that driver now?' Anderson walked forward to stand beside the Daimler. He stared at the big van still blocking Jarvis Crescent. 'The car was diverted into the crescent where it stopped because of that van blocking the street. The smaller van arrived behind and slammed into the Daimler effectively blocking it. Orwell was shot. The driver scarpers. I have a feeling this was a gangland contract murder or paramilitaries cleansing house. Orwell's driver would have set it up. The killers shoot Orwell and ferry the driver away.'

'What about the flower?'

Anderson turned and stared at his sergeant.

'An orchid, sir, in the front seat.'

The DI walked to the front of the Daimler and stared inside.

'Damn, I missed that. An orchid indeed. That creates a slightly different picture. You say Orwell was a drug dealer. Did he work for Brown, perchance?'

'I don't know for certain. It wouldn't be too hard to find out.'

'A pork chop against a pig's bollocks this is the same gang that robbed that betting shop a week or so back. Was this another robbery? Was Orwell carrying drugs when he was hit? Damn it, at least with the betting shop job we knew what happened. Here we can only speculate. Ask around for witnesses, but we know how fruitful that will be. Belfast is a city of blind deaf and dumb people. And find out if there's any connection to Brown.'

As the detectives were leaving the forensic team were arriving.

'Perhaps they'll find a fingerprint or two. Keep on top of this one, Gordon. We need to know if the car was carrying drugs and if the gun found in the car was the weapon that killed Orwell.'

Back at the station Anderson was walking through to his office absorbed in thought as he mulled over this latest orchid related crime. A photo-fit session was in progress. Anderson passed by but something about the bulk of the man crouched in front of the monitor attracted his attention.

The man had massive shoulders. His large meaty hands were placed on his knees as he leaned forward gazing into the screen before him. It was the face that drew the inspector's attention. His nose looked as if it had been gone over with a cheese grater and then patched up with sticking plasters. His chin looked no better.

'Cannibal Bates.' The detective put a name to the damaged face.

The big man looked up scowling. He did not return the detective's greeting. 'Are you using our equipment to find the latest victim of your brutality?'

The young WPC in charge of the photo processing equipment looked up nervously at the inspector.

'Mister Bates is here to identify the burglar who assaulted him last night.'

Anderson's eyebrows shot up. 'A burglar assaulted Cannibal Bates. Is the madman dead that tried to burgle you?'

Bates turned his head away from the inspector and stared stoically into the screen. Anderson flicked his head to indicate he wanted to speak to the WPC.

'When you get a result,' he said in a confidential tone out of earshot of the hulking form of Bates, 'bring me all the details. If Bates picks out his attacker, whatever you do don't reveal his identity. Tell the goon you have to check through the files to confirm all the details.

'Hope to see you in a cell soon, Cannibal!' he called cheerily, as he walked away.

It was late afternoon before his sergeant handed the forensic report to Anderson. While his chief was absorbed in reading the contents of the folder Sergeant White sat down and tackled a mound of paper piled on his own desk.

Taking a pen and a sheet of paper Anderson worked steadily at his composition. Pausing thoughtfully from time to time he pondered over the events of the last few weeks. At last he sat back and, putting his clasped hands behind his head, he stared broodingly into the distance.

'We were honoured by the visit of an esteemed member of the criminal fraternity this morning,' he said suddenly.

White looked across at his chief and waited for him to reveal the identity of the visitor.

'Cannibal Bates.'

'So we finally got something on that monster. Good thing too.'

'No.' Anderson was shaking his head. 'Bates was attacked by a burglar at Orchid Brown's club, The Tin Man, last night. The burglar used a fire extinguisher on Bates's face and he's now in competition with Hollywood stars for the remake of Frankenstein. I think he'll get the part. No make-up required. He came in at his own request to finger the fellow who attacked him.'

'Cannibal Bates bested in a scrap!' White whistled. 'I didn't know Mike Tyson was in Belfast. Did Bates identify anyone?'

For answer Anderson passed some papers clipped together to his sergeant. White started reading.

'Last night while on security patrol at the Tin Man I was attacked from behind and hit on the head by something heavy. I turned to grapple with the attacker and he smashed me in the face with a fire extinguisher. At that stage I passed out and knew no more till my boss Mr Brown found me. The attacker escaped but I got a good look at him.' White turned the page. 'Dennis Mallet.' He read silently for a moment before looking up. 'Mallet, he's got form – small time crook and car thief.' His eyes widened. 'That means Bates will go after Mallet. That kid's a dead man.'

'Not necessarily. I told the WPC not to reveal anything to Bates. He might have a face, but he hasn't got a name. But there's no reason why we can't pull in Mallet ourselves and work on him.'

'You're fitting it all together, aren't you, sir? We know from that report I just handed you Bates was Ben Orwell's minder. Bates was in that incident last night. It was no burglar he tangled with but the raiders who shot his partner, Orwell.' Sergeant White sat back, a gleam in his eyes. 'Bates didn't want us to know he was involved in the raid but he desperately needed to know the identity of the raiders. So he makes up that story about the burglary at the club so he can come in and find the fellow on our system. Wow!'

'Very good, Sergeant.' Anderson was nodding approvingly. 'With deduction powers like that when I retire you'll probably make superintendent. Right, we'll put out a general observation on Mallet. But he's a slippery little devil. He'll be hard to catch.' Anderson paused thoughtfully. 'Now there's an interesting tie-up. Remember the incident at the hospital when that young woman was abducted? Mallet and his associates and Tom MacLean just happened to be involved in that.' The DI stared off into the distance. 'Just what exactly is going on here?'

In another part of the building Detective William Moultrie was phoning an old acquaintance.

'Dennis Mallet,' he said softly into the mouthpiece, 'got form as a car thief. Last known address 227 Glenwall Heights. That's a block of flats at the bottom of Glenfield Road.'

30

There were three cars involved in the operation. Colin Thompson drove one, the usual 4x4. In the back were a couple of bouncers from the Tin Man. Rob Segal was at the wheel of vehicle number two accompanied by two more bouncers. Behind the wheel of the third car were Cannibal Bates and another man.

'There's the peelers going in now. They'll flush him out.'

All three were parked at vantage points covering possible escape routes from Glenwall Heights. They were parked outside the police cordon now moving in to apprehend the wanted man, Dennis Mallet

Glenwall Heights was only one of a series of dreary blocks of high-rise flats adrift in a wilderness of rubble and desolation. The bleak outlook was matched by the miserable prospects of the inhabitants trapped in their warrens by poverty and war.

Unemployment amongst the residents hovered at eighty per cent without any hope of lower figures in the future. Unruly gangs of youths roamed out-of-control, out of doors and out of work. These youngsters had known nothing, only war and unemployment. It was a fertile recruiting ground for the paramilitaries.

There was a frosty feel to the night air and it was chilly inside the vehicles. It did not help that windows had been wound down to prevent fogging on the glass. The men were tense, the strain of watching and the cold making some of them shiver. They stared intently into the neighbouring streets watching for movement.

A couple of kids came racing through, evidently spooked by the police presence. The watchers stiffened. They had all studied the police pictures of Mallet supplied to Brown by the bent detective, William Moultrie. The boys were too young. They ran, unaware they were under observation. A man and woman hurried out into the range of the watchers.

'Sam.'

Just one word spoken by Rob Segal and a man was out of the car.

'Excuse me, what's happening over there.'

'Dunno, mate, police raid or something.'

'Thanks.'

The bouncer coming back, shaking his head, this wasn't their quarry – the couple hurrying on.

Cannibal Bates was not having much better luck. Two teenage girls scuttled past giggling. They glanced at the car full of shadowy men and quickened their pace. An elderly man shuffled by clutching a plastic carrier bag. Two drunks came along carrying bottles in brown paper bags and talking loudly. It took all Bates's self-control not to get out and kick the men to death. He hated drunks.

It was the straggly ginger beard that gave them the clue. The young man came out of the entry and glanced back over his shoulder. He kept walking.

'That's got to be him,' Colin Thompson said tersely. 'Billy, Ted, get him.'

The two me got out and began to walk in the direction of the youngster.

Colin Thompson was talking rapidly into his car phone.

'He's come out our side. Close in and head him off in case he gets past us.'

Mallet glanced at the men walking towards him. He had a stolen Ford Capri parked in a garage nearby. That was where he was heading. When he saw the two men walking towards him his suspicions were roused. He quickened his step.

There was the slap of footsteps as the men began running towards him. Dennis did not hesitate. Years of living on his wits and dodging police and soldiers gave him quick reflexes. He took off running. The Capri was out of the question. With the men so close he would not be able to get the garage opened and the car started before they would be on him.

Colin Thompson started the 4x4 and accelerated along the tarmac. The roar of the car engine urged Dennis to run faster. Abruptly he turned down an entry. So quick was his movement the runners behind were taken by surprise. They stopped at the entrance to the alleyway and peered into the dim opening.

Thompson was talking frantically into the phone. The other cars were circling watching for Mallet fleeing towards them. A running form suddenly emerged into the street in front of Rob Segal's car.

'Got him!' he yelled into his phone and slammed the pedal to the floor. The screech of tyres was loud in the night. Their quarry turned again into a side street. Segal was an experienced driver. The 4x4 turned on a wheel spin and shot into the entry. The headlight picked up the running man. Then he was swerving and jumping for a six-foot wall.

His hands got a grip on the top and he was pulling himself up and over. Seconds later the car hauled to a stop and a man jumped out. He too clambered over the wall in pursuit. The car shot off again to the junction and turned left in an attempt to anticipate the fugitive's direction.

At the other side of the row of houses Dennis Mallet jumped into the street. Headlights dazzled him and he turned to run. A second set of headlights outlined him against the oncoming lights. Dennis was scurrying across the street seeking an opening. There was the sound of running feet behind him as the man who had followed him over the gardens emerged into the street and was coming after the youngster.

The headlights zeroed in on the fugitive. He fumbled with a tall narrow wooden gate – abandoned the attempt and jumped with outstretched hands for the top. His hands curled over the upper bar of the gate. The youngster yelled and let go as the razor wire cut into his flesh.

By now his pursuer was almost on him. Dennis pulled out his favourite weapon and whirled it round his head. The bicycle chain whipped across the man's face as he closed with him.

It was the bouncer's turn to yell with pain as the heavy links cut into his face. He put up his hands to protect himself. Dennis kicked him on the knee and the man stumbled aside. The headlights were full on and blinding him as he stood at bay. Men spilled out of the cars. They too had weapons.

One young man with a bicycle chain stood and defied a gang of thugs armed with an assortment of pickaxe handles and baseball bats.

'Give up now, son. You're going nowhere.'

'Wankers! I ain't done nothing! What you want me for?'

The ring of wooden clubs was closing in. Dennis swung his chain. It made a dull circle in the night air. A club was hurled out of the crowd. Dennis ducked – the chain wavered and then like lions harrying a wounded deer the thugs closed in. They didn't aim their clubs at his head. His hands were first, breaking the knuckles and his hold on the bicycle chain.

'Aaahhh. . . .' he screamed, as the chain fell to the floor.

They started on his knees next.

Another vehicle was approaching. Colin Thompson was leaning out of the window yelling.

'Don't kill him. Take him alive.'

It was easy after that. The moaning youngster was carried up to Thompson's 4x4 and dumped in the boot. One last punch in the mouth quietened him before the lid slammed down.

Dennis Mallet lay in his steel sarcophagus and whimpered in pain and terror. He believed he was the victim of the sectarian killers that roamed the streets of Belfast at night and picked their victims at random. The sadists would spend days and nights torturing their victims. No one ever survived. Their grim handiwork was dumped on waste ground.

The leader had shouted out to take him alive, Dennis wished now they had killed him out in the street.

31

Two of them carried the youngster inside the building. All was in
darkness. There was a pause while someone found the light switches. The
building was illuminated by rows of eight-foot florescent lights. The
effect was to bathe everything in an unforgiving pale brightness. The
inside of a garage workshop was revealed.

The men carrying Dennis cared not that he was in pain. They lugged
him inside as they would a sack of King Edward potatoes. The broken
bones in his legs grated together causing him unbearable agony. He
moaned constantly. No one took any notice of his discomfort. He was
dumped unceremoniously on the unyielding concrete floor. A huge figure
towered above him.

'Remember me, little man?'

Dennis tried to curl up but his busted legs caused him too much agony
and he groaned and stopped moving. Cannibal raised his foot and
brought it down on one of the broken limbs. Dennis screamed.

'When I ask you a question you answer me. Now, do you remember
me?'

'Yes!' the answer screamed out. 'Yes . . . I remember. . . .'

'Good. Once we've established a few rules you and I'll get on like a
railway carriage on fire. Now where did you and I meet?'

Dennis hesitated as if afraid to incriminate himself. The size fifteen
hovered again. Dennis screamed and tried desperately to twist away from
his tormentor. His broken hands were useless as he brandished them
ineffectively in the air. Pinned to the floor like a trapped insect his mouth
was wide open as he cried and moaned out loud.

'Now, once more with feeling,' his tormentor continued relentlessly,
'where did we meet?'

'Jarvis Crescent . . .' the words were a stricken moan.

'That's much better, Dennis. My name is Cannibal Bates. We've all night to get to know each other. I want to find out all about your friends. Those fellows you were with in Jarvis Crescent. You're going to tell me all about them – names, where they live, who their girlfriends are. What they like for dinner. That sort of thing.'

From somewhere in the pain and despair Dennis found a spark of defiance.

'Go to hell!' he suddenly moaned. 'I'll tell you nothing!'

Cannibal smiled a cold cruel smile and nodded. There was a pleased expression on his face.

'I love it when they say that. It makes my job more satisfying when you spill your guts at the end of our little session.' He turned away from his helpless victim. 'Now what music will we have? How about Iron Maiden, "The Number of the Beast"? That should do to start the entertainment.'

The heavy guitar riffs punched into the quiet of the spacious workshop. Satisfied with his choice Cannibal turned back to his work.

Like most garages the workshop was fitted with an electric hoist. This was used to raise and lower the heavy engines or gearboxes during repairs. The mechanism moved on runners and could be shunted from the vehicle to a bench for convenience of working.

The loud music drowned the hum of the motor as Cannibal operated the hoist. A robust metal hook swung heavily at the extremity of the chains suspended from the girders. Totally engrossed, Cannibal positioned the hook in the vicinity of his victim. He knelt down beside the suffering youth.

'You know when you have a chicken for the oven you tie its legs together with twine to keep the shape intact, or maybe it's to keep the stuffing inside. I can't remember which. I have to do the same for you. Only I haven't got no twine. I have to use this.'

Cannibal produced a length of electrical cable and with quick practised movements he twisted the wire around one ankle. The big man ignored the feeble struggles and moans of his victim as he finished wrapping the wire around the second ankle effectively lashing them together.

'There, how does that feel?'

He gave the cable an experimental tug. The bond held and Dennis screamed as the fractures in his legs jarred. It was a short reach for the big man to grab the hefty hook swinging on the dangling chains and clip it to the youngster's feet.

Ignoring the pleas of his victim Cannibal stood upright and pressed the green button on the hoist control. Bit by bit the links of the chain tightened.

Up and up, higher and higher till his torso was raised with only his shoulders making contact with the floor. Dennis sobbed out his anguish. The music blared out. The hook rose further till at last his body swung free off the floor – and began to oscillate.

As the youth hung upside down he stared wildly round him. His body twirled and his surroundings rotated around him. The hoist ceased its whirring. Movement caught his attention and he craned his head as far as he was able to watch his tormentor pushing a trolley towards him.

'Did you enjoy that, Dennis? There's even better to come.' Cannibal waved a hand over the trolley. 'Look here, Dennis, at all these tools. There's spanners, screwdrivers, pliers, hammers, electric testing apparatus.' There was a hiss of compressed air. 'A pressure hose for pumping air into the . . . well, I'll leave that bit to your imagination. A blowtorch, soldering iron . . . if you're unlucky I get to use them all on you. Just think of it. We've all night and all tomorrow and, if you're up for it, all the following day. Now let's see. Where shall we start?'

Before continuing his gruesome work Cannibal Bates turned up the volume on the music. Dennis pleaded then screamed. The screams blended with the music and blood began to drip on to the unforgiving concrete floor.

32

'The body of a man was found early this morning in Foundry Lane. Though police will not confirm these suspicions the crime has all the hallmarks of a sectarian attack. So horrendous are the wounds inflicted on the body even police officers, hardened by years of atrocities, are shocked. So bad is the mutilation, police at present are unable to make a positive identification. The RUC are appealing for help. If you know or suspect of anyone missing in the last few days contact police with details. Anyone who saw anything in the vicinity of Foundry Lane, please come forward. If you think you can help you may want to use the confidential police phone line.'

While the news reporter was saying his piece his camera crew were panning along a road. The road was bordered by hedges and decrepit looking garden sheds. Police stood guard at the entrance to the lane. Further into the lane a large tented structure could be seen where the police had erected a scene of crime enclosure. A man emerged from the tent and walked purposely along the road towards where the police vehicles were parked.

'That looks like Detective Inspector Anderson coming to make a statement,' the reporter informed his viewers.

The TV crew and the detective moved closer to each other. The police officer became the focus for the cameras.

'Detective Anderson, can you tell us anything more about the victim?'

Anderson held up his hand and shook his head. 'There's nothing more I can add to the original statement. A young male with extensive wounds on his body. Dumped sometime late last night or early this morning. We still haven't put a name to the body.'

'Inspector, in your opinion is this a sectarian killing?' the reporter asked.

The detective frowned. 'At this stage it's hard to say. Certainly it has all the characteristics of a sectarian murder, but until the victim has been identified we can only speculate as to the motives for this horrendous killing. Anyone, I repeat, anyone with the smallest piece of information please contact the police. The killer or killers of this young man must be brought to justice. As you know we have a confidential phone number. I ask you out there: help us rid our streets of this sadistic murderer. No matter how insignificant you feel your information is, please phone us. It just might be the vital missing piece of the jigsaw that will help put this killer behind bars.'

'Do you think it's a gang murder, Inspector?'

Anderson shrugged and spread his hands wide. 'Like I say we don't know anything at the moment. The investigation has barely begun. As soon as we know more we'll release the information. Thank you.'

Anderson fended off any more questions and made it through the television crew to his car. Inside the vehicle his sergeant was sitting at the wheel. Looking pale and distraught, he was starring fixedly into the windscreen.

'Gordon?'

Sergeant White blinked a couple of times and turned his stricken eyes to his chief.

'There's . . . I . . . it was. . . .' He stopped then started again. 'I'm sorry, sir. . . .'

Anderson held up his hand. 'There's no need to apologize, Gordon. If it helps, I felt the same as you when I saw the body. Years of coping with the aftermath of such sick work helps a little, but not much. One never gets used to it. If I ever feel nothing on coming across something like that I think it would be time to give up policing and take up some less arduous line of work. Would you like me to drive?'

'N-no sir, I'll be fine and thank you for your kind words. Nevertheless, I made a fool of myself. I suppose forensic were sniggering when I had to rush outside and puke up my breakfast.'

'No one was sniggering back there, Gordon. The only reason more weren't joining you is that most of us have seen it all before. Experience doesn't make it any easier but it helps a little.'

Sergeant White started the car and under the guidance of a police officer watching over the site reversed out on to the road. They were driving away when the sergeant spoke again.

'You think it was him, sir?'

'Yeah, it was him all right. I recognized the poor fellow from the police photo we were privy to the other day. They hadn't mutilated the face. My guess is they wanted Mallet recognized. It's a signal to the gang that they know who they are. The thing that bothers me is how Cannibal got to know the identity of Mallet. I told the WPC not to release those details to Bates.'

White shot his boss a startled look then turned his attention back to the road.

'You think Bates did that to Mallet?'

'What do you think, Sergeant? Orchid Brown sends Bates down to the station with a busted face making a complaint about a burglar. Cannibal Bates identifies Mallet. I ask the WPC to keep mum about Mallet's identity. Mallet's mutilated body is found a couple of days later. My guess is that Brown or Bates or both, kidnapped Mallet and tortured him to obtain information. But who passed the ID of the victim on to Brown's organization?'

'Perhaps the WPC accidentally let slip the information.'

Anderson was shaking his head. 'I know WPC McNulty. She's a good officer. It's very unlikely she would make that sort of mistake.' He took a sideways look at his driver. Colour was seeping back into his sergeant's face again. 'Would you be up to a visit to the club where Brown says the break-in took place?'

'The Tin Man – I know it, sir. Won't take a jiffy to get there.'

The doormen were reluctant to let the policemen inside till Anderson flashed his police card. The detectives waited in the entrance hall filled with mirrors and florescent lights while the heavies eyed them with hostility. Eventually Brown made an appearance.

'Detective Inspector Anderson, what an honour to have such a distinguished figure visit my humble establishment.' Orchid Brown exuded good will and clouds of cigar smoke. 'Come inside. Sorry my boys have kept you waiting out here.'

The nightclub owner ushered the detectives into a large dance area. As in the entrance hall the walls of the room were lined with mirrors. Coloured spotlights swirled from overhead fittings creating a multicoloured interior of reflections and illusion. Adding to the light confusion was noise confusion. Loud dance music pounded from speakers mounted around the room. On a stage, three girls, all but naked, swayed and gyrated to the music. Brown made a signal with his hand and the music was muted.

'How about some refreshments gentlemen?'

'This isn't a social call, Brown. We're investigating a break-in. Your man, Bates came in a couple of days ago and reported an incident in which he was injured.'

'Yeah,' Brown answered cautiously. 'You took your time about coming.'

'I apologize for the delay. We've been very busy. Can I see the site of the break-in?'

'Huh.' Brown looked disconcerted for a moment. 'There's nothing to see. The intruder broke a window and crawled inside. Bates discovered him and the fellow attacked him and escaped.'

'Why would Dennis Mallet want to break into your club?'

Brown's eyes flickered momentarily then shuttered down. He frowned thoughtfully. 'Dennis Mallet, is that the fellow's name? Never heard of him. I take it you've caught him.'

'Oh yes, we caught him all right. Unfortunately it was too late for us to save him from your thugs.'

The two men stared at each other. It was Brown who looked away first.

'You talk in riddles, Inspector. How could we interfere with someone we did not even know existed?'

'That's what I intend to find out. Who's your snout down at the station?'

Suddenly Brown laughed. 'Snout at the station! That sounds like a Duran Duran number. Oh, Inspector Anderson, you slay me.'

Anderson's face swelled with rage and took on a puce colour. He took a step towards the nightclub owner. Brown blinked but held his ground. Anderson felt his arm being gripped. He turned to look at his sergeant holding on to him.

'Sir, we're due down at the station.'

The detective turned his gaze back to Brown.

'One day, Brown, one day, you'll make the wrong move and I'll be there to take you down. . . .'

Whatever else the inspector said was drowned out as the music suddenly erupted into the room. Detective Anderson stared long and hard at the club owner. He had an insane urge to pound his fist into that complacent face.

Orchid Brown held his gaze. While the rage surged within him Anderson also knew there would be no mileage in starting a brawl. He motioned with his head to Sergeant White and the two detectives turned and walked back to the exit.

Inside the car Anderson sat while he got his temper under control. He put his fingers to his temples and massaged for a moment. With a sigh he sat back in his seat.

'Let's go, Sergeant. I think a mug of canteen tea might wash some of the foul taste away.'

33

The hammering on the door was persistent.

'For God's sake, John, keep your hair on.'

MacLean stood up and made an exaggerated gesture of exasperation to Roshein. She made a face back at him and shrugged.

John had phoned earlier to tell them he was coming over. He had sounded excited but would not tell them what his concerns were. Tom disappeared downstairs to let John in. For security reasons members of the gang would phone ahead to let the couple in the house know whom to expect.

When MacLean opened the door John pushed past him and took the stairs two at a time. Surprised by the youngster's abrupt behaviour MacLean scanned the street carefully. Nothing untoward caught his attention. Thoughtfully he closed the front door and made it secure.

Upstairs he found Roshein with her arms round John. He sat hunched on the settee his face pale and haggard.

'What is it, John?'

Roshein turned to him her face distraught.

'They found Dennis.'

'What do you mean, found him?'

Roshein's face crumpled. Tears ran unheeded down her face. She shook her head unable to answer.

'Turn on the TV,' John spoke in a toneless voice.

Somewhat annoyed at the lack of explanation MacLean went over and switched on. 'What am I looking for?'

'News channel.'

MacLean looked at the clock mounted on the wall. He fiddled with the controls, came back and sat down. The screen came alive as he settled. Armed police could be seen standing guard at the entrance to a rutted lane.

'The body was found early this morning by a man walking his dog. Police have not identified the body yet and are appealing for information.'

MacLean was staring at the screen with a growing sense of dread. As the newsreader's voice droned on describing the scene John spoke up.

'It was Dennis. The police won't release his name for some reason. I was listening in to the police broadcasts when his name was mentioned in connection with the body found this morning.'

'Dear God!' MacLean breathed.

'He was tortured, can't you see? Who would do it?' John began to sob.

'Who indeed?' MacLean was silent for some moments staring at the TV screen. 'Cannibal Bates, did he get a look at Dennis that night?'

John was staring at him. He was wiping at his eyes.

'It's possible. Dennis was in the road waiting for the Daimler. Bates might have seen him then.'

'Somehow Bates found out who Dennis was. They picked him up and did that to him. If that's the case it was partly revenge for Orwell and partly to find out who else was on the raid with him.'

MacLean went over to the TV and switched it off. Roshein still had her arms around John. She was holding him close against her. He had started sobbing again. Roshein's face was wet with tears.

'Where's Charlie?' MacLean asked.

'He's on his way. I phoned him before I phoned you.'

MacLean slumped back in his chair. He stared bleakly into space, thinking about Dennis. Thinking of the youngster at the hands of Cannibal Bates. He breathed deeply trying to remain calm, listening to John sobbing while Roshein held him.

'I'll make a drink,' he said more for something to do – trying to blot out the image of Dennis lying naked in a lane with horrific wounds on his body. He knew how they worked. Had seen the end results of savages like Cannibal before.

The Shankill Butchers they called them. Fiends. A pestilence released on the people of Ulster for their sins. Innocent men plucked at random from the streets and subjected to days and nights of torment. Knives from an abattoir the instruments of torture. Knives that had sliced and worked on animals used to carve and mutilate live human flesh. Death of a thousand cuts. They had taken that ancient ritual and refined it for their own fiendish ends.

He boiled the kettle, his own anger boiling up within. Stirred the coffee in the cups while the need for revenge stirred inside. Added large measures of brandy to each cup and carried the tray back into the living room.

John was sitting with a handkerchief pressed against his eyes, Roshein's comforting hand on his shoulder.

'Drink,' MacLean commanded.

John took the mug, his eyes red and swollen. MacLean handed a second mug to Roshein. She thanked him with her eyes, too choked up to speak. Before he could start on his own drink the banging on the downstairs door announced the arrival of Charlie.

When he let the newcomer in MacLean handed him his own mug of coffee and went back in the kitchen for another. When he rejoined them Charlie was sitting with white face.

'It can't be true,' he whispered barely audible. 'Perhaps they've made a mistake.'

'John seems pretty sure. He heard them name him on the police radio.'

Charlie threw back his head. 'Dennis my poor boy Dennis.' The words came out in a low moan. 'Damn them anyway! Damn them all to hell!' His voice was rising. 'Damn the murdering sadistic bastards!'

'They'll know about us now,' MacLean cut in. 'Who we are and what we're doing.'

'No,' Charlie was shaking his head. 'Dennis wouldn't betray us.'

MacLean looked at him pityingly, but did not bother to contradict him. 'It beats me how they put the finger on him. Was Dennis known to Bates?'

Both John and Charlie shook their heads. Neither of them believed Dennis and Cannibal Bates were acquainted.

'Someone fingered him that's for sure. Before the raid none of us knew Orwell or Bates. It's a sure bet they didn't know who we were. Somehow Bates or Brown found out about Dennis and were able to pick him up. My suspicion, they had inside information. Remember that night at the hospital. DI Anderson knew all about us. He was able to name all of you. It's quite possible he pointed Bates in our direction. Dennis is the first. They'll come for us one by one and pick us off.'

They stared at him, alarm in their eyes. Rage was roiling like a live thing inside him. He tried to speak calmly, rationally.

'We'll have to assume he did talk.' He could have added that everyone broke under the torture Dennis had endured, but he did not want to add to his companions' distress. After all, they had known Dennis much longer than he had. 'I think it would be safer to assume everything Dennis knew about us will now be known by Brown and associates. The thing is what are we going to do about it?'

They sat in morbid silence sunk in their own dark thoughts. MacLean sighed and made an attempt to overcome the inertia into which the dreadful news had plunged the little group.

'We must make plans. Like I said, in view of what has happened the best thing to do is to assume Brown knows all about us. It's no reflection on Dennis or his ability to hold out against his tormentors. It's just a sensible precaution. We must take steps to protect ourselves. It means going to ground. Our home addresses will be compromised. So we have to go into hiding. That's the first thing.'

His companions were staring fixedly at him. Their scrutiny made him feel uncomfortable. He ploughed on regardless. In all probability, he was the only one in the room who realized the true extent of the group's parlous situation.

'That's step number one. After that we must decide what next to do. In order to be completely safe we would have to flee Belfast. We can go abroad into Europe or to England, or down south to the Free State.' He stared back at each one in turn. 'We have money enough from the robberies to go into hiding and lie low. The decision of how or where is entirely yours. Anyone got any suggestions or comments?'

The silence was profound as they pondered his words. It was Roshein who broke the silence.

'Before we run, why don't we have one more raid on Brown?'

34

The discussion that took place after Roshein's shock announcement was long and heated. At times three voices were articulating opinions at once. MacLean waited for the arguments to run out of steam. He sensed the hysteria in the group and guessed the trauma of Dennis's fate had pushed his companions to the limits of their fears. At last he called a halt to the debate.

'Look, as far as I can see we've got three options. One, we can split up and go our own ways and hope to elude Brown and his gangsters. Two, we can just go into hiding and wait for things to cool down. Or three, we take up Roshein's suggestion and redeploy and plot another raid, a hit that will really hurt Brown. Maybe we ought to vote on it.' He waited for their agreement before continuing. 'OK, option one, we go our own ways.'

Negative shaking of heads.

'Option two, we go into hiding and wait for things to cool down.'

No.

'Option three, plan one last raid.'

The agreement was unanimous.

'Let's hit that bastard Brown.' Charlie spoke for all of them.

'Right, we'll have to assume Brown knows about this place and where John and Charlie hang out. We need a safe house to operate from. Anyone know of such a place?'

They sat in silence deep in thought. One by one they shook their heads.

'OK, here's my suggestion. Phoenix is lying idle. We should be able to hide out there if we don't draw too much attention to ourselves; keep a low profile and keep the place locked down as if it is still empty.'

There was a general nodding of heads.

'Sounds good,' Roshein said. 'There's plenty of space around it and we can keep the CCTV rolling to give early warning of an invasion if Brown does turn up. There's a whole estate of warehouses and workshops around the place. We can retreat out the back and make our escape in an emergency.'

'That's good,' MacLean nodded approvingly. 'All agreed?'

Again there was consensus.

'I want you to start immediately. I suggest you don't go back home for any reason. There's a good chance they'll be looking for us even now and someone might just be watching your place. My guess is that they'll pick us up one by one and deal with us.' He didn't add that meant the same fate as Dennis. 'How did you get here, Charlie?'

'I came by car. It's parked a few streets away.'

The crash from downstairs made them all jump. MacLean was on his feet immediately.

'That's them!' he yelled. 'They're breaking the front door. Can we get out the back?'

There came another crash and they felt the house shudder from the violence of the assault on the front door.

'Through the roof space,' Roshein told him, her voice trembling. 'It runs above the houses to the end one and that's empty. It'll get us out into the street. We got a bit of time. The front door is reinforced.'

Another loud crash shook the floor.

'Go! Go! Go!' MacLean shouted.

He ran to the front window and stared down into the street. The 4x4s were parked along the street. The steady pounding on the door continued. He ran back into the living room. Roshein and her companions were in the bedroom pulling down a ladder from the opened trapdoor in the ceiling.

There was a splintering sound from downstairs and MacLean knew the door was breaking up. He ran back through the rooms and looked down the staircase. The splits in the reinforced door were letting in light from the street.

'They're almost through!' he yelled, and the top of the door collapsed as the next blow smashed out a whole panel.

He glimpsed the blunt head of the sledgehammer as it was withdrawn ready for another wallop. Back in the living room he glanced around for some means to delay the attackers. His eyes lit on the large TV squatting in the corner.

Quickly he jerked out the plug and the aerial. The set felt reassuringly heavy in his arms as he carried it to the head of the stairway. The sledgehammer was now being used to smash away the bottom half of the door. Pieces of wood flew as the door disintegrated under the battering. The way was being cleared for the attackers.

MacLean waited patiently hardly noticing the weight of the TV he was holding. Behind him he heard Roshein calling his name. He ignored her shouts. He stepped back from the head of the stairs out of sight. With a quick bend of his knees he hefted the TV and pressed it above his head. He smiled wryly to himself as he remembered doing similar exercises in the gym. Clean and jerk.

He stood easy and balanced, listening to the voices cursing and shouting below. Waiting for the right moment. Wanting to inflict as much damage as possible on the men coming after them. The shouts of triumph echoed up the stairs. Though he could not see from his position he was listening carefully. From below came the crunching of feet on splintered wood and still he waited.

'Tom,' Roshein was calling again.

He could not answer for fear of alerting the men below. There was the bustle and noise of men pushing through the ruined door. Then steps on the stairs. Still he waited. Gruff male voices shouting encouragement to each other as they mounted the stairs.

Now.

He stepped forward and tossed the TV like it had no more weight than a pillow. His silent delivery took them completely by surprise. The bulky set sailed out and down. The leading gangster saw the dark shape swooping towards him and put up his hands to defend himself. The TV brushed his arms aside and punched him squarely in the head. He toppled helplessly back down the stairs.

The TV carried on smashing into the men crowded into the hallway. They had nowhere to run. They twisted round in a vain attempt to evade the hurtling object. Smashing down among them splintering the cabinet – exploding the tube like a small grenade going off. Yells of pain and rage rose up from the stairwell.

MacLean was running through into the bedroom. The ladder was in position. The anxious face of Roshein was peering down.

'Go!' he yelled and swarmed up after her.

It was but a moment's work to pull the ladder up and slam the trapdoor shut behind him. The roof-space was dim with faint light filtering in from the eaves of the sloping roof. He felt Roshein's hand on his. She was pulling him along. He went willingly wondering how many of Brown's soldiers he had put out of commission.

143

No matter how many he had injured there would be plenty more to take their place. Of that he was sure. They had won a minor skirmish but the real war was yet to be fought.

Orchid Brown had killed one of MacLean's soldiers. MacLean was not one to forgive and forget. He wanted revenge. But first he had to regroup and plan his next attack.

Roshein led him into a rubble filled backyard and out through a broken door into the street. The shouts warned them something was wrong.

MacLean saw the men gathered around Charlie. He was backed up against a gable wall. John lay on the ground squirming in agony. One of the thugs had his baseball bat raised ready to hit Charlie. The emergence of MacLean and Roshein distracted him. MacLean started running.

35

The batsman turned with a snarl on his face and swung his weapon at MacLean. He ducked and went in under the club. MacLean was moving, fast. His target was static. He heard the whoosh as the wooden weapon missed his head. He straightened up and the top of his head cannoned into the batsman's chin. There was a grunt and they both went down. MacLean's hand grabbed for the bat. He wrenched it from the suddenly slack grip of the gangster. Just in time.

The bats met in mid air as he countered the second thug's attack. He drove up with the blunt end punching his attacker in the stomach. The man bent over and grunted but recovered enough to swipe again at MacLean. Then the thug had more to contend with. A pair of arms wrapped round him from behind as Roshein grabbed him. She was clinging to his back while trying to bite his ear.

The thug swung about and brought his weapon over his shoulder. The blow glanced from the side of Roshein's head. She yelled with pain but still didn't let go. Charlie took a hand then and kicked the man in the knee. The thug turned on his new attacker and swung at Charlie. He was badly hampered with Roshein still clinging to him. As Charlie ducked MacLean stepped in. He had all the time in the world and there was no mistake. The bat he wielded hit the man solidly in the teeth. With Roshein strangling him and MacLean's calculated strike, the man crumpled to the pavement. Roshein released her hold. She was rubbing at her head as she glared at the man on the ground. Then she kicked him.

'Bastard!'

'Come on! Let's go!'

MacLean was anxiously watching the street expecting more of Brown's thugs to appear. John was on his feet bleeding from a cut on his head. Charlie took him in tow and ran across to the adjoining street.

Pausing only to whack the first thug who had gone down under his

145

initial attack and was showing signs of reviving, MacLean grabbed Roshein's arm and followed Charlie across the street to the car.

Breathlessly they tumbled inside. Charlie wasted no time starting up. With tyres screeching they hurtled down the street.

John was in the front passenger seat holding his hands to his injured head, traces of blood on his fingers. MacLean was in the back seat with Roshein. He was turned around, keeping a lookout through the rear window for signs of pursuit.

'Slow down, Charlie,' he called. 'We don't want to attract the peelers.'

Charlie eased off the accelerator and the car slowed to a more reasonable speed. Roshein was holding MacLean's hand. She was squeezing tightly. He gave her a reassuring grin.

'What kept you back there in the house, Tom? I was worried you were going to stay there and hold them off on your own.'

'I was trying to get them interested in the TV. Figured it might delay them a bit.'

'The TV?' She looked askance at him. 'What the hell are you talking about?'

'Promise you won't hit me.'

'Hit you! If I have to, I'll knock some sense into you. Stop talking in riddles.'

'I gave them the TV as a down payment.'

Her face was screwed up in bewilderment. 'You gave them the TV! Has all this flipped your brain?'

'Well, you owe Brown a lot of money. I thought they might just appreciate something on account.'

'On account! Tom, would you tell me properly what's going on?'

He was grinning crookedly at her. 'I wasn't sure they would accept the gift in good faith so I chucked it down the stairs to them. Unfortunately they didn't catch it. It knocked them about a bit and then the cathode tube exploded.'

Her eyes opened wide. 'My TV! That was almost new. I only bought it a couple of months ago.'

'Couldn't you claim it on your house insurance?'

She let go his hand and aimed a punch at his midriff.

'Hang on.' He was trying to defend himself. 'I couldn't lift the fridge so I used the TV. There was nothing worth watching on it anyway.'

She was still seeking a way through his defence.

'Tom MacLean, you owe me for a new TV.'

He managed to grab her hand and pull her close. By accident or design their lips met. The fake fight dissolved into a kissing diversion.

'Mmm . . . don't try to get round me,' she murmured in his ear. 'You'll have to make it up to me in some other way.'

'Would you two stop spooning in the back? We have a mob of gangsters up our ass. I'm trying to drive carefully so as not to draw attention, and you two messing about isn't making it easy for me.'

'Keep your eyes on the road, Charlie,' Roshein said, not releasing her hold on Tom. 'You shouldn't be watching us anyway. Did you hear what this gombeen did with my TV?'

'Ach, sure the man has no culture. You can take the price of the TV out of his cut of the loot.'

Eventually they reached the vicinity of the Phoenix Fancy Fare warehouse. Roshein had snatched up her handbag before she fled the house. The bag contained the keys to the padlocked gate and the warehouse. In a very short time they had driven around the back, relocked the big gates and gained entrance to the warehouse.

'What are we going to do for food?' Charlie asked.

'This place is coming down with crisps and chocolate and packets of nuts. There's tins of dog food from when I had a dog.'

'Huh,' Charlie grunted. 'That seems appropriate enough. We'll all be barking mad after we've spent a few days cooped up in here.'

'Cans of pop,' Roshein continued with her list of consumables, ignoring Charlie's gloomy prediction. 'There might be some tinned sausages. I'll have to check the shelves though they're probably out of date. It was a line that never really sold.'

'Crikey!' John interrupted, his injured head forgotten for a moment. 'It'll be just like Christmas; sweets and nuts and pop.' They had arrived in the tiny utilitarian kitchen by now and John discovered the little cooker. 'Look, we can have proper cooked meals. I could do potato crisps and grilled sausages. That'll be like a nutritionally balanced meal.'

Nobody felt like endorsing this menu.

'We'll have to keep the lights out at all times,' MacLean speculated. 'Can't take a chance of them being seen or someone's bound to come and investigate.'

'There's plenty of hand torches and millions of batteries. If we use them carefully the light from those shouldn't be seen from outside.'

'What about sleeping arrangements?'

'Mmm. There should be blankets on the shelves. Some can sleep in the office and some in the kitchen. There's little electric fires we can use also

147

if it gets too cold. There should be a batch of inflatable mattresses somewhere.'

'Right, we seem to have all our orders. Anyone for lunch?'

They feasted on crisps and salted nuts with bars of chocolate for desert. John discovered a tin of powdered milk and they were able to wash down the grub with hot mugs of coffee.

'Oh, I enjoyed that,' observed John. 'There's some advantages to being on the run.'

'Yeah, that's all very well, but we have to figure out some way to hit back at Brown. John, you're the brains, have you anything in mind?'

John was happily munching on a chocolate-coated peanut bar. He hastily swallowed to clear his throat then took a drink of fizzy pop.

'As a matter of fact I have. It'll be difficult. But I think I've figured a way to pull it off.'

'Yeah, go on then, tell us.'

'I've discovered a gambling den run by Brown. It's illegal, but somehow he keeps it open in spite of that. Must be well in with the peelers and city councillors. Anyway he runs it with impunity. What do you think?'

'A gambling den!' MacLean whistled. 'If I know anything about gambling houses there'll be big money involved. Knowing Brown he doesn't go in for peanuts. And as well as that, you may be sure it'll be crooked. Brown never ran anything straight in his life. If we can pull off something like that it will net us a fortune. Have you any details of how the place is run?'

John pointed to a duffle bag he had been hauling round since he called that morning.

'It's all in there – blueprints of the building, security systems, personnel working in the place, times of shifts. Everything you need to know about that place is in a folder in my bag.'

They sat in silence staring at John. He chewed on his chocolate and stared back at them complacently.

'If we can pull this off it will be a small act of revenge for poor Dennis.'

'In that case we have to pull it off. Let's put our all into this final job. It would indeed be a fitting memorial to a brave comrade.'

Solemnly they nodded their agreement. In the silence that followed they heard a noise somewhere in the depths of the warehouse.

36

'They've followed us,' hissed Roshein.

In the intervening silence they strained to listen.

'Could be rats,' whispered Charlie.

'Rats don't knock over buckets.'

That's exactly what it had sounded like, a tin bucket rattling on a hard floor.

'Come on.' MacLean moved to the door of the office where they had congregated to discuss their plans. 'Spread out and keep quiet. No heroics. Yell if you see anyone.'

They dispersed into the interior of the warehouse.

MacLean headed for the back door. Daylight was filtering into the interior of the building. Shadows filled the gangways. He stepped carefully – eyes scanning every nook and cranny. The shelves lining the aisles of the warehouse piled high with merchandise.

Arriving at the rear entrance he carefully tried the door. It was unlocked. He paused and listened. The faint sounds and movements within the building were confusing. He was beginning to believe his companions prowling about in search of the intruder were making the bulk of the noises he was hearing. As he turned to retrace his steps the express train came out of the tunnel.

MacLean went down, bowled over by the speed and mass of the fast moving figure that emerged from behind a pyramid of children's toys. He caught a glimpse of a bulky form and then he was on his back, the wind knocked out of him. He rolled over on his front, urgently sucking in air to his shocked body. Painfully he got to his hands and knees, paused a moment, as he felt himself recovering before getting back on his feet.

The intruder was at the back door. MacLean yelled out a warning to alert his companions, but also to challenge the intruder who was intent on escaping from the warehouse. The man fumbled for a moment at the door and then pushed it open.

In desperation MacLean launched himself forward. He hit something solid. The man staggered forward with MacLean clinging frantically to his back much as a parent gives a piggyback to a child.

There wasn't much MacLean could do to stop the forward momentum of his captive. The man seemed as strong as an elephant. He was staggering forward with MacLean clinging to his back. MacLean was helpless to stop the fugitive from running on indefinitely. For the time being all he could do was hang on.

The mysterious runaway was heading for the rear gate that was always kept locked. It was imperative the man was stopped. If he escaped he would warn Brown of the gang's whereabouts.

MacLean began to slide down the broad back. He knew he was seconds away from losing his grip altogether. He kicked hard at the legs of his mount. It was a fortuitous strike and the man stumbled, arms swinging as he tried to keep upright. With the burden of MacLean on his back it was a losing struggle. The runaway went down on his knees with a grunt of pain as he hit the rough surface of the yard.

MacLean went instantly on the attack. When he felt his mount going down he released his tenuous hold and smashed a hard punch to the man's kidneys. He might as well have hit a sandbag for all the impact it had.

The intruder was wearing a duffle coat that hid most of his form. He ignored the punch and was intent on clambering back to his feet again. MacLean tried another track. Swiftly he moved to one side and kicked the man in the head. His victim grunted but the kick did not prevent him from getting on to his feet. MacLean kicked again and a large hand reached out and grabbed his foot. With a quick jerk MacLean was tossed on his back.

It was MacLean's turn to grunt as the fall punched the wind from him for the second time during his encounter with the mysterious intruder. While he was readying himself for another assault, there was the noise of footsteps in the yard and his companions steamed to the rescue. The intruder backed up against the chain-link fence and faced his attackers. Both Charlie and John were wielding pickaxe handles they had picked up in the warehouse.

'All right, fellow, better come quietly or we'll beat you to a pulp,' Charlie said aggressively.

MacLean was looking with some curiosity at their captive. He looked large and bulky in his duffle coat. A bloated, pale face stared out at them from eyes sunk in rolls of fat.

No wonder my punches didn't have much effect, he was thinking. This guy's built like a whale with layers of blubber to protect him. He peered more closely suddenly realizing the face was quite young, albeit he was solidly built, but nevertheless only a youngster.

'Careful what you're about, mister. I could take that stick away from you and push it up your ass, then toss you and the stick over this fence.'

Roshein had arrived on the scene. 'What were you doing in that warehouse?' she yelled. 'That's private property. I've called the peelers. They'll be here any minute.'

'Fuck you and the peelers! I won't be here when they arrive.'

'Who's paying you for watching this place?' MacLean suddenly asked.

The puzzled look in the youth's eyes told him he had made a significant discovery.

'Ain't no one paying me. All I did was take a few eats. I didn't damage anything.'

'How'd you get in?'

'Locks ain't no barrier to me. I just picked them. I don't need to mangle locks to open them.'

MacLean remembered the youth fumbling at the rear door after he had been bowled over. He had relocked the door after finding it open. The fugitive took only seconds to undo it and make his escape out into the yard.

'Whatever Brown's paying I'll double it,' he said.

Again that puzzled look. 'Brown, who the hell's Brown?'

'Let's just beat the shite out of him.'

Charlie was getting impatient. He shook his pick-axe handle menacingly. John moved up as well. Duffle Coat said nothing, watching for a chance to grab the weapon and do what he threatened to do with the stick.

'Hold it.' MacLean held up his hand. 'I have a notion this fellow has nothing to do with Brown. I think he's just a common burglar.'

'I ain't no burglar! I . . . I just needed somewhere to stay for a day or two . . . that's all.'

'You been living in the warehouse?' MacLean asked.

Doughboy stared out at him with his blackcurrant eyes but said nothing.

'Let's go inside and discuss this,' MacLean suggested. 'We'll attract attention if we all stay out here. We'll call a truce for now. You promise not to run and we promise not to gang up on you.'

For a moment it looked as if the youth might refuse then he shrugged and splayed his podgy hands. Warily keeping an eye on the stranger the little group trudged across the yard and back inside the warehouse.

37

Once inside MacLean began to quiz the youth. The others gathered round and stared curiously at him.

'You say you only wanted a place to stay. Are you homeless?'

For the first time the youth looked discomfited. He had pulled back the hood of his duffle coat exposing a large head. His dark hair was plastered flat on his skull. He looked even younger with his head exposed. The youth shifted his feet and looked down at his hands.

'It's only temporary. I had a row with Samantha. She threw me out.'

'Samantha, she your girlfriend?'

He nodded and a brief unhappy expression stirred on his face. 'It's only for a little time. We had a bit of a disagreement. I was cruising round looking for somewhere to stay. I already knew about this place being closed for a few weeks. I didn't think no harm in living here till Samantha took me back.'

Roshein moved forward. 'I'm sorry. We took you for someone else. What's your name?'

'Liam Doherty.' He stared at her shyly. 'I lost my job, you see. That's when the trouble started.'

'Let's go back in the office. We can talk there.'

They spread themselves around the office on chairs and desks and stared curiously at the robustly built youngster. Haltingly he told them his story.

Steve Quinn, an elderly clockmaker and locksmith, had taken Liam on as an apprentice. Quinn had him stripping locks and clocks almost as soon as he had joined the old man in his tiny workshop. Once he was trained, Liam was sent out on emergency calls, a duty old Quinn hated.

'It was so good. I just loved to drive around the city sorting out problems. People locked themselves out. Sometimes a householder wanted the locks changed to prevent another party from having access.

Properties were broken into and locks smashed in the process. When I was out on a job I met Samantha.'

On Liam's own admission he never had much luck with women.

'I don't blame them for avoiding me. I'm five foot six and eighteen stone.'

Samantha was a kindred soul for she was, like Liam, overweight. They discovered they had a lot in common. He loved junk food, as did Samantha. They instantly bonded and Liam moved in with his new girlfriend. All might have been well except something happened to change Liam's fortunes. The old locksmith had a heart attack and the shop closed down throwing the young locksmith out of a job.

Life on the buroo was not good. The pittance the British state paid an out-of-work locksmith was hardly enough to keep Liam in doughnuts and fizzy drinks, never mind pay rent and keep Samantha in iced buns. MacLean sympathized. For the few weeks before finding the job at Phoenix he had done the same as Liam and tried to subsist on the same meagre amount.

Liam continued his tale of woe. Last week Samantha showed her true feelings. She kicked Liam out of the flat they shared. The stricken look on Liam's face said how much the rift with his girlfriend had hurt. The monologue ground to a halt. There was complete silence in the office. Suddenly Liam looked up with a sudden unease on his countenance.

'You said you called the peelers. I don't want to be mixed up with the no peelers.'

'Relax,' Roshein assured their guest. 'I didn't ring anyone. I just said that to put the wind up you.'

'I . . . I don't want no trouble. When I get a job again I can pay back what I took from here. It was just food I was taking.'

'Looks to me like we're all in the same boat here,' Charlie said thoughtfully. 'We've just been made homeless ourselves. The only thing is we can't afford to let anyone know we're here. The people who made us homeless are a violent pack of gangsters. We can't have you wandering off and letting out our whereabouts.'

Instead of looking worried by this remark Liam's face brightened.

'I don't mind being here,' he offered. 'I was sort of getting used to crisps and peanuts and chocolate. In fact, that's the kinda food I really like.'

Charlie looked around at the others and somehow found this funny. He suddenly began to titter then tried to turn it into a cough. It was too late. His mirth triggered a response in the others and the gang dissolved into helpless laughter. Even Liam became affected and joined in the laughter not quite understanding but nevertheless suspecting, he was the focus of the joke.

MacLean watched them with an indulgent air. He knew they were letting off steam. The laughter was a safety valve against the affects of the tension and worries over the last few days.

'Oh well, Liam,' Roshein managed through her mirth. 'It looks as if you have joined up with us whether you like it or not. Maybe when you've found out what you've let yourself in for you might not be so keen.'

Liam grinned at her his broad face lighting up with pleasure.

'To tell the truth I was getting a bit lonely here on my own. It'll be good to have a bit of company. What are you guys running from anyway?'

'We crossed swords with a gang boss,' Roshein said carefully. 'With the help of my sister I was running this warehouse.' She waved an arm to indicate her surroundings. 'Then this hoodlum came around wanting protection money. I didn't pay, so I had to shut up shop and go into hiding. Unfortunately he found out where we were living and came after us. Hence we've come back here to hide out in the hope he won't think to look for us so close to home.'

Liam's eyes widened. 'You ran this place! Wow! That's cool. There's masses of good stuff in here. I know what you mean about protection. When I was on my rounds sometimes it was to repair damage inflicted by protection gangs. Those gangsters must be raking in thousands.'

'Didn't your boss pay protection?'

'Nah, he only had a little workshop. We weren't worth bothering about. They mostly went for big businesses like yours. Builders were popular with the gangs. I don't think any building went up in Belfast without paying protection. If they didn't pay then the gangs went to the site, smashed the locks and stole equipment, or set fire to the place. It was my job to make good again the locks that were damaged. The builders usually paid the gangs in the end. Those guys didn't mind beating up the workers or destroying their transport. You can't win against gangsters.'

'I guess you're right,' MacLean said heavily. 'That's what we're finding out.

'Charlie, why don't you take Liam and sort out the sleeping arrangements. It looks like we'll be here for a while. Roshein and I have some things to discuss.' MacLean was making signals to Charlie who nodded understandingly.

'Come on, Liam, show us where you were kipping down.'

As soon as the youth was out of hearing MacLean turned to Roshein and looked at her questioningly.

'What do you think? Can we trust him?'

'He is sweet. I feel kind of sorry for him. Maybe we shouldn't tell him too much of our own situation though.'

'Yeah, that's what I thought. I think he's harmless enough. What about you, John? You any reservations?'

'Nope. He seems a bit of a sad case. It's almost as if he was glad we found him.'

MacLean nodded thoughtfully. 'What he said about knowing locks made me think. Perhaps we can make use of those skills.'

John's eyes widened. 'Hell, I never thought about that. You mean the gambling club job we were thinking on? Or is that all on hold now we've been turfed out of our natural habitat.'

'Not necessarily, this tubby locksmith might just be our lucky break.'

38

Sometime during the night while the gang slept, a bulky figure made its way to the rear of the warehouse. There was no sound as the door was unlocked and Liam slipped outside. Carefully he closed the door behind him. Keeping to the shadows he made his way outside the surrounds of Phoenix warehouse and into the industrial estate of which it was part. His objective was the public telephone situated a few streets away. When he had finished his call he crept back to the warehouse and was soon tucked up in the small kitchen where Charlie and John slept peacefully unaware of their guest's midnight ramblings.

Wrapped in each other's arms MacLean and Roshein were sleeping also. In deference to their relationship the other members of the gang had graciously allowed the couple the privacy of the office. The stock of inflatable mattresses they unearthed ensured the inhabitants of Phoenix Fancy Fare rested in comparative comfort during their sleeping hours.

The following day started slowly. No one was eager to face the chilly atmosphere of the large building to which they had fled for refuge. So they lay wrapped up in blankets that had also been filched from the Phoenix stores. In the end it was hunger that drove the refugees from their resting places.

John was first in the kitchen where he heated water for coffee. When he went the rounds informing his companions the brew was ready, one by one they joined him.

'Afraid there's not much in the way of breakfast unless you want crisps again or biscuits.'

There was a universal groan. Last night the snacking had taken on a party atmosphere but in the cold light of morning faced with the prospect of crunching into salted peanuts and crisps it was not so appealing. The only one undaunted by the bizarre diet was the newest member of the gang.

'Great,' he enthused pushing half a packet of potato crisps into his mouth.

Roshein nibbled on fig rolls and tried not to look at the chubby youth as he tucked into the snack food.

'We ought to get some proper supplies in,' she remarked. 'Right now, a plain loaf and half a dozen eggs seem like a gourmet meal.'

'Yeah,' agreed Charlie. 'A few days of this fare and we'll be suicidal.'

He glared resentfully at Liam, peeling the wrapper from a large chocolate bar. Liam broke off four squares at a time and cheerfully pushed the confectionery into his mouth. The youth caught his look and grinned, showing of his chocolate-coated teeth.

'Want a bit?'

'No I do not! I'll try one of these fig rolls. You're right, Roshein we have to stock up on proper food. Just the basic staples like bread and milk along with cheese and cereals would be a good start.' He bit his fig roll in half and chewed. 'Mmm, not bad but no substitute for a sausage roll.'

'Maybe if we wait till it gets dark, one of us can slip out unnoticed for the groceries,' John suggested. 'Any volunteers?'

MacLean was shaking his head. 'Much as I agree with you about food we can't afford to take the chance of being seen. Just remember Dennis.'

That immediately sobered them.

'Who's Dennis?' Liam asked opening a large bag of peanuts.

MacLean looked speculatively at Liam wondering how far they could trust the youth. He had been working on plans for the gang's next job. If they could pull it off, robbing the gambling den would net them a large quantity of money.

'He was a friend of ours,' he ventured. 'He was murdered by the gang running the protection racket Roshein told you about last night. We think they'll pick us off one by one if we venture outside.'

Liam had stopped chewing. He crumpled the empty snack packet and it joined the growing pile at his feet.

'Gee, that's too bad. Would you like me to go shopping for you?'

MacLean watched, fascinated, as the youth reached for a large bottle of fizzy pop and put it to his head. When he returned it to the vertical half the contents had disappeared. Liam burped noisily and unabashedly apologized. He grinned cheerily across at MacLean.

'Good 'ere, ain't it!'

MacLean waggled his head bemusedly and looked over at Roshein. 'What do you think, should we sent Liam out for groceries?'

She cast her eyes upwards and shrugged. 'Don't look at me. I'm as hungry for decent food as the rest of you.'

In the end they decided to trust Liam. He was to leave the warehouse as soon as it was dusk and go shopping.

'No junk,' admonished John who undertook to write out a shopping list. 'Stick to the things I have written down.'

'I got no money.'

'That's all right, we have plenty.'

As the night gathered over the city Liam slipped out from the warehouse and made his way through the small industrial estate of which Phoenix was a part. He left behind an anxious MacLean.

'Hell, I can't just sit here. I'm not sure we've done the right thing letting that eating machine loose. I'm going to prowl around outside till he comes back in case something goes wrong.'

In the tool section he found a large spanner, which he slipped inside his jacket. Thus armed he set out to patrol the area round the warehouse.

The object of MacLean's concern was leaning against the bar of the Gridiron pub. Liam Doherty sipped his pint of Guinness while anxiously scanning the other patrons. He had finished his second pint and the barman was pouring his third when he saw the man he was waiting for.

'Evening,' he greeted the newcomer.

Detective Inspector Anderson nodded his greeting. 'A whiskey hot,' he ordered, and added, 'I'll pay for my friend's pint.'

The barman poured a measure of whiskey into a glass, spooned sugar into it and added hot water from a copper kettle. He put a small spoon in the drink and pushed it across to the detective. He then finished pouring the Guinness for Liam. Anderson paid with a ten-pound note. When he stowed away his change he turned to Doherty.

'Well, young man, what have you got for me?'

'Would you be interested in bagging an IRA cell?'

39

The detective thoughtfully stirred his drink making sure the sugar had dissolved before sipping at the mixture. He nodded in satisfaction.

'Whoever invented the whiskey hot should be awarded the Nobel Prize for innovation. There's nothing like a whiskey hot to warm a body up on a cold night. An IRA cell . . . sounds fine. We'd certainly like a crack at that one. And where should we be looking?'

Before replying the overweight youth sank his lips into the froth on top of his glass. After a long draught he wiped at the foam on his upper lip.

'You know better than that. What about remuneration?'

'Remuneration! That's a big word after six pints of Guinness. Would twenty buy it?'

Liam looked suitably pained. 'Give me a break, master. What would twenty buy these days?'

'Fifty then and it had better be good.'

'When did I ever bring you duff information?'

The detective made no answer and sipped at his drink. Though they each knew the other's identity neither man used names when together.

Liam was a snout for Anderson. His tale to the gang at the warehouse had been a complete fabrication, carefully rehearsed, that had earned him sympathy in previous similar tight situations.

Liam's profession was burglar. Not only did he snout for Anderson, but the detective also used him for other dubious purposes. When intelligence was needed that could not be obtained by legal means the fat youth was sent to get hold of it by fair means or foul. This, more often than not, meant a break-in. In this way they fed off each other. Anderson got his information while Liam, in return, received immunity from prosecution for his criminal life.

'Phoenix Fancy Fare. It's off Slaneys Lane on an industrial estate. I was inside when the team arrived. I nearly got away, but they cornered me. I gave them a cock and bull story about being homeless. I could have gone during the night while they slept. But I thought when they discovered me missing they would do a runner. Because I was on my best behaviour they sent me out for food.'

'Any names?'

For answer Doherty took out a piece of paper and handed it to the detective. Anderson unfolded it and noticed it was headed notepaper with the token bird and flames of the Phoenix. He tried to hide the little shiver of excitement when he recognized the names on the list.

'What makes you think they're IRA?'

'Why else would they be hiding out? You know how they work. They go to ground when some big operation is being planned. Then disappear when the job is done. They tried to tell me some big gangster has them in his sights and they're hiding out from him. I overheard them mention the name Brown. Does that mean anything to you?'

Anderson had to turn and bury his nose in his drink to hide his excitement. The connection with Orchid Brown and the gang gathering to plan a job was too obvious. When he was in sufficient control of his emotions he turned back to his informant.

'What about weapons?'

'No sign of any. I had a good look around before I phoned your fellows. You know as well as I do they'll pick up the shooters on the way to the hit. If you raid them tonight you'll catch them all together at the warehouse.'

Anderson's mind was working overtime as he tried to figure out how much it was safe to let his snout know.

'Listen, if there's no weapons we can't really charge them with anything. You have to find out what the job is and let me know in advance.'

'What? You mean you want me to go back there? No way am I risking that. You know what happens to snouts.'

The youngster was shaking his head. To calm his agitation he put his glass to his head and drained it in one go. With a regretful sigh he sat the empty glass on the counter. Anderson signalled the barman for a refill.

'You think you'll make me drunk enough to say, yes. Well, the answer is, no – drunk or sober – no thank you! I want to go on living.'

'Five hundred.'

Anderson made the offer and saw he had blundered. Immediately a cunning light flickered in the burglar's eyes.

'The answer's still no!' Doherty was wondering what had made the detective so keen.

Anderson sighed. 'They're not IRA. From what you've told me I think they might be a gang who's been hitting Brown's organization. We've named them the Orchid Gang for they've hit Orchid Brown on at least two occasions. Also, each time they strike they leave an orchid at the scene of the crime. They robbed a bookies belonging to Brown and were involved in a drug dealer heist. The dealer was one of Brown's employees.' The detective decided to leave out the murders of Dennis Mallet and Ben Orwell. 'If they're planning another job it'll be against Brown again. Of that I'm fairly certain. You just have to go back there and pretend you want to join them.'

Liam listened with some interest to the detective. He drank half his pint and stared into the glass wondering what advantage he could prise from this situation.

'What's in it for me?' he said at last.

'Five hundred and me locking away a file on you that would put you in Crumlin Road Prison for a decade at least.'

Doherty laughed and drained his glass for the fourth time and without asking Anderson waved the bartender over. The detective downed the remains of his whiskey.

'Same again.' Anderson waited till he had paid for the drinks before speaking. 'Here's to our continuing friendship.' There was a slight edge to his voice as he spoke. 'I need the goods on that gang. With them harassing Brown he might be suckered into making a mistake. They're the only people who've made a dent in his organization. I just might turn this to my advantage. With a bit of luck I'll nail two birds with one snout. Whether you like it or not you're going back in there. Failing that, you'd better prepare yourself for a long incarceration at Her Majesty's pleasure.' There was something flinty in Anderson's smile as he gazed at his companion. 'There's fellows in there doing time that would like to know who it was that grassed them up.' He shook his head regretfully. 'Nasty things happen in Crumlin Road – very nasty things.'

'You bastard! After all I've done for you. Anyway, I want that five hundred now.'

'You know I don't carry that sort of money around. You'll get the reward, never fear, but not till you bring me the info, my fat friend. Only when I have those villains in my sights.'

'Sometimes I wish I'd never met you,' Doherty said bitterly.

40

The Roof Proof Gaming Club was situated in an old distillery. Since the end of its days as a brewery, the place had been converted into a hotel. Many of the artefacts from the heyday of the brewing industry had been salvaged and used to give the rooms a unique atmosphere of bygone days when whiskey was distilled on the premises. The name of the club was derived from the common name used by the man in the street for the dark amber liquid produced by the brewery.

It was reputed that after one drink of the robust liquor the roof of the imbiber's head lifted off. So Roof Proof was what it was called amongst the heroic men who had downed the potent brew. That was the legend and who knows, the managers of the distillery might well have made up the yarn themselves in order to enhance the desirability of their product.

The Roof Proof was one of the businesses owned by Orchid Brown. Making the most of the gambler's appetite for thrills and excitement, a brothel was situated on the top floor. Between the betting tables and the girls many thousands of pounds found its way into the safekeeping of Orchid Brown and his partners. The revenue thus earned was deposited in a large iron safe. It was this safe that was the object of intense interest by the Orchid Gang.

Many hours had been spent planning and gathering intelligence regarding the club. Windows, doors, fire escapes, roof access had all been explored. The new recruit to the gang had proved invaluable in planning the proposed raid. With John's expertise at hacking into radio and security links they had a good idea of the protection installed.

'We need someone to go inside the club when it is open and gamble a little of our money,' MacLean proposed. 'That way he can check out the layout of the club and note the number and position of bouncers. He would have to circulate all through the club and memorize everything that might be of relevance.' He looked around at his little team. 'Brown and some of his associates might know me. Twice I've crossed them in a punch up. That one time here at Phoenix and again when we were running from Roshein's house.' He hesitated, for he knew full well his face was well known in Brown's criminal kingdom. After all, when he came out of prison Brown had offered him Tennant's job. 'Are there any volunteers?'

'Perhaps I would be the one to carry out that task,' offered Charlie. 'Though there was that scrap coming away from Roshein's. Would anyone recognize me from then?'

'There is a chance of that for sure. The only one we're fairly certain is not known is Liam.'

The crew turned and looked at the chubby youth sitting in on the discussions. Since his decision to throw in his lot with them they had taken him fully into their confidence. They had even told him about their former compatriot Dennis Mallet and his fate. The self-styled locksmith had just shrugged and agreed to take his chances with them.

'What about the rooms upstairs?' he asked, solemn-faced. 'Shouldn't I case out that part of the club?'

'Liam,' Roshein exclaimed, 'what about Samantha, or have you given up on her?'

Liam managed to look shamefaced. 'It was just an idea. We need to know if there's bouncers upstairs as well as down.'

'Damn it, maybe I should go after all,' Charlie interposed. 'I have a much more mature outlook on these things. Can't have our youth corrupted.'

'Hang on,' John interrupted. 'Why can't I go? I would have a better idea of what to look for in the way of alarms and suchlike.'

'Oh, for God's sake,' Roshein spoke tartly. 'Men! Why don't you all go and sample the delights of the whores of Babylon?'

MacLean couldn't help grinning at her expression of disgust. 'That sounds very much like a quote from one of Ian Paisley's sermons.'

Liam surprised them all by suddenly standing up. 'My fellow Ulstermen, the Harlot of Rome is poised on the borders of our beloved province,' he began in an excellent imitation of the notorious preacher. 'Guard your loins against the insidious invasion of Papist idolatry. The Papist devil-spawn, as well as worshipping the Devil is also contaminated with communism and socialism. We must guard the last bastion of our Christian heritage. These gaudy and vulgar creatures are an abomination in the sight of God. Ulster stands as the last bulwark against the Whore of Babylon. Do not soil your souls with base surrender to the false prophets of Beelzebub. Ulster says no!' As he bawled out the last statement Liam brandished his fist wildly above his head.

With the exception of Roshein, still looking miffed by the eagerness of her compatriots to visit the brothel, his audience laughed uproariously and applauded as the youngster bowed and sat down again.

MacLean called the meeting to order. 'OK, let's have a bit of serious discussion about this. Whoever goes in for the reconnaissance can use their own discretion whether to visit the upper rooms or not. If anyone is squeamish about paying for a sexual encounter you can always suggest the idea and then make some excuse not to go any further.'

His audience had the grace to blush while casting covert glances at Roshein. She kept her gaze on MacLean, her tightened lips and the twin spots of colour in her cheeks an indication of her disapproval. It was Liam who suggested a way out of the dilemma.

'How about we play cards between us to see who goes in? Winner takes all.'

'Mm. . . .' MacLean nodded. 'That could be a solution. Everyone agreed?'

There was a general nodding of heads. Amongst the goods of Phoenix Fancy Fare were packs of playing cards. They broke open a pack and Liam took it on himself to shuffle. He performed the operation with great dexterity, which made MacLean wonder what other skills their latest recruit possessed.

'Are you in on this?' Liam asked MacLean who shook his head. 'OK, then you cut the deck.'

When the cut was made Liam gestured at Charlie and John.

'You guys go first. Highest card wins.'

Charlie split the deck and palmed a card. He held it up. Ten of spades. John was next. He pulled the six of diamonds.

'Damn!'

Liam passed his hand over the deck of cards a couple of times while intoning some gibberish.

'Omega char shish pell-mell the card that comes is the card that is.'

His companions were grinning at the fat youth's antics.

'Black magic, I reckon,' murmured John.

'Ah-ha!' As he spoke Liam pulled a card and held it so no one could see it. 'Damn!' he exclaimed echoing John's epithet.

Charlie tossed his ten of spades to the table. He was grinning triumphantly when Liam turned his card round for all to see.

'Ace of clubs.'

'Damn!' It was Charlie's turn to swear. His eyes widened as he stared at the card in Liam's podgy hand. 'The Ace of clubs – that's supposed to be the death card.'

41

The detective and his snout met at a different venue. In Belfast it was always best not to establish patterns. This time they choose a pizza parlour. Liam was vandalizing a large pizza. The menu stated it would feed a family of four. But then Liam never went by what menus and recipes asserted regarding portions; his own instincts guided him. Appetite was everything. If he was hungry he ate. If that meal didn't fill him he ate some more.

Anderson slipped into the seat opposite. Liam grinned at him and pushed the last of the cheese and dough into his mouth and chewed.

'I see you've eaten,' Anderson observed.

'You should try the three melts. It just drips with full flavour. Order me one while you're at it.'

'I haven't come here to eat. What you got for me?'

'You have no soul, master. Cockroaches and peelers are the only creatures that can go all day without food and still keep on the move.'

'It's amazing you're as slim as you are,' Anderson said ignoring the insult.

The sarcasm was lost on his companion. Liam caught the eye of the waiter and ordered another pizza.

'You want a drink?' he asked his companion.

'I'll have a coffee.'

'Bring me a large Coke. Eating pizza always makes me thirsty. Must be all that cheese on it.'

'Cheese, anchovies and all the other shite you pile on.'

'Now, now, master, don't speak disrespectfully about food, at least not in front of me,' Liam chided placidly.

'To get back to my original question, what have you got for me?'

'You were right; this gang is the one you mentioned to me at our last meeting.' The fat youth was speaking low in deference to the presence of other diners in nearby tables. Uninspiring music played incessantly and easily drowned out the conversation that might be overheard. 'They're planning another job against the man you told me about, Brown.'

His companion nodded non-committally. 'Good. What is the job?'

'Roof Proof.'

The detective blinked in surprise. 'The gambling den? Christ, that's a hell of a job to undertake. What makes them think they can pull a stunt like that and get away with it?'

The drinks arrived and Doherty took a long slug of the fizzy drink before replying.

'Don't forget they've got me helping them.'

'You're an arrogant pig and a fool to boot! There's no way they can rob that place. The amount of money they're raking in there they must have a safe to keep it in. And guards! Most of those bouncers will be heeled. It'll be suicide. Orchid Brown is no amateur like you and that gang you're hanging out with. He's a professional criminal and he has a gang of killers working for him.'

'That's the whole point. They're not supposed to succeed. When the robbery is underway and the shooting starts your lot come in and take the criminals into custody. Think of all those guns about the place. Christ, you'll not have cells enough to put all those villains in.'

Anderson was biting his lip and frowning. The new pizza arrived. Doherty immediately tucked in, pushing large portions into his mouth with evident relish.

'What's the plan anyway and when do they do it?'

'This fellow MacLean who leads this bunch and his bird Roshein will go to the club. They're to dress up for the occasion. I've been out doing the shopping for the clothes.'

'Hell, he can't go in there. He's well known to those guys.'

'He thinks he can. As I say, I've been doing the shopping for them. His bird ordered some stuff from the make-up shop. She reckons she can disguise him so he won't be recognized.

'There's a brothel on the top floor. He requests a girl and goes up to the brothel. Once up there he opens the fire door and there's me waiting on the fire escape. I go in. We make our way to the office where the safe is. MacLean is the brawn and takes care of any bouncers who might get in the way. While that's happening, another member of the gang breaks into the basement and, at the appropriate moment, sets off the alarms. Meanwhile, we've cracked the safe and tossed the loot out into the alley. The fellows outside grab the lolly and drive back to the rendezvous. In the confusion caused by the alarms suddenly going off MacLean makes his way downstairs, collects the woman and leaves.'

Anderson reached out, tore away a small piece of pizza and put it in his mouth.

'When is all this to happen?' he said chewing.

'They haven't set a date yet. When everything's in place then they'll move.'

'This MacLean, I found out something about him,' Anderson said glibly. 'He's done time in Long Kesh.'

For a moment Doherty stopped chewing. 'How so? What was he in for?'

'At the time he was suspected of being a hit man. He was their top assassin. From what I heard he took out British Special Forces. Killed several top rankers. Nothing could be proved against him. In the end he was pulled in on suspicion of being a member of an illegal organization. It was all they could pin on him. During the two years he was in prison, fatalities among the elite forces dropped dramatically. Now that he's out, the army are training a top team to assassinate him. They tried to do it in prison, but he managed to escape two attempts on his life.'

Doherty was staring at the detective with a worried frown.

'How do you know all this?'

'I'm a DI, for God's sake. I began digging into the man's background when you passed his name to me.'

Which was a lie, for it had been Anderson's task to track down the assassin who had been causing so much havoc amongst the Special Forces. It had been Anderson who had trumped up the charge that had taken MacLean out of the killing fields.

'You mean he's that good?' Liam's pizza lay temporarily forgotten on the plate as he absorbed this information.

'He's the best – the best they ever had. The army want him dead. They're biding their time till he makes contact with his old associates. They have a mole high up in the organization feeding them information. MacLean is playing it smart. He hasn't joined up yet with the organization. My bet is that the money from the robbery will find its way into the coffers of the IRA. Once he's back with them again the informant will let the security forces know. When MacLean goes active the army intends to take him down.'

The worried look was still on Liam's chubby features. The neglected pizza slowly congealed on the plate.

'Oh my God, what have I got myself mixed up in? If he finds out about you and me then I'm dead.'

'Calm yourself, the only people who know about you and me are you and me. No one else is involved.' Anderson did not let on he suspected there was a leak at headquarters. That would really have freaked out his fat informant. 'I keep my sources close to my chest.'

Liam looked down at the plate of pizza. Slowly he pushed it away. 'I think I've lost my appetite.'

'Don't you chicken out on me now. I need to know about that raid. This is the closest I've ever come to nailing that murdering bastard, not to mention that gangster, Brown. You're my only lead on them.'

'I'd better get back. I'll phone when I know more.'

Liam eased his bulk from behind the table built for slimmer bodies than his own obese form.

'I'll not let you down.'

Detective Inspector Anderson nodded his farewell. 'I'll be waiting for your call.'

42

Liam Doherty walked away from the meeting at the pizza shop with much to think about. In view of the revelation regarding MacLean, the fat youth began to worry for the first time about being able to survive in the twilight world he lived in.

His main source of income was the burglaries he carried out. Of minor consequence were the bribes he received from Anderson for information. The most important benefit from the alliance between the police officer and the burglar was the implied protection from prosecution offered within the partnership. Now his confidence regarding such an arrangement was rattled.

At their last meeting Anderson had threatened to throw Liam to the wolves by removing his immunity from prison. Not only that, the detective had also warned him he might expose his role as a snout. Liam knew quite well what happened to snouts. On top of all these considerations, it now looked like he was teamed up with a notorious assassin.

Liam walked through the streets of Belfast, his sharp mind pondering his options. If he carried out his promise to Anderson and informed the detective of the date of the raid and MacLean escaped the trap, then Liam would be exposed to even greater danger. It would not be hard for MacLean to work out who had betrayed him. Liam found it difficult to associate the mild-mannered man he had come to know and like over the last few days with the notorious assassin the detective had described.

Anderson had claimed the money from the raid was to finance the IRA. That being the case, not only would MacLean be after his hide, but he would have all the resources of the organization behind him. The more he thought on these matters the more apprehensive he became.

'Damn you, Anderson,' he swore out loud. 'And damn the curiosity that led me to break into that blasted warehouse.'

Liam wondered if he could jump on a plane and flee to London. He had never been outside his native Ulster, but he imagined he could lose himself in the vastness of that famous metropolis in England. Then he speculated if he did that and cut himself off from all his contacts, would he be able to survive in a strange environment? His options were limited.

He needed funds to do a runner. Money, that's what it all boiled down to. Where could he get that sort of money? The more he pondered the problem the more limited his options seemed.

'I need a big job that'll pull in enough loot to keep me comfortable,' he muttered.

Suddenly he stopped walking. The idea when it came was so startling in its simplicity he stood in the street turning it over and over in his head.

For a moment he felt dizzy at the audacity of the plan. Slowly but slowly a smile began to form on his chubby face and little by little replaced the worried frown he had worn since his encounter with Detective Inspector Anderson.

'All it will take will be steel nerves and luck,' he said to a dog pishing against a lamppost.

The dog ignored his observation and stepped back to sniff his handiwork. Liam gave a little laugh and with a lighter step began to make his way back to his friends in the Orchid Gang. Suddenly he punched the air with a clenched fist.

'Doherty, you're a genius!' he yelled, then looked around guiltily.

The only witness to his strange outburst was the dog who had left off its affair with the lamppost and was now watching him warily from a safe distance.

From outside the warehouse appeared deserted. No lights were visible. Inside was a hive of industry. MacLean sat at the desk in the office with a dismantled handgun in front of him. He was busy with rags and oil, cleaning and lubricating the mechanism. Liam Doherty was watching him at work.

'You seem to know what you're doing with that gun,' he observed.

'Where I grew up there were guns galore,' MacLean replied smoothly. 'Kids were used as carriers to ferry the weapons to a hiding place, or to take them to the man who was to use them. In the quiet times we retrieved the guns and played cops and robbers with them. I also watched the gunmen handle the weapons. The gun was a well-cared for tool in the hands of a soldier. His life, as often as not, depended on the reliability of his gun.' He smiled wryly. 'Just imagine you confronted the enemy and your gun jammed because of a bit of grime in the mechanism. You could find yourself very dead as a result.'

'Did you ever shoot anyone?'

MacLean gave his interrogator a sharp look then shook his head. 'No!' He indicated the weapon he was working on. 'This is just for show. When I wave this little beastie around even the bravest bouncer will back off. If I have to fire it I'll aim at the ceiling. The noise and smoke is usually enough to stop most people.'

Liam looked suitably relieved. 'Thank goodness for that. I don't want to go down on no armed robbery charge.'

MacLean looked shrewdly at his companion. 'You scared, Liam, about what we have to do?'

The youth gave a weak smile. 'Shite scared!'

MacLean smiled back at him. 'At least you're honest. Most men won't admit to fear. Even when they're shaking in their shoes.'

'What about you? Are you scared also?'

Before replying, MacLean began to fit together the weapon.

'A bit, but once the action starts usually you don't have time to be scared.'

'You've done this sort of thing before?'

'Sure, dozens of times.'

The gun was assembled. MacLean sighted along the barrel and pulled the trigger. He grinned disarmingly at his companion and Liam had to look away to hide the unease in his own eyes. The door opened and Roshein looked in.

'Tom, come in the kitchen. I'm ready to do your disguise.'

'OK.'

She seated him on a chair and studied his face for a moment or two. Arrayed on the table was a box of grease paints and various wigs and false moustaches and beards.

'You sure you know what you're doing?'

'Of course. I was in the amateur dramatic society. In one part I played Ophelia. The critics raved about it. Said I was the definitive tragic heroine.'

'Mad as well as suicidal, yeah, I can see that. Come on then. And I don't want to look like a clown when you've done.'

'Is that so? In that case I'll have to obliterate most of your face.'

He grinned up at her. 'You going to be all right with this caper?'

'Don't worry about me. I'll keep my end up.'

She picked up a brush and began to apply shading beneath his eyes. 'Give you shadows beneath your eyes. Makes you look older.'

She worked for some time on him stepping back occasionally to admire her work. Finally she handed him a pair of wide-lens spectacles. While he pulled the glasses on she held up a mirror. He frowned at the older man in the mirror. Greying hair and puffy eyes along with a small dark moustache changed him completely. Slowly he nodded.

'Pretty good. Even I wouldn't know myself if I met me in the dark.'

'Change into your suit. You'll look like an accountant who's embezzled the company's funds and is out to gamble the lot away.'

He stood up and pulled her to him. She felt the bulge of the revolver pushed into his waistband.

'Is that a gun in your pocket, or are you just pleased to see me?' she murmured.

He laughed and pushed her away. 'Only I'm afraid to mess up my make-up I'd show you how much I'm glad to see you. When this is over we'll take a long Caribbean holiday together.'

He took the gun out and laid it on the table then turned to the dark-brown pinstripe suit hanging behind the door. While he changed into the suit Roshein was putting the finishing touches to an excess of garish make-up. While he watched she adjusted a curly blonde wig. He nodded approvingly.

'You look like the accountant's whore who's trying to help him gamble away his illicit earnings.'

She smiled beguilingly. 'Do you prefer me this way, big man?'

'I've always thought the ideal situation for me would be a woman who was wild in bed, a woman who was a fantastic cook, a woman who loved cleaning and tidying around the house and a woman who was good with money. The trouble is, how would all those women live in harmony under one roof.'

'You arrogant bastard!' She stuck out her tongue at him.

He watched as she shrugged out of her coverall. Underneath she had on a tight-fitting, pale-blue silk dress. Looking at him seductively she hiked up the hem of the dress till he could see she was wearing a broad black garter around one creamy thigh. In spite of the seriousness of the situation he felt a tug of desire as he viewed her fine-looking legs. She picked up the gun and wedged it into the garter. Dropping the hem of the dress she experimented walking. He regarded her quizzically.

'If anyone tries to grope me they're in for a shock.' She picked up a blue leather handbag.

'Just remember,' he instructed her, 'if things start to go wrong just leave. Whatever happens we'll all meet back at the warehouse. Then its Donegal here we come.'

43

The detectives watching Phoenix Fancy Fare were on the top floor of a disused factory. They were equipped with cameras, night-glasses and radio. Like all police officers in Ulster they were also armed. They watched the figures slip through the gates and disperse in different directions.

'What the hell do we do now? DI Anderson said the raid was not to take place till the twenty-second. This is the only the twentieth. Where the hell are they all going?'

'You're right, Anderson's informant confirmed the robbery would be on the twenty-second of the month which is not for another two days.'

'Maybe they're just fed up with being cooped up in that place. Perhaps they've only gone out for the evening.'

'Hell, we'd better call in and let them know what's happening.'

They made the call. Detective Inspector Anderson could not be located. The detectives left a message for Anderson to contact them with further instructions. They went back to watching and waiting.

'Whose turn is it to fetch the kebabs?'

'What about a good old-fashioned fish supper for a change?'

'OK, toss you for chips or kebabs.'

In spite of the Christian disapproval of gambling, it had always been popular in Belfast. Illegal pitch and toss games went on in back alleys with youngsters betting their pennies and halfpennies. Then there were the older youths who used silver coins instead of copper. Card schools flourished in the back rooms of pubs and clubs. No district, from the poorest to the more affluent, was without its betting shops. Punters flocked to greyhound races. Hare coursing, dogfights or badger baiting was popular in the more rural parts.

Orchid Brown knew quite well the hunger for gambling amongst his fellow Ulstermen and his gaming clubs were designed to tap into this lucrative source of riches. He had three gaming clubs in and around Belfast. The richest and most popular of these was the Roof Proof.

There were three floors and a basement. Former dining areas and kitchens from the days when the building had been a hotel had been gutted and converted into gaming rooms. Roulette tables and baccarat and pontoon games were scattered in the large spaces created. Bars served drinks at all hours of the day and night.

Other floors housed a series of cosy rooms where card games and other indoor sports were played at levels to suit every wallet. The very top floor was a series of bedrooms where gamblers could take the weight off their feet and relax in the horizontal with high-priced female participants.

The Roof Proof was a place where the rich and the not so rich came to relax and have a good time. Punters chasing fortunes sometimes lost their shirts and every time money changed hands lots of it went into the big iron safe housed in Orchid Brown's office.

MacLean circulated amongst the crowds on the ground floor. He held the obligatory handful of chips and wandered from table to table betting only enough to keep him mingling with the crowds. MacLean was watching Roshein. She flicked her eyes towards the rear of the room. Casually he followed. He watched her disappear through a door signed: Ladies Powder Room then wandered across to the bar and ordered a Bushmills. He winced at the price he had to pay for the drink, then consoled himself with the thought that the money he paid out was part of the proceeds from the raid they had made on Ben Orwell and Cannibal Bates.

Roshein come into view a few paces from him. He turned and smiled at her. 'Can a fellow buy a lady a drink?'

'Sure, I'll have whatever you're drinking.'

She moved close holding her handbag between them. It was hanging invitingly open. With swift sleight of hand he transferred the gun to the waistband of his trousers. Everyone was frisked on the way into the gambling club. Males were fair game for frisking. However no bouncer would dare put his hand up a lady's skirt to search for weapons. The only thing they got their paws into were the bags carried by the female clientele. MacLean glanced at his watch.

'Nice meeting you. I must see a man about a dog.'

Her smile was slightly strained as she nodded and moved away from the bar with her drink. MacLean purchased his token for the top floor where the rooms of sexual entertainment were located. Again he parted with a considerable amount of money. He consoled himself that it was a good investment. If everything went according to plan the money spent would bring huge returns.

With just a cursory glance at the sex-token the pair of bouncers opened the door and ushered him through. MacLean found himself in a wide hallway. There was a broad flight of stairs leading upwards and, at the end of the hall, he could see lift doors. MacLean decided to go for the stairs. He wanted to see as much of the building as possible.

On the next floor two bouncers were conversing in low tones. They eyed him curiously. He flashed his token and they stared at him till he disappeared up the next flight of stairs. If John's information was correct one of these rooms housed the safe. Liam was confident, given the chance, he could crack it.

'There's not a safe that's made that can keep me out,' he had boasted.

MacLean was suddenly assailed with doubts. They had nothing but the fat burglar's word that he was an expert safecracker. Damn, it was too late to start worrying now.

He was glancing at his watch. Two more men were patrolling the top corridors. Wall lamps threw a reddish glow into the hallway. A door opened and a middle-aged man with a paunch emerged.

'Bye, darling,' a female voice called after him.

The man gave MacLean a sheepish look. MacLean ignored him. His gaze was on the two bouncers. He walked hesitantly down the carpeted corridor trying to look as nervous as a man coming to a prostitute for the first time. His hand was inside his jacket as if he was massaging his stomach.

The bouncers tried to ignore the newcomer, waiting for him to disappear into one of the rooms. He reached the first man who looked at him indifferently. MacLean showed his token.

'I've never been up here before. Which girl would you recommend?'

'There's a number on the token,' the man said. 'That's the number of the room you should go into. Yours has a seven on it. That means room seven.' He turned sideways and pointed along the corridor. 'Three doors down.'

'Show me.' MacLean's voice sounded diffident and nervous.

The man looked pityingly at MacLean. He sighed and began to walk towards the door he had indicated. Though bigger than MacLean most of it was fat. MacLean figured he was in his fifties. He had an enormous gut. The other bouncer looked equally big but younger and fitter. He was looking down the corridor wondering what his companion was doing with MacLean.

The fat bouncer arrived at a door and pointed to it. MacLean waited, not making any move. The fat man sighed patiently and reaching out twisted the knob on the door of number seven. MacLean nodded and smiled then grabbed the big man and pulled him bodily inside the room.

'What the. . . !' began the bouncer, and then saw the gun. His mouth clammed shut.

44

A buxom blonde girl was lying on the bed staring wide-eyed at the two men. MacLean put his finger to his lips.

'If either of you make a noise I'll start shooting.'

The girl cowered in the bed pulling at the bedspread to cover her nakedness. There was a rapping on the door.

'Martin, what the hell's going on?'

'Tell him I'm sick,' MacLean hissed.

'It's the punter; I think he's sick or something.'

'Jesus!'

The door opened. MacLean was to one side out of sight. He waited till the man was almost in the room and then slammed the door hard against him. At the same time he swiped the fat bouncer hard across the face with the gun.

The man staggered back across the room blood spurting from his nose. MacLean grabbed a handful of jacket and jerked the second man all the way into the room. The younger of the bouncers was not slow on the uptake. He swung a punch at MacLean as soon as he saw what was happening. The swing missed as MacLean ducked. At the same time he shouldered the door to.

The younger bouncer was about to go on the attack again when he saw the gun in MacLean's hand. Slowly he backed further into the room.

'Wise move,' MacLean grunted. 'Both of you lie flat on the floor. Any shouting or trying to raise the alarm and I start shooting.'

The gun looked lethal and menacing in MacLean's hand. The men did as they were told and lay on the floor. MacLean put the gun away and pulled a handful of plastic fasteners from his pocket. In a matter of moments both men were helpless with their wrists bound behind their backs. He frisked them and pulled out a couple of Lugers from shoulder holsters. It was but a moment's work to eject the ammunition clips. The guns he tossed under the bed and ammunition clips he stored in his pocket.

He smiled at the girl as he approached the bed. She was staring at him with wide, terrified eyes.

'Just stay quiet and you won't be harmed.'

He pulled a blade out and she gave a little squeal of terror. MacLean ignored her and began shredding the bed sheets into strips.

'Damn you, mister, you're dead,' the younger of the men growled as he twisted his head to watch MacLean. 'This place belongs to Orchid Brown. He'll cut you into little pieces and feed you to his dogs.'

Further words were lost as MacLean gagged him with the strips of bed sheet he had cut. He did the same to the second man then bound their legs with more strips. Testing his handiwork he nodded in satisfaction before turning to the frightened girl. She looked so young MacLean was tempted to ask her was she still at school.

'I'll have to tie you up, honey. Wouldn't want you setting these two goons free.'

She was too terrified to make any resistance as he tied her to the bed. Even though she was so young he couldn't help being stirred by her voluptuous well proportioned body as he worked.

'Who are you, mister?' she finally asked in a trembling voice. 'What are you going to do to me?'

'I'm a member of the SAS,' he replied solemnly. 'That stands for Sex and Sin. My mission is to save young girls like you from a life of prostitution. Just you lie there quietly and pray for salvation. I promise you no harm will come to you.'

He went to the door and looked out. All seemed quiet. At the end of the corridor he saw the doors leading to the backstairs and the fire escape where hopefully Liam should be waiting. He glanced at his watch. Running ahead of time. That was good.

As he stepped through the doors at the end of the corridor he saw the flight of bare wooden stairs that ran down towards the rear of the building. The fire doors were to his right off the small landing. They were made of grey painted plywood with iron security bars running across the middle. He tried the handles and at first they resisted his efforts.

'Damn!'

Steadily he put pressure on the bars. With a loud screech they moved.

'Shite!'

He kept pulling. More squealing from dry metal rubbing over dry metal.

'Shite!' he said again and the door began to open.

Now the hinges creaked noisily. It was obvious the fire doors had not been opened in a very long time.

'Tom!'

So keyed up was he that the hissed sound made him jump.

'Yes, who the hell did you think it was?'

Liam reached out and began to help with the door. When it was wide enough the youngster slipped inside. He was carrying a large carryall and wearing a pair of navy-blue coveralls. Quickly he stripped off the coveralls to reveal a dark-grey suit with shirt and tie.

'Come on.' MacLean ordered. 'Walk behind me. Look as if you belong here. Or look sheepish as if you've just left a bed of lust behind.'

'I wish. . . .'

Liam picked up the carryall and followed MacLean. Swiftly they walked down the corridor and reached the main stairs and lifts. MacLean pressed the lift button. There was a clanking and whirring as the mechanism geared up. Doors slid open. Fortunately the compartment was empty.

'One floor down,' MacLean said unnecessarily as Liam stepped inside.

The lift deposited them on the floor below. If John's intelligence was correct this was the floor where the safe was housed.

The two big men on the landing stared curiously at the newcomers in the lift. MacLean smiled at Liam and stepped to one side to let him exit the lift first.

'After you, pal.'

Liam nodded his thanks and stepped out. MacLean lingered watching the two heavies closely. They were staring at Liam. Their faces indicated something was amiss. A man carrying a bag was not quite right in the Roof Proof. They stepped up to Liam as he turned to walk down the corridor. Fifth door along according to John.

'Hi there, mister.'

Liam smiled a greeting and kept on walking.

'Hang on a minute.' The man grabbed Liam by the arm and stopped his progress down the corridor. 'Where are you off to?'

'Where the hell you think I'm going?' Liam looked indignant and tried to shrug off the big hand holding his arm. 'This is a gambling club. I'm looking for a card game.'

The big man was not easily put off. 'What's in the bag, mister?'

'What the hell you want to know that for? It's my own personal belongings.'

The second bouncer was moving forward and then seemed to notice MacLean.

'You with this guy?' he asked.

MacLean shook his head. 'Never saw him before. We just come down in the lift together. What's going on?'

'Never mind, just keep going. We'll sort this out.'

By now Liam's bouncer had grabbed the bag.

'You're going nowhere, mister till I see what you've got in there.'

Liam looked at MacLean. 'What's with these guys? I got a few personal belongings in here.'

The bouncer was not letting it go. 'I gotta see what's in the bag.'

'Damn it, I'm a diabetic. I need to inject to keep stable. If I don't I'll go into a coma.'

'I still gotta see it.'

MacLean had his hand inside his jacket holding the revolver, waiting. The bouncers seemed to have forgotten him. All their attention was on the diabetic fat youth with the bag. Liam sighed deeply.

'OK, if you must. But don't touch anything. If the needles are contaminated they become useless.'

Liam unclipped the clasp of the bag and dug his hand inside. He brought his hand out and released his grip on the bag. As it tumbled from his grasp the big man interrogating him reached forward to save it falling to the carpet. He had not anticipated the piece of lead pipe Liam brought out.

Liam slammed the cosh hard against the man's forehead. The bouncer yelled and fell against the wall. Though he was groggy from the blow he was slipping a hand inside his jacket. Believing the man was going for a gun Liam kicked him hard in the stomach. The stricken man folded over groaning.

In the meantime his fellow bouncer started forward to the rescue. Momentarily forgotten, MacLean was directly behind him. By now he had his gun in his hand and smashed the weapon into the back of the man's head. The bouncer grunted and went to his knees. MacLean hit him again. He collapsed on the carpet, twitched a moment or two and then went still.

Liam used his cosh again and his victim settled quietly beside his companion.

'Christ!' Liam expelled the word with an explosion of breath.

MacLean was anxiously watching the corridors. Amazingly nothing stirred within his vision.

'You did well, Liam. We got to get these goons out of sight before someone comes along and sees them.'

'In the lift,' Liam suggested.

'They'll be discovered in there. Then the alarms will go off.' MacLean was looking round desperately.

'Not if we disable the lift.'

'You can do that?'

'Piece of pizza.'

They each took a body and dragged the two men inside the lift.

'Stand in the doorway and keep the doors open,' Liam ordered.

While MacLean did as he was told Liam took out a screwdriver and began work on the control panel. The steel plate came away revealing a mess of wires. In a moment or two he stepped out of the lift leaving the plate dangling on the end of the wires.

'Come on.'

When MacLean joined him he pressed the lift button. The doors slid shut.

'It'll stay there till the maintenance men can get in to repair it.'

They padded along the corridor and counted five doors down.

'This is it.'

Liam knelt before the door and peered into the keyhole. He pulled a bunch of keys from the bag and selecting one inserted it in the lock. MacLean stood leaning against the wall. His hand was inside his jacket gripping the revolver, which up to now he had used only to cosh people.

He watched the corridors both ways listening to the faint sounds of Liam working beside him. Other than those slight noises the corridor was eerily silent. A click and a grunt from Liam and the door swung open. Liam darted through. With one last look along the corridor MacLean followed.

45

It was late in the evening when Detective Inspector Anderson phoned in.

'Any messages for me?'

'Sergeant White phoned to say he wouldn't be in till lunchtime tomorrow. He has a dental appointment in the morning.'

Anderson grunted acknowledgement.

'The surveillance team at PFF phoned in to say the party had gone out for the night. They are standing by and will report in when they return.'

Anderson's antenna twitched.

PFF was the acronym used to identify Phoenix Fancy Fare. In view of the leaks coming out from the police station Anderson was worried the operation to net the Orchid Gang and with it the excuse to gatecrash one of Brown's business ventures would be compromised. The men assigned to help him were sworn to secrecy. Every precaution was being taken to foil the mole at headquarters.

He knew quite well the Roof Proof was an illegal gambling club. Brown was untouchable for he was protected by high-ranking police officers and political figures. The gang's raid on the club would provide an opportunity for some heavy-handed police action inside the club and perhaps provide material for future prosecution.

He phoned the team who were watching the Phoenix warehouse. The phone at the other end rang and rang. Anderson's worry factor increased considerably. He was not to know a series of simple coincidences resulted in Anderson ringing when the lookout team were not at their posts.

Detective James Clements was in his late twenties. A small moustache on his upper lip was an effect to make him look older. Alcohol was strictly forbidden on duty. However stakeouts were notoriously tedious and drinking helped pass the tiresome hours.

His companion on the watch was Detective Martin Keys. In his mid forties he was running to fat and had the customary middle-aged paunch and bloated red face.

'Now we've reported in I'll get the beer up from the car.'

'Good man! I have a thirst you could sharpen a chisel on.'

After a consuming a few tins of lager, Key's appetite began to gnaw at him.

'Who's going for the kebabs?' he asked, contentedly burping.

'I'll jump in the car and go,' Clements volunteered.

He was glad to get out of the room to give him a break from Keys. Aside from the older man's internal wind problems he was also addicted to telling crude and unfunny jokes and then laughing uproariously and spraying spittle as he gave the punch line.

Clements would take his time fetching the food – the longer the better as far as he was concerned. And anyway nothing was happening. If the people in the warehouse had gone out for the evening they probably wouldn't return till late. After all, the main action was not to take place for another few days. He could safely waste time on his errand.

The younger man was gone about an hour when Keys felt the need to relieve his bladder.

'Where the hell is that skitter?' he muttered aloud. 'I badly need a pish.'

In the end he abandoned his station and went downstairs to use the toilet on the ground floor. While the phone rang and rang upstairs the floodgates opened and Detective Keys sighed and thought he would never stop pishing.

The alarm bells were ringing for Anderson. He had been at home when he rang the station to check his messages.

'The twenty second of the month,' Liam Doherty had informed him. 'That's a firm date for the raid on the gambling club. If anything changes I'll contact you.'

There was still two days to go, but the birds had left the nest and, more worrying, Keys and Clements were not answering their phone. Anderson knew how dangerous MacLean was. All sorts of possibilities were coursing through his mind.

Had MacLean found the police surveillance team and cancelled them? There was the distinct possibility the former gunman had terminated the detectives assigned to watch him.

What if MacLean had discovered Doherty's betrayal? With the discovery that Anderson was on his tail MacLean may have gone on the run. Another possibility crossed Anderson's mind. It was quite feasible MacLean had fed the fat burglar false information to mislead the detective.

Cursing silently, Anderson grabbed his jacket and car keys. He was going to Phoenix to find out for himself what was happening.

Oblivious of the anxieties he was causing his boss, Detective Keys zipped his member safely inside his trousers and returned upstairs and resumed his watch. Idly he picked up another can of lager. Nothing had changed. There was nothing to watch.

'What the bloody hell's keeping Clements? He should have been back ages ago.'

Detective Clements had found himself behind an alluring young brunette in the queue at the kebab shop. He began chatting to her. They were beginning to discover they had a lot in common. Her eyes were sparkling as she weighed up the young stranger. Except for the silly moustache she was quite attracted to the presentable young man showing such interest in her. It was not long before they felt confident enough to exchange telephone numbers.

Detective Clements was well pleased with himself when he finally got his order for the food and jumped in the car to return to duty. That was until he got to the car-park behind the disused factory they were using as a base. His boss, Detective Inspector Anderson was just pulling in at the same time as the young policeman parked his car.

When he saw who it was James Clements knew not only were the kebabs cooked but so too was his goose. He lost his appetite for his supper as the DI jumped out of his car and stalked over. The young policeman was trying to push the takeaways under the seat when the door was wrenched open. Detective Inspector Anderson bodily dragged the young detective from behind the wheel.

'What the bloody hell is going on here?' The DI slammed a terrified Clements against the car. 'This is a stakeout not a bloody picnic.' Anderson's face was inches from Clements. 'Mister, you're back in uniform. And where is that asshole, Keys, while you're out fetching and carrying? I suppose he's down the pub filling his fat gut with Guinness.'

'I . . . I . . . he should be upstairs, chief I . . . I . . . only nipped out a minute ago. . . .'

'Shut up! Have I given you permission to speak?'

Anderson hauled the unfortunate detective around and pushed him towards the factory. 'Get up them bloody stairs. If this operation is cocked up I'll see you thrown off the force.'

Upstairs, Detective Keys sipped at his lager and cursed his companion for taking so long.

'I'll give him what for when he gets back.'

He opened another tinnie.

46

MacLean was watching Liam stuffing the holdalls. The bag the fat burglar brought with him and had aroused the suspicion of the security guards contained another couple of bags along with the obligatory potted orchid and, of course, the piece of lead pipe he had used to bludgeon the guard. When the raid was being planned no one had any idea how much loot the safe might contain so MacLean had opted for the extra bags.

'It'll all be cash,' was MacLean's guess, 'notes of all denominations. We will need something to carry it away.'

Now Liam, with one bag already filled, was rapidly filling the second with bundles of banknotes. It had been an impressive performance. The youngster had taken all of five minutes to crack the safe.

'Old model,' he explained to MacLean when the heavy steel door swung open under his skilful tinkering. 'Easy as opening a box of breakfast cereal.'

There were stacked bundles of cash inside the safe along with papers and deeds. Liam had given these later a cursory examination.

'Mostly IOUs and deeds against money owed,' he told MacLean.

Finally the bags could take no more. Some of the top banknotes ripped as Liam forcibly zipped the bags closed.

'Ready,' he stated as he set the orchid inside the plundered safe. 'I'll carry the bags. You'll need both hands free to handle any trouble.' The safecracker stood and followed MacLean to the door. 'Take a look outside and make sure the coast is clear.'

MacLean cautiously opened the door and poked his head outside. He did not see the youth behind him set down the bags he had been holding. Nor did he see the piece of lead pipe that Liam took from his inside pocket.

He was turning as Liam brought the cosh down with all his considerable strength. Had the blow landed properly the back of

MacLean's head would have caved in. As it was the pipe swiped along the side of his head with sufficient force to stun. With a low animal sound MacLean went down.

The youth knelt beside the unconscious man and with a grunt turned him over. MacLean flopped on to his back oblivious to everything. The burglar fished inside his victim's jacket and extracted MacLean's gun. He transferred it to his own waistband.

Armed with the cosh and pistol Liam began to feel more confident. Carrying the two bags of money he walked briskly along the corridor.

He almost panicked as two men in suits came out of a doorway. However he kept walking conscious of the weight of the gun in his waistband. He did not want to have to use it but now he had come this far he was determined nothing would stop him. The men would have been patrons of the club for they only stared curiously at Liam but made no attempt to speak or interfere.

By now he was at the lift where another two gents stood futilely pressing the call buttons. They glanced at Liam hoping he was one of the club's personnel and would come to their assistance, but the fat youth ignored them.

Liam was sweating by the time he arrived at the doors leading to the fire escape. He wondered how long it would be before MacLean was found. Once the open safe was discovered all hell would break loose.

Liam hauled the fire doors open and slipped outside. Casting wary glances below he began to descend. As he reached the bottom of the steps a figure loomed out of the darkness. Liam dropped the bags of cash and pulled the gun.

'Liam.' Charlie's voice was loaded with anxiety. 'Everything all right?'

'Like hell it is! MacLean copped one. He's up there injured. We'll have to go back up and rescue him.'

'Shite!'

'I'll give the signal to John to start the alarms. You go on up there and give MacLean a hand. When I've stashed the loot in the car I'll follow.'

'You got into the safe!'

'Sure, Charlie.' Liam hefted the two weighty bags. 'We're rich. Now hurry before someone finishes MacLean.'

Muttering profanities Charlie took the steps two at a time. Liam watched him for a moment then went looking for the getaway car. It was parked at the end of the next street. Liam tossed the bags into the rear seat. He climbed into the driver's seat, took a handset from the dash and spoke to John.

'John, set those alarm bells ringing. We're ready to go.'

Liam peeled a large chocolate bar, took a huge bite, started the engine and drove away from the vicinity of the Roof Proof Gaming Club. He did not hear the alarm go off within the building. He did hear the police sirens in the distance. Liam pressed a little harder on the accelerator.

'Not too fast. Don't want to attract any attention to myself. Not now that I have a fortune in cash in the car.'

Suddenly he began to laugh. Chocolate dribbled from the corners of his mouth. He was still laughing when the police cars passed him going in the opposite direction. He wondered briefly where they were going in such a hurry.

'Goodbye, Detective Inspector Anderson, goodbye, Orchid Gang,' he chortled. While Detective Anderson and his team waited in vain for the gambling club heist to take place in two days' time Liam would be long gone.

Charlie reached the top of the fire escape to find the doors into the building lying open. He crashed through not knowing quite what to expect. The doors banged back and Charlie saw on one side a set of wooden steps leading towards the rear of the building. On the other side were doors that obviously led into the club. Suddenly warning bells sounded throughout the building as John received the signal to set off the alarms.

Charlie pulled the doors open and found he was looking into a carpeted corridor dimly lit with red wall lamps. Doors were opening along the passage and heads peering out cautiously.

There was some shouting and a group of burly men appeared from the bottom end. Two of them were supporting a third person between them. The man they were half carrying was evidently disabled, for his feet were dragging along the carpet. Charlie couldn't see the face of the person being hauled along but he guessed it was the man he was seeking.

'Clear the way there,' one of the men was shouting.

'Everyone out! You're to assemble downstairs.'

'No need to panic! Everything's under control.'

The men carrying the injured man were elbowing their way along the corridor as it became crowded with men and women emerging from the rooms. Most of them were in some stage of undress. The men with the injured MacLean were coming rapidly towards Charlie. He stood undecided. Then they spotted him. Charlie was obviously out of place in a bomber jacket and jeans. Everyone else was dressed in suits.

'Hey, you! What the hell are you doing there?'

Charlie chose flight over valour. He turned and fled back the way he had come. There were shouts behind him and the thud of muffled feet on the carpeted floor.

Charlie pushed his way back out through the doors again. His only thought was to escape. Once through and on the landing he slammed the door behind him. Something heavy banged into it and the doors flew open again. A burly form crashed through.

Charlie lunged for the fire doors. Fortunately he had left them open. Once through he tried to pull them shut after him but a big hand grabbed hold of the edge and wrenched them from his grip. Charlie turned to flee. Something crashed into him and he was rammed against the railings of the fire escape.

He punched wildly at the man grappling with him. His attacker grunted and pushed hard against him. Charlie felt his feet go from under him. The railing was riding hard against his buttocks. He tried to push his attacker away. There was a rending, screeching noise and Charlie felt the railing move.

Charlie screamed and grabbed at his attacker. Unaware of Charlie's dangerous position the man punched with one hand while holding Charlie with the other. There was another rending screech of fractured metal and the rail pressing into Charlie's back gave way. There was nothing to keep the two men on the platform. For a moment they teetered on the edge, then the laws of gravity kicked in. Charlie yelled out in blind fear as he tumbled out into space. The man he was clinging to was yelling also.

47

Inspector Anderson was not a happy man. After a night of fruitless searching through the Roof Proof gaming club, nothing had been found that could prove useful in any prosecution against the owner of the place. The only tangible evidence that something untoward had happened were the two bodies found at the rear of the premises. One of the bodies had been identified as Charlie Mitchell.

According to Doherty, Mitchell was a member of the gang plotting the robbery on the gaming club. The finding of the body of one of the gang had suggested the raid by the so-called Orchid Gang had gone ahead as planned, though something had obviously gone very wrong.

Evidence of a struggle and the broken railing at the top of the fire escape told its own story. Charlie Mitchell had obviously been apprehended during the robbery and, while trying to escape, fell to his death along with one of the club's bouncers.

According to the men running the club nothing was stolen. Anderson shook his head in frustration. No matter how he permutated the events of the night he could make no sense of anything. He needed to talk this one over with Sergeant White. But that would have to wait. His sergeant was not due in this morning. He was having some dental work done.

'Two heads are better than one,' he was fond of telling his sergeant. 'Even if one is only a sheep's head.'

Once he realized the Orchid Gang were on the move, he had rustled up a team of cars to raid the Roof Proof in the belief he would find the suspects in the act of the robbery. In the end the whole operation had been a wasted effort. All they had found was the dead Mitchell and nothing incriminating against the gang boss, Orchid Brown.

His phone rang. He listened to the voice on the other end. It was Detective Keys from the stakeout at the Phoenix requesting to speak to him. Anderson had forgotten all about his team on watch. He should have sent a replacement team but the events of the night had overtaken him.

Serve the bastards right, he thought, thinking how they had let him down. Keys was probably wanting to know when Clements and he would be relieved. Anderson toyed with the idea of leaving them in place for another twenty-four hours.

'Yes, put him through.'

As the voice spoke to him Anderson suddenly became very alert.

'You're sure about that? They're back in the warehouse again! Damn it, stay on it! If they leave you get after them. Don't let them out of your sight. I'm on my way.'

Pausing only to leave a message for Sergeant White, Anderson ordered a car and was soon racing through the streets of Belfast to the vicinity of the Phoenix warehouse.

Detective Keys and Clements eyed their boss warily when he joined them at the lookout station.

'We could see only two people – a man and a woman.'

'And they're still there?'

'Yep, no one's left since.'

Anderson peered through the binoculars at the warehouse. He could see no sign of activity.

'Could you identify the couple?'

A noticeboard nailed up by the window held police photos of the people hiding out in the warehouse.

'The man was John Lamb.' The detective pointed to a picture of Lamb with long hair and looking too young to be a hardened criminal. 'I'm sure the woman was Rafferty.

Anderson nodded thoughtfully. 'Roshein Rafferty. Brown put pressure on her to pay protection. When she defied him he had her lifted and they shaved her head.'

'Looked like she had a full head of hair when we spotted her.'

'A wig, Clements. She would wear a wig till her own hair grows.' Anderson suddenly came to a decision. 'Clements, you stay here on watch. Keys, you come with me. We're going into that warehouse. Make sure your gun's loaded and working.'

Anderson took out his own weapon, a heavy Ruger pistol and checked it over. All police officers, no matter what rank, went armed in Northern Ireland. Beside him Keys took out his weapon and tried out the mechanism.

'Bring the break-in kit. We might need to force an entry.'

'Are you sure you want to do this, sir?' Keys asked, as he slung the haversack with the tools. 'Should you not request backup?'

Anderson eyed the detective with a cold stare.

'You're my backup, Keys. You'd better not let me down. If you do this right I might think of not downgrading you pair for last night's fiasco.'

His two subordinates gave a sideways glance at each other.

'Yes sir, we'll not let you down.'

'Watch our backs, Clements. There are still two members of the gang not accounted for. Liam Doherty and Tom MacLean are still roaming around out there. One of the others, Charlie Mitchell, was killed last night at the Roof Proof club. You see anyone as much as look like they're heading for that warehouse you buzz us straightaway.'

They took a circuitous route that brought them behind Phoenix. A dilapidated Ford Transit van was parked up near the building. Keys used a large pair of bolt cutters to cut the chain securing the gate. The two detectives crept cautiously to the rear doors of the building. For a few moments they stood and listened. No sound could be heard from within. Anderson nodded to Keys.

The detective wedged a jemmy into the middle of the double doors. Slowly he began to put some pressure on the lever. There was a sudden crack and the door sprang ajar.

Again they paused and waited for some reaction from within the building. Nothing seemed to be stirring.

'Are you sure they're still in there?' Anderson whispered.

'Positive. There's no way they could have got, out again without us seeing them.'

'OK, let's go.'

The hinges of the jemmied door creaked loudly. Anderson had his Ruger out. Keys dropped his jemmy by the door and took out his own weapon. The two men stepped inside, every sense alert, pistols at the ready. Anderson waved Keys to the left while he went right.

The two men moved into separate aisles that ran towards the front of the building. They crept along between piles of haberdashery. Nothing seemed to be stirring in the warehouse. As Anderson came to what seemed an intersection in the aisles he heard a faint noise behind him. He turned swiftly.

The movement saved him taking a pickaxe handle on the back of the head. Instead it hit him on the shoulder. The force of the blow was such his arm went numb and his gun tumbled to the floor. He did not waste time looking for his gun but instead launched himself at the man wielding the improvised club. They both went down with Anderson on top. He slugged the man on the side of the jaw. He could see the man's face and realized he had John Lamb on the floor, one of the Orchid Gang.

The youngster yelped and tried to bring his club around in a futile attempt to hit the detective again. The weapon was too unwieldy to handle effectively while lying on the floor and especially with a fifteen-stone detective inspector sitting on his chest.

'Police!' Anderson yelled and hit Lamb once more to discourage him.

The sound of a shot going off in the warehouse startled both of them.

'Don't move,' Anderson hissed.

He saw his gun a few feet away and clawed it to him. The detective stood up, grabbed a handful of shirt and hauled the youngster to his feet.

'Move,' he mouthed, pointing the gun in the direction of the gunshot.

He was pushing the youngster in front of him and at the same time listening for sounds of a struggle. Then he caught sight of Keys. The detective was standing holding his service revolver on a pale-faced young woman. In spite of the wig, Anderson recognized her. It was Roshein Rafferty.

'Keys, what happened?'

'It's all right, sir, I had to fire a warning shot.'

'Read them their rights, Detective. These two are nicked.'

48

The music was thumping hard and heavy. A raw hoarse voice cawed out the words.

Pain and Hate.
Pain and Hate.
Blood and tears.
Blood and tears.

The words didn't make any sense. His head was aching too much; agonizing coarse pain throbbing in his head and coursing through his body. The return from the blessed dark was beginning. He cringed from the hurt. Please! No more pain. No more hate. No more blood. No more tears.

Consciousness was returning and along with the awareness came the pain. Deep lacerating pain. Making him scream. Making him want oblivion.

'Hello, hello, anyone in there?'

While the voice was asking, something hard was being hammered against his skull the pain jarring and intense. He prised his eyes open.

'Ah, there you are, MacLean. Don't go to sleep on me again.'

Cannibal Bates tossed the hefty metal rasp he had been using to hit MacLean to the oily floor of the garage. The loud rock music thudded incessantly.

Bates stood back and admired his handiwork. His victim was hanging by his bound hands from a metal hook on the end of a hoist. He was naked and covered in blood. There were numerous cuts and abrasions on his body from which the blood seeped and dripped to the greasy concrete floor.

'Now, MacLean, I have to admit you've stood up to the treatment

197

better than most men I have worked on. Much, much earlier than this they would have told me where the money from the safe is. I'm going to give you another chance to tell me. Then if you don't co-operate, I'm going to get really mad at you. I've been gentle up to now but I am beginning to lose patience. So as you know exactly what I want, I'm going to ask again. Where is the money you took from the safe?'

The agony in his arms was unbearable. He had been suspended from the hook for . . . he had lost track of time. Had he been here days? He had passed out several times from the pain. His body was a festering mess of pain. He tried not to think of the damage Bates had inflicted on him. It would soon be over.

Soon I will be dead and it will be all over. Poor Dennis. He had endured this same torture at the hand of this foul creature and told all. Was it any wonder? I would tell but I know it will not ease my suffering. Even if I knew where the money was I would not tell.

Liam. Liam has double-crossed me. It doesn't matter for I am a dead man now. It is but a matter of time. If I tell them anything they will have won. The fact that they are still questioning me means that they don't know who else was with me.

Roshein, don't let them take Roshein. Set me free for a few moments and put a gun in my hand. The Browning 9mm parabellum. That would put a big hole in this monster. In the guts. Make him suffer. Then go after Brown. Damn them all to hell! For that's where I'm headed. . . .

'You're a stubborn bastard, MacLean. You'll tell in the end. Everybody does. Who was with you on this caper?'

The man hanging on the hook tried to lick his lips. They felt like pieces cut from a rubber tyre and glued on his teeth.

'What's that, MacLean? Are you trying to speak?'

The big man's face was close. MacLean stared into those mad, staring eyes.

Was it true what they said about Bates? Had he had eaten a man's brains? MacLean could believe it. Perhaps he would eat MacLean. This was an abattoir. Hanging on a hook. Suddenly the thought he conjured up was too real. He imagined the butchers critically examining his carcass.

There's a MacLean cadaver. Should carve up nicely. Roast pork.

'No, you're not going to speak.' Cannibal shook his head. 'If you persist in this stubbornness then it looks as if I'll have to do a bit of roasting.'

Bates was gone from him for a few moments. He heard vague clanking and banging as the man searched for his next implement of terror. There was the acrid smell of some chemical. Bates was holding up a five-litre can in front of him. He shook it and a liquid sloshed around it.

'Gasoline,' he informed his victim. 'Recipe for the barbecue from hell. Take one stubborn son of a bitch and add petrol.'

Bates was tipping the can so gasoline ran out into a small metal dish. With a flick of his hand he splashed the contents of the dish on the torso of the naked, bleeding man. The petrol stung the wounds on his body but MacLean was too far gone to flinch from this fresh torment.

He tried to arch his body, but the agony in his wrists was too great. Instead he sagged in despair. His eyes were wide open now as he bit down the moan he wanted to let loose. He watched his tormentor set the petrol can down behind him. The screw top spun away as he bent to reseal the canister.

MacLean watched the top roll along the floor and under a car parked close by. The car's bonnet was up and mechanic's tools were scattered around it. Bates cursed and bent to retrieve the top, but decided it was too much bother. Instead he turned his attention to the small portable bench on which was placed the instruments of torture he was using to torment his helpless victim. When Bates turned back to MacLean he was holding a blowtorch.

'I watched a guy do toast with one of these once,' Bates remarked conversationally. 'It seemed strange but it worked. The toast tasted good, crisp and dry.'

The big man fumbled in a pocket and took out a cigarette lighter. With a flick of his thumb the small flame ignited. He passed the lighter across the front of the blowtorch. There was a hissing sound and a fierce bluish flame jetted from the small round nozzle. Bates grinned at MacLean.

'Anyone for toast?' he asked and laughed uproariously.

MacLean stared at the flame. He knew he would not withstand this new treatment. He would tell all.

Bates was before him grinning. He waved the blowtorch in front of MacLean's face. MacLean could feel the heat on his skin. His eyebrows sizzled.

'Are you ready to tell me now? Where is the money? Who has it? Name all those involved in the robbery.'

The torturer waited, a smile of cruel anticipation on his face. The longer he waited the more terrified became the victim.

MacLean stared at the flame, the hissing blue flame as thick as a man's penis was waving back and forth before him.

Bates was shaking his head. 'I do believe you are still doing your stubborn act. If I don't get answers Mr Brown will be very disappointed. He told me in no uncertain terms: "Don't come back till you have the names of those bastards that robbed me and the location of the loot." I don't like to disappoint my boss. So start talking now and I might just go easy on you.'

It was agony. It was forlorn. It was the last reserves of a dying man. What was it Charlie had said? *The last kick of a dying rat is always the worst.*

MacLean jerked upwards. The cords that held him bit cruelly into his wrists. His body was a mass of suppurating pain. He knew he was dying but he kicked out with the last of his draining strength.

Bates was close. The knees came up into his crotch. Bates was a big man and strong as an ox. But an unexpected knee in his privates from a helpless victim came as a shock.

The big man jerked backwards, his heel catching the can of petrol he had discarded minutes before and upsetting it. He stumbled, lost his balance and went over backwards landing on to the square container, his weight crushing the tin. Petrol gurgled from the open neck spewing across the greasy floor. Some of it soaked into the clothes of the big man.

Bates grunted as the petrol can dug into his back. With a curse he twisted away from the sharp hurt. His elbow struck the hard concrete floor momentarily paralysing his arm. The flaming blowtorch jerked from his grip and fell to the floor. Bounced and rolled into the free-flowing petrol. The flames were slow at first, a mere flickering. They licked tentatively at the petrol-soaked coat of the big man, flickered across the floor chasing the liquid rippling from the overturned can.

At first Bates did not notice his jeopardy. He was cursing vehemently as violent men do and rolling over to get to his knees. His rage was building.

'Bastard!' he screamed.

The flames worried eagerly at his coat then reached up to lick his chin. Bates clambered to his feet suddenly realizing the danger. The swearing grew louder. He beat frantically at the flames on his jacket. The fire was really getting hold now. The back of his jacket was in flames as well as the front. Bates was yelling as the conflagration took hold.

'Help me!' he screamed.

He tugged at his jacket as he tried to strip it from him. His trouser legs had caught now. The petrol from the can was running freely on the floor and spreading. Beating madly at his flaming clothes the big man staggered back. He screamed for help, but there was only MacLean to hear his cries and MacLean was hanging helpless, his wrists lashed to a hook, not able to help himself.

Closer and closer to the pit where the mechanics stood and repaired motorcars the big man danced in frenzied agony, all the time beating frantically with his bare hands at the engulfing flames. So engrossed and terrified was the big man as he battled with the conflagration on his person he did not see this new hazard.

One foot went over into space, his arms flailing wildly as he tried to retain his balance. Slowly he toppled backwards. Engulfed in flames like a tree in a forest fire he was outlined momentarily, the branches waving crazily as he tried to keep from falling. Like the doomed tree he was helpless against the rampant force of the flames, now raging unchecked around his body as he crashed into the pit disappearing from sight.

The spilt petrol from the overturned can flowed after him spilling into the crater in the floor. The flames were leaping high. A shape highlighted in flames rose out of the blaze then disappeared once more. For some agonizing moments black misshapen paws clawed at the edge of the pit. More and more petrol flowed into the well.

MacLean watched the pantomime of death through pain-dimmed eyes. He caught glimpses of the dark shape rising from the flaming pit almost making it over the edge but then sliding back again. The screaming diminished and eventually ceased but the flames continued unabated.

MacLean closed his eyes. He could die in peace. Cannibal Bates was dead. Roshein and the rest of the gang would be safe.

The heavy metal music thudded loudly inside the burning building. Oily rags caught fire and spread to the parked car that had come in for repair. The smoke crept across the workshop and poured out the vents.

49

The cell door clanged open. Roshein looked up in anticipation. After a night in a police cell she was feeling distinctly unglamorous. A young police constable with blond hair glowered at her from the doorway. Roshein suspected she was getting the guilty criminal treatment. The constable looked too young to be a policeman.

'Come. DI Anderson wants you in the interview room.'

He led her through dingy corridors painted pea green. She felt slightly nauseous. She wasn't sure if it was the effect of the painted walls or the fact that she had been arrested and put in a police cell.

The young constable put her into the room with a grey Formica table and steel-framed uncomfortable chairs with dark-blue plastic padding. He stood by the door, folded his hands across his crotch and stared at a point above Roshein's head.

Half an hour later Anderson arrived. He had his sidekick with him. When he questioned her yesterday after she had been arrested, Anderson had introduced the younger man as Sergeant White.

'Right, Miss Rafferty,' Anderson began, after the preliminaries had been observed. 'Your friend and accomplice John Lamb has told us everything. How you raided the Roof Proof gaming club with the intention of stealing a large sum of money from the safe installed on the premises. He has left certain gaps in his confession which I hope you'll be able to fill in.' He smiled encouragingly at the girl.

'I don't suppose there's any chance of a cigarette?' she countered.

She hadn't smoked since she was a teenager. Somehow a fag seemed the most desirable thing at that moment.

Anderson turned his head towards his sergeant. The sergeant pulled a box from his pocket and offered her the open packet. She took one and waited while he flicked a lighter for her. She sucked greedily at the cigarette and inhaled deeply and, unused to the smoke, coughed for at least a minute. The policemen waited patiently.

'I don't know what on earth you're talking about,' she wheezed, her voice strained after the coughing session. 'Gaming clubs and robberies! Sounds like some Hollywood film plot. What's it all about anyway?'

Anderson sighed. 'You can't fool me, Miss Rafferty. We had good information about the job. You see we had your place bugged and heard you discussing the details of the raid. Your accomplices were Tom MacLean, John Lamb, Charlie Mitchell, and Liam Doherty. So you see we know all about the plan. As I say we just need you to fill in a few details, like where the money is now and where MacLean and Doherty are hiding out.'

She frowned as if thinking over what he had said. 'Tom MacLean worked for me at the warehouse. This Liam Doherty I never heard of before today. John and Charlie are just good friends. I've known them since we were kids. There was no plan, there was no robbery and there is no money.'

'You're making this harder for yourself. If you give us the information things will go easy with you. Help us track down Doherty and MacLean and we can get you off with a suspended sentence. As it is you face charges of attempted armed robbery. You'll get ten years at least on that charge.'

'Is that what this here is all about, fitting up an innocent woman? I've heard the police do it all the time but I never suspected it would ever happen to me.' She chanced another drag on the cigarette. This time she didn't inhale. She blew a long plume of smoke towards the ceiling. 'When do you bring out the rubber hoses and start beating a confession out of me?'

Anderson had to admire her coolness. He sighed deeply before consulting a sheaf of papers on the table in front of him.

'We found Charlie Mitchell at the club.'

She frowned for a moment. 'I knew Charlie liked a flutter on the gee-gees but I never knew he went to gaming casinos.'

'He wasn't gambling. He was trying to rob the place as you know quite well.'

She pouted with her mouth and shook her head in denial.

'We know he was there to rob the club,' Anderson bored on. 'His body was found at the rear of the casino at the foot of the fire escape.'

He could see the news had shaken her. When she spoke again her voice was muted.

'I know the police tell lies to trap people into saying something incriminating but that's a terrible trick to play on anyone.'

'No trick, Miss Rafferty.'

He pulled a photo from his folder and pushed it across the table in front of her. She stared at the image of the dead man. Her face crumpled. Anderson pushed a packet of tissues towards her and left her to her grief.

'Order some coffee, Gordon,' he asked the sergeant.

Detective Sergeant White opened the door and spoke to someone on the outside. Roshein sat bowed over, sniffling into a paper hankie. The cigarette was propped in the ashtray, now forgotten.

'I know nothing about this,' she said in a muffled voice. 'I have no idea what Charlie was doing at the club. What happened to him? Was he murdered?'

'I was hoping you would help me with that one. You see I know for a fact you were at the club the night the robbery was carried out. What went wrong during the operation we're not too sure about. I speculate the gang fell out and there was a fight. MacLean murdered Charlie and probably Doherty is dead also. MacLean scarpers with the money. He doesn't have to share with anyone. That's how it looks to me. I need to find MacLean before he kills again.'

'You got the wrong man. Tom MacLean's not like that. He wouldn't kill anyone.'

'When he came to work for you, did he tell you what his profession really was? If not, let me fill you in. Tom MacLean was an assassin. His job was to kill members of the Special Forces. He was very good at his job. No one knows how many men he murdered. I don't suppose he knows himself.'

'You're lying.'

'There are none so blind as those who will not see,' the detective quoted. 'You don't want to admit the man you took as your lover is a killer. Oh yes, he is a very clever man. He fooled us for years. We knew there was an assassin working out of Belfast. Special Forces were his targets. In the end, to get him off the killing fields, we had him jailed on a trumped-up charge as a member of an illegal organization. When he was in Long Kesh Prison the number of murdered Special Forces soldiers fell dramatically.'

Roshein looked up at the detective. She seemed to have recovered from her shock at learning of Charlie's death.

'You can sit there and lie all you want. From what you're telling me you put Tom MacLean in prison for something he wasn't guilty of. I know you'll fit me up with something also. I'll probably go to prison for a crime I never committed just like hundreds of other poor innocent victims caught up in the wheels of justice. You'll tick me off as another result. Make your arrest record look good.'

Anderson slammed the flat of his hand on the table, the sudden noise making Roshein jump.

'You stupid bitch, can't you see you'll never see that killer again? There's just you and Lamb to carry the can. MacLean's got off scot-free. He's laughing all the way to the Cayman Islands with the money from the robbery while you rot in prison. How many more men do you want murdered before that killer is brought to justice?'

Roshein stared stubbornly back at him. Anderson knew at that moment he had lost her. Whatever loyalty she had for MacLean ran deep. She would not about to betray him, no matter what.

'Charge me and put me in a cell again,' she told him. 'But don't insult my intelligence by cooking up all these lies. Whatever MacLean might have been in the past is of no consequence to me. I had to go on the run because of Orchid Brown's threats. You saw me in hospital after his thugs kidnapped me. Where were the police then? I had to close my business and go on the run, hiding like a criminal while Brown walked free to harass me and my family. Why don't you go after the real criminals instead of taking the easy option by drumming up charges against innocent people?' She shoved her hands across the table at Anderson. 'Here, put the cuffs on. You have a ready-made victim here. It'll probably help your promotion to mark up another arrest.'

Anderson stared back at her. Before he could react to her tirade there was a knock on the door. While Sergeant White went to answer it Anderson sat shuffling the papers in front of him.

'I can lock you up for your own protection,' he said at last.

'Inspector.'

White had put his head back inside the door and was motioning to him. Anderson sighed and went outside. Roshein sat alone in the room and stared at her hands. After a few moments Anderson returned. He stood by the table looking down at Roshein. She stared back up at him.

'We've found MacLean. You'd better come with us.'

There was something in his face that frightened her.

50

'Wait here.'

They were in the hospital corridor. Sergeant White stayed with her. Anderson walked forward and talked to the man with the stethoscope dangling down the front of his white coat. A uniformed constable was standing outside a door. When Anderson and the doctor approached, the policeman saluted the inspector and opened the door for them, then went back to guarding that same door.

'What is it?' Roshein asked White. 'Is he bad hurt?'

White's shrug told her absolutely nothing. She went back to worrying. The door opened and someone spoke to the constable on guard. He turned and nodded to the man and woman waiting.

'The chief says to bring Miss Rafferty.'

When she saw the figure in the bed she gave a small gasp. The doctor nodded a greeting to her then walked past and out of the room. She was left with the two detectives and the motionless figure of the man in the bed. She walked forward fearful of what she would see.

She was right to be apprehensive. The oxygen mask hid most of the face. What was revealed was swollen and distorted with abrasions and bruises. She stood by the bed and reached out. A needle had been pushed into a vein in his hand. Tentatively she touched the skin. It felt warm and alive. She couldn't help the sob that broke from her.

'Tom.'

The eyes opened. His pupils were large and black.

'Roshein . . .' the voice was weak.

'What happened, Tom?'

'Can't remember. Everything's hazy.'

'Who did this to you, MacLean?' Anderson interjected. 'Tell us who did it.'

'Fell. Hurt myself on some steps.'

'Damn it, MacLean you were found hanging in a blazing building. Trussed up like the traditional turkey. You would have roasted too, only someone broke in and pulled you out. You're lucky to be alive. Now tell us who put you there.'

The door opened and the constable on duty outside poked his head inside.

'Sir, message just come through. I think you should listen to this.'

Anderson left the room. By now Roshein had managed to take MacLean's hand in hers.

'They're trying to make up some wild story about a robbery, Tom,' she said quickly. 'Tell me it's not true.'

His drugged eyes stared back at her. Sergeant White tried to intervene.

'Don't try to cover up. We know you're both involved. Miss Rafferty is under arrest for her part in the robbery,' he told the man in the bed. 'We just need to know where you stashed the money and where your accomplice Liam Doherty has got to.'

The door opened as White was speaking and Anderson walked across to the bed and stared down at the injured man.

'We've found Doherty. They've just pulled his body from the pit at the same garage where you were rescued. They haven't identified the body yet, but I know in my heart it's Doherty. Only you were strung up for roasting I would suspect you had a hand in his death. As it is you need to tell us who murdered Doherty and left you to fry in that burning building.'

'In the pit!' MacLean whispered so low Anderson had to lean over to hear the words. 'So that's where the fat git got to. Must have been some blaze with all that lard on him. I certainly wouldn't have wished that on the poor fellow.'

'Damn it, MacLean, who did this to you and Doherty? We need to catch them. It's probably the same people who murdered Dennis Mallet.

'I suspect Cannibal Bates but there's nothing to pin it on him. If you agree to testify against him we can put him away for a long spell in prison. Mad dogs like Bates need to be taken down. Will you help me put him away?' He sighed deeply. 'I suppose I can tell you this now that Doherty is dead. Doherty was keeping us informed about your plans. He was a police snout. We knew your movements all along.' A frown creased the detective's brow. 'Why did you bring the date of the raid forward? Doherty told us the twenty-second of the month yet you went on the twentieth. Why the change of date?'

The detective thought he detected a flicker of some deep change in

MacLean's eyes as he revealed the true nature of Doherty's duplicity.

'I have no idea what Doherty's game was,' MacLean responded weakly. 'Perhaps he had some agenda of his own and made up those stories about us for some obscure reason. Maybe he needed a smoke screen to divert your attention for some scam he was trying to pull. Anyway it's academic now. Doherty is roast pork, you said. Maybe we'll never get to the bottom of this.'

'Damn it, MacLean, don't you care who put you in this hospital bed? Just give me his name. I'll make sure he won't torture any more people. We have our suspicions it was the same man who murdered Dennis Mallet.'

MacLean closed his eyes. Anderson stared helplessly at the injured man.

'You're a fool, MacLean. The next time they come for you, you mightn't be so lucky. And don't forget they'll do the same to Miss Rafferty as they've done to you and Dennis Mallet and Doherty. How do you think you'll feel then when we pull her mutilated body out of a ditch?'

MacLean's eyes remained closed. Anderson guessed he was feigning. He sighed deeply.

One thing he hated were the sadistic killers who kidnapped random victims and tortured them. He would have liked the name of the man who had performed the torture on MacLean. He was certain it was Cannibal Bates, the same man he suspected of murdering Dennis Mallet in a similar sadistic manner. MacLean's eyes remained closed. Perhaps there was one way of getting the man in the bed to tell him who had tortured him and roasted Doherty.

'OK, if that's the way you want to play it. Miss Rafferty, you're free to go, for now. Don't go too far though. I might want to question you again. Oh, there is one thing. Don't go out on your own. Don't walk the streets at night. It's obvious someone is waging a vendetta against the Orchid Gang.' He held up a finger. 'First Dennis Mallet.' Finger number two. 'Then Charlie Mitchell.' Finger number three. 'Liam Doherty is the latest victim and our friend MacLean here is number four. There's only John Lamb, MacLean and yourself left. Unless you tell me now who is committing these murders I don't think any of you have much of a future.'

51

His body was a living wound. Every part of his skin where Bates had used the blades and the drill throbbed intolerably. His head was fuzzy with the painkillers the doctor had administered.

The drugs had blunted the pain somewhat, but had dulled his mind also. But not so much that he did not heed Anderson's veiled warnings when he promised to let Roshein go and then advised her to exercise caution when going out alone.

MacLean had not risen to the bait. Anderson had wanted him to break and name names to protect Roshein. But naming names would have implicated Roshein and him in the robberies they had committed as the Orchid Gang. Because of Liam Doherty Anderson knew everything, only the detective had no proof now that he believed Doherty was dead.

The detective was making wild guesses to explain the events of the past week or so. The body in the pit was that of Cannibal Bates not Doherty. That was Anderson's mistake. Because Anderson had been looking for Doherty and MacLean, he had assumed the roasted man in the pit to be Doherty. Because of that mistaken identity the detective, believing Doherty was dead, had revealed his treachery.

MacLean remembered ruefully the success of the safe-cracking episode. They had been about to leave with the money when Doherty had coshed him. After that there was the journey in the boot of a car and delivery to the garage into the hands of Cannibal Bates. He should have died there but for the small mistake on Bates's part.

He pulled the oxygen mask from his face. He had foxed the detectives into believing he had lost consciousness when in reality he had been alert to everything around him. He knew there was a police guard on his door. Without the mask his breathing became laboured and painful. He had inhaled smoke in the burning garage before being rescued. His memory of that rescue was foggy. He had been in so much pain he had passed out before being pulled from the burning building.

When he moved he felt the tug of the needle inserted into his hand. He pulled it free and a flow of blood spread across the back of his hand. Slowly he pushed back the bed covers, swung his legs out of the bed and sat up. That was a mistake. He should have moved more slowly. His head swam and he pitched out of bed on to the floor. The pain and shock of his head hitting the floor was too much for his abused body. As he lay there he swam in and out of consciousness.

When he surfaced again the waves of pain ebbed and flowed within his ravaged body. This time when he sat up he was more cautious. Eventually he managed to get to his feet. By holding on to the bed he was able to stay upright.

There was a glass decanter of water sitting on the bedside cabinet along with a tumbler. He looked around for somewhere to get rid of the contents. A metal waste bin made a convenient receptacle and he emptied the jug. Then he carried the jug and tumbler to the door.

He had to take short shuffling steps fighting nausea and dizziness. When he got to the door he rested against the wall and waited for his strength to return. He tucked the jug beneath his arm and held the tumbler in his right hand. Drawing back his arm he hurled the tumbler with all his strength at the wall above the bed and gave a hoarse shout. The glass shattered and showered down on the bed. He was leaning against the wall for support otherwise he would have fallen on his face when he flung the tumbler. He took the water jug in his right hand raised it above his head and waited.

The door opened and the policeman on guard duty came inside the room. MacLean brought the jug down with all his force on the back of the man's head.

The policeman went down and MacLean collapsed on top of him. His hand rose and again he brought the heavy glass decanter down on the back of policeman's skull. His victim grunted and went still.

MacLean lay on the unconscious policeman for several moments before he was able to roll over on to the floor. On hands and knees he crawled to the door and nudged it closed. Everything he did required great concentration and effort.

Firstly he pulled the blankets from the bed and spread them on the floor. Then with much sweating and grunting he rolled the unconscious policeman on to the blanket. He tied a knot in one end of the blanket trapping the man's feet. Finally he unbuckled the policeman's gunbelt and tossed the rig on the bed. Then he sat on the bed and dragged the blanket towards him.

Bit by bit he pulled and heaved at the dead weight of the burden. Often he had to stop to ease his breathing and relieve aching limbs. Inch by painful inch he pulled the unconscious man up on to the bed. At any moment he expected the door to open. When finally he had accomplished his task the unconscious policeman had now taken his place in the bed.

By now he was getting inured to the pain in his body and the agony in his lungs. It was a laborious task to undress the policeman. Once he had the outer garments removed he pulled on the jacket over his hospital gown. It was tight across his chest, but the trousers were a reasonable fit. Lastly he buckled on the gunbelt and pulled on the peaked cap. At a cursory glance the only thing that distinguished him from a normal police constable was the livid bruises and abrasions on his face.

He stood by the door and looked back at his work. The oxygen mask obscured the features of the man in the bed. A casual inspection would see nothing amiss. The patient was sleeping peacefully. The only thing missing would be the police guard on the door. MacLean took a deep breath and went out into the hospital corridor.

He walked as swiftly as his condition allowed stopping occasionally as the dizziness swept over him. His lungs were on fire. His body felt as if someone was poking heated needles through the skin. He passed hospital staff from time to time but no one thought it odd to meet a police constable with a ruined face.

A young nurse was coming towards him when he had to stop and lean against the wall of the corridor. Beads of sweat rolled down his face and he was not sure if he were going to pass out.

'Constable, are you all right? Gosh, you look a right mess. What happened to you?'

'I was in a car accident. Ran off the road. My mate is waiting out front to take me back to the station.'

'Can I get you anything?'

She was very young and very attractive. A dark strand of hair strayed from beneath her cap. Her face was filled with concern.

'I could do with something that would keep me awake for a couple of hours,' he answered. 'I have to go in front of the board of enquiry and answer some very awkward questions.'

'You poor man.' She looked both ways along the corridor. 'Come with me. I think I have the very thing for you.'

She turned and walked back down the corridor again. He watched her hips as they swayed in front of him. Then realized she was exaggerating the walk for him. If his lips had not been so sore he might have smiled.

She stopped by a door and turned to him. 'I won't be a minute.'

'Can you get me a box of plasters as well?'

She smiled and disappeared inside. When she returned she held out her hand. Nestling in her palm were three small blue capsules.

'Take one now. In another couple of hours if you need it, take another one. Whatever you do don't take more than one at a time.'

Her grey-green eyes stared up at him with a strange glow as she pressed a cardboard box of plasters into his hand.

'Come back and see me sometime, Officer. Ask for Nancy Rice.'

Then she turned and was walking away. He stood and watched those swaying hips as she departed. Just before she disappeared through the double door she turned and gave him a little wave.

'Goodbye, Nancy,' he murmured. 'You make a wonderful nurse.'

He found the nearest toilets and standing by the sinks one by one he put all three capsules in his mouth. A paper cup of tap water helped them down. He tried to ignore the nightmarish face reflected in the mirror above the row of sinks.

By the time he reached the car-park his head was clearing. A buoyancy was invading his body and he began to feel strong again. It was a moment's work to break into a dark-coloured Ford Cortina.

Removing the peaked cap and the tunic jacket he tossed them into the passenger seat. The weight of the gunbelt around his middle was reassuring. Dusk was coming down and he switched on the headlights. He drove steadily through the darkening streets of Belfast.

It was still too early for the Roof Proof to be busy. He parked the Cortina in the street and sat watching the cars arriving at the gaming club. He was waiting for darkness to come down properly. He was also watching out for Orchid Brown to arrive. The black Bentley limousine drew up and MacLean watched as the two bodyguards stepped on to the pavement and examined the surrounds as the gang boss disembarked.

MacLean opened the box of plasters and emptied the contents on to the seat beside him. He spent some time fixing various shaped plasters on his face. When he had finished he doubted if even Roshein would have recognized him. He got out of the borrowed Cortina and once more donned the police jacket and cap. When he had adjusted the gunbelt to his satisfaction he turned and marched confidently towards the club entrance.

His steps were steady as he advanced, his strength returning as the drug the nurse had given him took effect. He felt a surge of energy in his body. His vision sharpened, his senses felt honed and ready. He was keyed up and ready for action. This was what he had trained for; this was what he was good at.

52

The two large men in suits looked with some interest at the policeman waking into the lobby of the gaming club. He walked confidently as if he was a regular visitor.

'Can I help you, Officer?' There was a faint frown on the bouncer's face as he asked the question.

'I have business with Brown.'

The big man was staring at the policeman with the ravaged face. He could not contain his curiosity.

'What the hell happened to you?'

MacLean shrugged. 'I was called out to a riot. Some guys grabbed me and had me on the ground kicking the blazes out of me before the snatch squad got to me and pulled me out.'

The big man shook his head. 'Looks like you're lucky to be alive.'

MacLean pointed to his face. 'You call this lucky?'

'What's your business with Mr Brown?'

'I have some information for him. I was told to go directly to Brown. It's for his ears only.'

The second security guard was talking into a wall phone. He nodded to his partner. 'Send him up. Brown will see him.'

'You know the way?'

MacLean knew the way. 'Yeah, I've been here before.'

He walked through to the rear of the games room. There were not too many punters at the tables. The night was still young.

The bouncers on the door nodded him through. MacLean decided to take the lift. He needed to conserve his energy for the task in front of him. In the lift he unbuttoned the flap of his holster.

There were two men each end of the corridor scrutinizing him as he stepped out on to the carpeted hallway. Brown must have beefed up security since the robbery.

The men kept watching as he walked to the door behind which was the safe he had so successfully raided.

How many nights ago was that? He had lost track of the days. He stopped in front of the door and knocked. His hand was on the butt of the revolver. He did not pull it for he did not want to attract the attention of the heavies guarding each end of the corridor.

The door opened. Colin Thompson peered out at him not recognizing the man in the uniform of a copper. MacLean pulled the gun. Thompson was Orchid Brown's top security man. As he saw the gun recognition dawned. He was fast. Before MacLean could barge through Thompson slammed the door in his face. Maclean wasted no time in trying to force it open. He stepped back and fired two rapid shots into the centre of the door.

The guards at the ends of the corridor were reacting also. There were shouts and they were pulling at guns concealed beneath their clothing. As he fired into the door MacLean then stepped to one side and flattened against the wall. The door was splintered again as someone inside returned MacLean's shots. Plaster erupted from the wall opposite as the bullets hammered into it.

MacLean was sighting across his body at the nearest security guards. They were getting into the action and bullets began to hum along the corridor. Nothing hit him and he fired deliberately at the large targets presented by the guards. One man threw up his hands and fell backwards through the double doors behind him. His companion went down clutching at his chest. His gun fell unheeded to the carpet.

MacLean whirled and concentrated on taking out the remaining guards at the other end of the corridor. Before he could fire the two men turned and crashed through the doors behind them. Seeing their comrades go down under the gun of the policeman they fled. Still with his back to the wall MacLean ejected the spent cartridges and reloaded from the ammunition pouch on his belt.

'Billy – Joe,' someone was shouting from inside the room behind him. 'What the hell's happening?'

'It's all right, boss,' MacLean yelled. 'We got him. He's bleeding like a stuck pig out here. Do you want us to finish him off?'

'Hell no, keep him alive. I want that son of a bitch. He has some questions to answer.'

The door opened. MacLean moved fast, shouldering the door and throwing the man inside off-balance. Then he was inside and moving very fast. Hardly pausing, he shot the man by the door. He had just time to recognize Bob Segal as the bullet from his police gun punched a hole in his face. Then he dropped on one knee and fired a few shots into the interior of the room.

'For God's sake stop firing! I'm not armed.'

Behind the large desk Orchid Brown was sitting with both hands raised in the air. Sitting on the floor with his hands clasped across his stomach was Colin Thompson. There was blood leaking through his fingers. He was grey-faced staring at the intruder with lacklustre eyes.

Slowly MacLean stood keeping his revolver trained on the gang boss.

'MacLean. I should have killed you that day you turned down my offer. I thought you had died in that garage. Who was roasted in the pit? I figured it might be Bates.'

Still keeping his gun on Brown, MacLean moved across the room.

'The mistake you made was picking on Phoenix. When you kidnapped that young woman and shaved her head you set of a chain of events that leads right to this confrontation. All I want now is the name of the detective who has been passing on information to you.'

Brown began to lower his hands.

'Keep them up!' MacLean snapped. 'I want to see your hands at all times.'

The gang boss was frowning. 'What the hell is the bent detective to you? Are you going after him as well?'

'No, I have no interest in him only as a damage-limiting ploy. I have a straight cop up my ass name of Anderson. I figure when he takes me in again I might have a slight bargaining edge when I offer him the name of the traitor in the police in return for clemency.'

To MacLean's consternation Orchid Brown began to laugh.

'You want the name of the bent cop down at the station!' he spluttered. 'Oh boy, MacLean, just turn around. See if you recognize him.'

MacLean shook his head. 'An old trick, Orchid. First I'll shoot you in the shoulder. Each time you refuse to answer my questions I shoot you again. None of the shots will be fatal. In the end as you bleed to death like your bodyguard Thompson here, you'll tell me.'

'Pull that trigger and it's the last thing you'll ever do.'

The voice came from behind. MacLean went still. Brown was grinning from ear to ear.

'Can I lower my arms now?'

53

'Shall I plug him now? You can claim you shot him in self-defence. After all there's several dead bodies he has accounted for lying all over the place.'

MacLean stood regarding the rogue police officer. The man's hand was very steady as he held his revolver. MacLean's own weapon now lay on the floor.

Detective William Moultrie was a good six feet tall with the figure of an athlete. His face was covered with designer stubble. MacLean guessed he was about thirty years of age. He had dark wavy hair and deep-set eyes that stared coldly out at his captive.

'Hell no, I need to keep him alive. He stole my money. I want it back. Bates was supposed to handle that but somehow he bodged the job and this cookie is still roaming free with my money stashed somewhere. How the hell did he get the uniform? It looks like the real McCoy.'

'That's an interesting question. The last time I heard, this guy was in hospital after being rescued from a burning garage. I was just coming to tell you where to pick him up. I was in the mood to taste the delights on offer here. So I came in person. Good job I did.'

'Good job indeed. We have to get him out of here. That shooting will bring in the peelers for sure. I don't want that asshole Anderson rooting around here again.'

'Don't worry about that. I told your fellows not to let anyone use the phones. They're telling the punters some fireworks you were storing for a big party went off accidentally. Anyway in this old building the noise doesn't travel far. How much did he snatch, anyhow?'

'My accountant reckons there's more than seven hundred grand missing. I need that money back.'

Moultrie whistled. 'Three-quarters of a million! That would make a nice little nest egg. OK, if you take him upstairs or wherever, I'll handle this end of things. I'll reassure the punters and tell them the police have everything under control. That way you won't get any interference from the force. You can take your time interrogating this fellow. Right, MacLean, start walking, unless you want to save yourself a lot of pain and grief and tell us now where you hid the money.'

'I can't tell you where it is, but I can take you to it.'

The detective laughed out loud. 'When Orchid's men are slicing bits off you, remember my offer.'

They walked down the corridor with Brown trailing behind holding a pistol on MacLean. Moultrie had gone to assure the patrons of the club that everything was under police control.

At the end of the passage the man MacLean had shot was sitting against the wall. He was groaning and his shirt front was covered in blood.

'Hang on there, Noel,' Brown called to him. 'We'll get you to the hospital as soon as we take care of this joker.'

'You have to stanch the blood,' MacLean said and stopped.

He could see the Luger on the floor beside the wounded man. Brown was too far behind to see the gun. MacLean tugged a handkerchief from his pocked and knelt down.

'Here, let me help.'

'Damn it, MacLean, keep moving.'

The hand holding the cloth obscured MacLean's other hand reaching for the Luger.

'Watch him, boss. . . .'

The wounded man's shout was too late. MacLean was swivelling with the Luger in his hand. Brown fired too hastily. The man with the bullet wound in his chest died from a bullet in the head from Brown's weapon.

MacLean fired from his kneeling position. He put two bullets into the gangster's upper torso. Brown staggered back under the impact of the bullets. He managed to fire again into the wall and then he went down. His legs kicked for a spasmodic second and the gun fell from his hand.

MacLean staggered back down the corridor in the direction the detective had taken. He felt like hell, but he knew his job wasn't finished yet. He had to take care of the crooked cop, Moultrie. As he reached the double doors at the end of the passage leading to the lifts and stairs, a wave of dizziness suddenly overcome him.

'Damn. . . !' he managed, as his legs gave way.

He tried to stop but crashed helplessly through the doors. He fell awkwardly and the hand holding the Luger folded beneath him.

The shots rang out shockingly loud in the confined space of the corridor. The bullets meant for him punched holes in the wood of the door above his head. MacLean was on the floor struggling to bring the pistol from where it was trapped beneath his body. Moultrie was by the lift doors lining up his weapon on his target.

'Damn you, MacLean, what have you done with Brown?'

'He's gone to join that other devil, Cannibal Bates. They're roasting in Hell right now, waiting for you to join them.'

'I'll spare your life, MacLean, if you tell me where the money is. Seven hundred grand is too much for one man to hoard to himself.'

'You bastard! You gave Dennis Mallet up to Cannibal Bates.' MacLean was guessing, but he saw he had hit home.

'I had no idea they were going to do that to the kid, otherwise I'd never have done it.'

'You murdered that kid,' MacLean said bitterly. 'I hold you responsible for the terrible death he suffered. You're no better than the scum you feed information to.'

'I think it's time you died, MacLean. It's a pity, for I could have done with that money you stole from Brown. I take it you killed him.'

'I told you he's rotting in Hell with that other sick bastard, Bates.'

'It feels funny to shoot a man in my own uniform.'

MacLean tried for the pistol again. He knew it was futile, but he was not one to go down without a fight. Moultrie would not miss at that distance. He was a trained marksman as were all RUC. The shot rang out.

MacLean flinched as finally his hand with the pistol came free. Somehow the detective had missed with his shot. MacLean got his gun up and stopped. Moultrie was sagging against the lift doors. Beyond him in the stairwell was another figure with a smoking pistol in his hand.

'Put the gun down, MacLean. You won't be needing that where you're going.'

MacLean stared in disbelief.

'Anderson. . . .'

The detective inspector walked slowly forward. He kept his weapon trained on MacLean. Detective William Moultrie was now sitting in front of the lift. His head was tilted to one side and a little trickle of blood leaked from the corner of his mouth.

'One thing I hate more than an assassin is a crooked policeman,'

Anderson observed as he walked past the dead detective. 'Are you going to put that gun down, MacLean, and come quietly, or do I have to shoot you also?'

54

Roshein stared resentfully at the two policemen.

'I'm his fiancée,' she said stiffly even though this was not true. 'Surely I must be allowed in to see him?'

'I'm sorry, miss.' The policeman spoke firmly. 'Our orders are to permit no one to communicate with Mr MacLean.'

'Stuff you and your orders, I only want to make sure he's all right.'

'Ahem.'

She turned at the sound and stared at the man who had come up unnoticed behind her.

'Detective Anderson, I want to visit Tom and these morons won't let me in.'

His lips were pursed as he regarded her steadily.

'Tom MacLean is under arrest and charged with a host of serious crimes. No one is allowed to visit him without the express permission of the chief superintendent.'

'I . . . I need to see him.' Her face worked as she tried to keep back her tears. 'I need to make sure he's all right.'

'I can assure you he's being looked after. As soon as it's possible you'll be able to see him and reassure yourself as to his condition. Now if you'll just be patient and wait here quietly without making a nuisance of yourself, I need to go in and see him on police business.'

Her shoulders slumped. 'Would you give this to him?' She handed him a small pot plant wrapped in gift paper.

A sour smile touched his lips as he regarded the gift.

'An orchid.'

She gazed innocently at him. 'That's all right, isn't it?'

'Quite appropriate. Now if you'll just move aside I have official business to conduct with the prisoner.'

MacLean was propped up in the bed. The oxygen mask lay beside him on the bed covers. He glanced up as Detective Inspector Anderson entered. A slight frown creased his brow as he noticed the pot plant in the detective's hand.

'An orchid if I'm not mistaken. I didn't know you cared, Inspector.'

Anderson ignored the jibe. 'Miss Rafferty is outside. She asked me to give you this.

The detective crossed to the bed. He placed the small colourful bloom on the cabinet. With some deliberation he took a document from his inside pocket and placed it beside the orchid. Then he pulled a chair up to the bed, reversed it and sat astride it. He folded his arms across the backrest and sat staring at the man in the bed.

The swelling on MacLean's face had all but disappeared and the bruises and abrasions were less livid. Both men regarded each other silently.

'Why couldn't Roshein deliver the orchid in person? Even a condemned man is allowed visitors.'

'You're facing thirty years, MacLean.'

MacLean's eyebrows lifted. 'Thirty years, why so lenient?'

'You have a string of murders to answer for. Ben Orwell, a known drug dealer, Orchid Brown – a gang boss, along with four of his henchmen. There is also the murder of Detective William Moultrie.'

'Moultrie, so that was the bastard's name. You're going to hang that one on me as well. I should have guessed. Maybe I should hire me a good lawyer and plead insanity.'

'You did commit all those murders.'

'Funny thing is I don't know any of those men I'm supposed to have murdered – Ben Orchid, or Orwell Brown, or whatever,' answered MacLean.

Anderson was staring down at the floor. 'There is a way out of this for you,' he said, not looking directly at the man in the bed.

'You're going to leave a loaded pistol on the bed and leave me alone for five minutes.'

Anderson reached inside his coat and for a moment MacLean thought he was indeed about to pull a gun. Instead the detective took out a stainless-steel Parker pen.

'Sign that document,' he nodded to the paper he had placed by the bedside when he first walked in, 'and you might save your skin.'

Slowly MacLean reached out and took up the paper.

I, Thomas Aloysius MacLean freely and voluntarily make this statement of the known facts as stated below.

When I came out of prison Detective William Moultrie recruited me to help in obtaining evidence against a notorious criminal commonly known as Orchid Brown. I agreed to help the detective in this work. On the night of 24 inst. he provided me with an RUC uniform. I was to go to the Roof Proof, a gaming club, where he suspected certain illegal activities were being carried out. My task was to cause a diversion while Detective Moultrie gained access to Brown's office to get evidence of these illegal activities.

Brown became suspicious and ordered his men to take me from the club and murder me. Before they could carry out these orders Detective Moultrie came to my rescue. He confronted Brown and told him he was under arrest. Brown and his bodyguards pulled their guns. During the ensuing gun battle Detective Moultrie managed to gun down Brown and his bodyguards before being fatally wounded. It is my opinion that Detective Moultrie saved my life. In spite of the terrible odds against him, he showed extraordinary bravery that night. In my estimation Detective Moultrie died a hero.

MacLean looked up from the paper. 'Why is Moultrie so important?'

Anderson was staring down at his hands and did not answer immediately.

'If it was left to me I would put you behind bars, MacLean, and throw away the key,' he said with a note of bitterness in his voice. 'The powers-that-be don't want this to go to court. Moultrie is to be awarded the Queen's Medal for bravery and buried with full honours.'

'What's to happen to me?'

'As soon as you sign that confession you're free to go.'

MacLean did not hesitate. He reached out his hand for the pen. There was complete silence as MacLean sat with the pen in his hand poised over the paper.

'Will I be shot trying to escape?'

'Just sign the bloody confession!' Anderson snapped.

MacLean signed. Anderson snatched the paper and glared at the signature before folding it and placing it in his pocket.

'There's no need to tell you, MacLean, this goes against the grain. I should have shot you that night in the Roof Proof.'

'That would have been a mistake. You need an independent witness.'

For a moment MacLean thought Anderson was about to strike him. Instead he pulled open the drawer in the bedside cabinet and extracted a copy of the Gideon Bible that is placed in numerous hospitals and hotel rooms throughout the world.

'Swear on this Bible, MacLean,' he said, through clenched teeth.

Warily MacLean placed his hand on the book.

'I swear on this holy Bible never to reveal to anyone the events that occurred in the Roof Proof gaming club nor the private conversation we've just had. So help me God.'

MacLean repeated the oath. Anderson sighed deeply and replaced the Bible in the drawer again.

'Goodbye, MacLean. Don't expect this to change anything. I'll be watching you. I'll have no hesitation in shooting you down like the mad dog you are when I catch you in your next act of villainy. The only good thing to come out of this thing was the removal of that monster and his evil crew, Orchid Brown. Oh, and by the way whatever happened to the money you stole from him?'

'You really don't know?'

'Why would I be asking if I knew?'

'Your snout, Liam Doherty legged it with that little lot. I suppose he gave you your share before he went into hiding.'

Anderson ignored the implied slur on his honesty. He was frowning.

'Doherty! I thought he died in the garage fire. We found his body: it was burnt to a crisp.'

'That wasn't Doherty, that was Cannibal Bates.'

Anderson's eyes widened. 'Bates! Then where's Liam Doherty?'

'When you find him let me know.'

'Liam Doherty.' The detective shook his head. 'The dirty little twister. No wonder he gave me the wrong date for the robbery.'

Anderson turned abruptly, went to the door and opened it.

'Let Miss Rafferty through,' he said to the guard outside.

Roshein brushed past the detective and ran across to the bed. She squealed and flung herself on top of MacLean. The detective could see MacLean give a wince of pain as Roshein hugged his tortured body. It was small satisfaction for the detective. He wanted MacLean back in prison where he belonged.

Detective Inspector Anderson slammed the door behind him.